STRICTLY MY HUSBAND

Also by Tracy Bloom

No-One Ever Has Sex on a Tuesday
Single woman Seeks Revenge
I Will Marry George Clooney (By Christmas)
No-One Ever Has Sex in the Suburbs

STRICTLY MY HUSBAND

TRACY BLOOM

For Bruce.
For being the kind of husband who will drink wine with me and then dance around the kitchen like no-one is watching. You are a legend.

Prologue

Midnight, the kitchen

Laura cranked the music up to full volume, kicked her high heels across the tiled floor and then moved into position in front of the sink to attack the vast line-up of dirty wine glasses. She tapped her foot in time to the song whilst wondering, as she did every time she cleared up after a dinner party, how on earth they had got through so many damned glasses and how long would it be before she broke one. Moments later, however, she was rescued from washing-up hell as she felt Tom's hands snake around her waist. She smiled to herself and let her head drop back on to his shoulder.

'Are you ready?' he whispered in her ear.

'For what?' she asked, a bigger smile spreading over her face.

'Tango time!' exclaimed Tom, spinning her round and clutching her in an expert ballroom hold.

'Seriously,' she said, laughing.

Tom nodded. 'Seriously. You've nearly got it. You were brilliant the other night. Now listen to the music. It really helps, as I keep telling you.'

Laura pricked up her ears, instantly recognising 'Eye of the Tiger' blaring out of the speakers. Tom must have changed the song.

'We're going to tango to *this*?'

'Oh yes,' replied Tom. 'We are going to take this kitchen floor by storm. Are you ready? In one, two, three, four.'

Laura let Tom thrust her down the length of the kitchen cabinets, past the cooker and then they took a sharp left-hand turn at the fridge-freezer. She stuck her chin high in the air and set her face in a hard glare just as Tom had shown her; but she caught sight of his determined mouth out of the corner of her eye and started to giggle.

His rigid face softened momentarily as they glided past the breakfast bar where he reached down and squeezed her backside before recovering his solemn air.

'Cheeky!' She smiled, kicking her leg in the air and flicking her head from left to right as they turned again to strut back towards the utility-room door.

She managed to regain her composure and just about kept up with Tom's expert guidance throughout the rest of the dance until they gave a last flourish with a dramatic double-dip finale in front of the goldfish tank at the end of the kitchen counter. He carefully lifted her back up, and held her hand so that they could bow and curtsey to their aquatic audience.

'Fantastic, you're definitely getting it,' said Tom as Laura struggled to catch her breath.

'I'll never be as good as you though,' she gasped, bending double again.

'I've been doing it a lot longer than you, that's all. It's just practice. Now, shall we see what the judges have to say?'

Laura nodded and laughed. They both leant forward and peered into the fish tank.

'I think Darcy is clearly saying *wow*, that was amazing,' said Tom, scrutinising a bright orange fish. 'And Anton Du Beke, well, he looks beside himself with joy as always.'

'It's a shame he isn't a judge then, isn't it, because I think Craig Revel Horwood is saying *woeful*, over and over again. Look, watch his mouth,' said Laura. They both watched the jet-black swimmer open and close his mouth several times.

'Craig clearly doesn't know what he is talking about,' said Tom, turning to sweep her up in his arms again. 'Shall we give him our waltz, so he knows where to stick his woeful?' He darted off to go and find the right track on the iPad.

Moments later the familiar bars of Elvis's 'I Can't Help Falling in Love with You', filled the room and she was back at her wedding day, five years ago, being waltzed around the room by her new husband. She'd thought initially it was a terrible idea doing a proper dance at her wedding given that Tom was a trained dancer and she was a market research analyst who couldn't dance for toffee but he'd somehow managed to persuade her. Come their wedding night she'd felt like a princess gliding around the dance floor in her husband's arms, happy to follow his every move as their guests oohed and aahed around them.

She melted into him now as they cruised the kitchen, knowing she would probably never do it in public again but very happy that after some limb-loosening refreshment she and Tom could often be found waltzing to Elvis Presley around their kitchen floor after midnight.

CHAPTER ONE
LAURA

Two weeks later...

'Where have you been?' asked Laura, flinging open the front door in exasperation. She looked up, gasped, and then immediately slammed the door shut again. There was a moment's silence as she stood stock-still before laughter exploded on the other side of the door.

Had she really just seen what she thought she'd seen? That was definitely female laughing inter-twined with her husband's, wasn't it? A female who had appeared to be attached to her husband's arm. Time stood still. She grabbed hold of the table in the hall to check that it was real and she wasn't simply trapped in her worst nightmare.

'Aw, let us in, Laura?' came Tom's voice from the other side of the door. 'I must have left my key at work.'

'Or in the pub,' cackled Tom's unknown female accomplice.

Laura threw open the door again to be greeted by two happily grinning faces. One she had thought she knew inside out; the other was a total unknown. She took a moment to assess the stranger. She was tall, maybe five foot eight, with cheerleader-blond hair in a high bouncy ponytail and long, fit legs encased in Lycra. She was young, maybe early twenties, around ten years younger than Laura at a guess, but it was hard to tell beneath the layers of dramatic make-up. Yes, she was definitely Laura's worst nightmare. Oh, and she looked really good next to her handsome husband. In her book, glamorous, six-foot-tall men who worked in entertainment rarely had five-foot-two short-arsed wives with wayward brunette hair and limited cosmetic ability. No matter how many times Tom told Laura he preferred her girl-next-door natural beauty she couldn't help but think that the in-your-face obvious attractiveness of the girl standing in front of her now was what people expected someone like Tom to be with.

Tom and the mystery blonde both looked at her expectantly, as if it was her job to explain the bizarre tableau that had erupted on the doorstep of 25, Lime Avenue at seven thirty on a Friday night. As if she didn't already have enough to do. The ice-cream dessert experiment had failed spectacularly, the table hadn't been laid and she wasn't sure they had enough red wine unless she could persuade Jerry to stick with white instead of guzzling the red as he usually did. It was only quarter of an hour before their guests were due to arrive and here she was standing on her own doorstep staring at her husband who had arrived home attached to some kind of Barbie doll.

'You missed your appointment with the dental hygienist this morning,' was all she could think of to say, fixing her gaze on Tom and hoping that if the woman were out of her eyeline, she might somehow magically evaporate.

'And,' she continued, taking a deep breath, 'Anton Du Beke is dead. I told you he didn't look well this morning.'

Tom and his accomplice gasped; the mystery woman looked as though she might cry.

'Oh my God,' she said, forcing Laura to look at her. Then, to Laura's horror, she rushed forward and engulfed Laura in her arms. 'I can't believe it,' she declared, somewhere way above Laura's head. 'He wasn't that old, was he? And you knew him? You must be in total shock.'

By this time Laura was being smothered by the woman's fake purple fur coat, and was feeling deeply uncomfortable in close proximity to so much Lycra.

'She means our goldfish,' Laura heard Tom announce before collapsing into hysterics. 'Luckily we still have Darcey Bussell and Craig Revel Horwood. I always thought Anton would be the first to go. It was a bad idea to put a professional in with the judges.'

'Really?' shrieked the woman, springing away from Laura. 'I thought...I thought' – she gasped – 'I thought you meant...' She started to howl with laughter.

It's Friday, Laura was thinking. He's knows it's Friday, and he knows it's our turn. And he's standing here laughing over the demise of Anton Du Beke, who was still floating on the surface of the fish tank because she couldn't bear to look at him never mind touch him. She'd hung a tea towel over the tank since getting home and waited impatiently for Tom to return from work and do the deed before their dinner guests arrived. But now he was helping the blonde off with her coat and hanging it up in their hall. What the hell was going on? She found she couldn't speak, which often happened during high-stress situations, meaning she had to resort to her usual way of communicating with her husband when she was too cross to get the words out.

Eyebrows.

She stared at Tom, shooting them to the top of her forehead. He didn't respond. She put them through a full gymnastic routine until Tom finally appeared to recognise her distress.

'Sorry, Laura,' he said. 'So this is Carly.'

He stopped there, as if giving Laura Carly's name explained everything. That once armed with this information, it would be perfectly OK for him to arrive home tipsy with an attractive young blonde woman on their regular dinner party night.

Laura fought hard for a few moments to find the appropriate response. But, conditioned after years of having good manners drilled into her by an obsessed mother, she merely stuck her hand out stiffly and muttered politely, 'Laura.'

As Carly laughed and shook her hand, Laura wondered what was stopping her from shoving Carly out into the cold and slamming the door in her face. Oh my God, she's taking off her shoes. This really has gone too far now, Laura thought as she watched the blonde dump her silver Converses on top of Tom's muddy trainers.

'Oh, don't let them get dirty,' she cried, reaching down to move them before she could help herself and placing them on the other side of the hall, well away from the gathering of marital footwear.

She stood up and glared at Tom and something in the fierceness of the look must finally have got through.

'Oh my God,' he cried, slapping his forehead. 'You've not met Carly, have you?'

Oh my God, you are such a twat, Laura wanted to scream. In what universe would I have met this … this … 'No, I don't believe I have,' she squeaked.

'I meant to call you,' he continued. 'I tried to call you but I left my phone at home.'

'But you left your phone at home,' said Laura at exactly the same time.

'You see,' cried Tom, turning to Carly whilst throwing an arm over Laura's shoulder. 'This is what I was saying. This woman is the business. She can even finish my sentences.'

'Sooooooo cute,' cried Carly. 'You are adorable together, do you know that?'

Tom grinned down at Laura. Laura grimaced back.

'So,' said Carly. 'This is totally embarrassing. You have no idea what I'm doing here. Unbelievable. What must you be thinking?'

Best you don't know, thought Laura.

'So, let's rewind, shall we?' announced Carly. She stood up straight and did a jerky backwards robot dance whilst making squeaking noises that were presumably supposed to sound like a tape rewinding.

'She's very funny,' Tom mouthed to Laura.

'Hello,' said Carly. 'I'm Carly.' She stuck her hand out for the second time.

'Still Laura,' said Laura, without offering her own hand.

'Your utterly wonderful husband is mending my broken heart,' Carly explained, smiling adoringly at Tom.

'Well,' said Tom, 'I'm just doing what I can.'

'You are a knight in shining armour,' declared Carly. 'And you...' she said, pointing at Laura.

Are the stupid mug who has no idea what is going on, thought Laura.

'...you are my fairy godmother,' finished Carly.

Excellent, thought Laura. Usually old, wrinkly, overweight and inappropriately dressed for her age.

'Shall we rewind back to this morning?' Carly asked Tom.

'Allow me.' Tom copied the backwards robot dance, much to Carly's delight.

'Picture the scene,' said Carly, dramatically waving her arms around.

I'd much rather not, thought Laura.

'I arrive at the audition with a suitcase—'

'Exhibit one,' interrupted Tom. He shuffled back through the front door and reappeared moments later – to Laura's horror – with a suitcase.

'And the first person I see is your Tom,' continued Carly.

'I could see she was upset,' Tom told Laura gravely.

This was too much. He could identify when someone he'd only just met was upset, could he? Laura practically had to put a sign over her head wrapped in fairy lights and with cans of beer hanging off it for Tom to recognise when she was upset.

'Me and Gordon have broke up,' announced Carly.

'Gordon!' Laura spluttered.

'He came home and said he couldn't live with me any more.'

'Your boyfriend is called Gordon!'

'Noooo,' said Carly. '*Was. Was* called Gordon. It's over. We are no more.'

No one was called Gordon these days, especially anyone young enough to be Carly's boyfriend.

'Loaded,' Carly added tearfully, by way of further explanation. Laura now understood completely.

'He said he couldn't live with me any more,' she continued. 'He said I was messy and selfish and self-ob...ob...ob...'

'Self-obsessed?' Laura added helpfully.

Carly nodded. 'Yes, that's it. But I don't think I am. Do you think I am, Tom?'

'No,' said Tom, shaking his head vigorously. 'Not at all. Is she, Laura?'

'I – don't – really – know – do – I?' said Laura slowly. Because I don't know who this complete stranger, wrapped in purple Muppet fur, standing in my hall with a suitcase, *is*.

'So then Tom...' Carly faltered, her eyes now brimming with tears, '...Tom said he'd give me a lift to the Red Cow after the audition—'

'She got the part, by the way,' interrupted Tom, as though Laura had been waiting with bated breath for this information. 'One of the best auditions I've ever seen at Wonderland.'

'Really?' said Carly, wide-eyed.

Tom nodded. 'Really.'

'And what happened next?' urged Laura, unwilling to pause for admiration just now.

'Well,' continued Carly. 'We got to the Red Cow and they had no rooms left, a funeral or something, so we had a drink and then Tom had a brilliant idea.'

Tom nodded again. 'I did.'

I very much doubt it, thought Laura.

'Tom said I could come and stay with you – just while the show is on. You know, rent your spare room.'

Laura felt her jaw slowly drop as Carly flashed her a watery smile.

'Brilliant, eh?' said Tom, moving to put his arm around Laura's shoulders. 'We were only talking the other night, weren't we, about getting another lodger?'

'We were,' said Laura slowly. It was true they'd had a discussion about it. They'd not had a lodger since Laura got a big promotion at work, meaning they no longer needed the extra money to help pay the mortgage. But they'd been talking about starting a family and knew that at some point they wouldn't be able to rely on Laura's income. A short-term lodger seemed a good solution to building up their savings.

'Carly says she'll pay us two months' rent up front even though she only needs to stay for four weeks,' gasped Tom, grinning as though he'd just won the lottery.

'It's cheaper than a B & B,' said Carly. 'And much nicer,' she added, glancing round the hall approvingly.

When they'd discussed having a lodger again Laura had envisaged someone similar to Rory, their previous tenant. She had happily overlooked his appalling dress sense and chronic dandruff since they rarely saw him – he worked all hours in one of the restaurants at the theme park during the open season then moved out over the winter to cook in a chalet in the Alps. Somehow Laura knew that Carly would not be as easily overlooked, even if it was only for four weeks.

'I'm so grateful,' said Carly, launching herself at Laura and engulfing her in another bear hug. 'I've had the worst day and I can't believe it's all worked out so well. Come on' – she pulled Tom's arm – 'group hug.'

Laura felt Tom's arms tighten around the two of them as she was suffocated by Carly's celebrity scent.

'It's all going to be OK,' Tom said above their heads.

'Do you know what I can't believe,' said Carly, abruptly pulling away. 'The bastard left me on a Friday. Ruined my entire weekend.'

CHAPTER TWO
TOM

Earlier that day…

How he was already at this roundabout, he had no idea. In fact he had no idea how he had got out of bed, got breakfast, got changed, got into the car and was already just ten minutes from work doing the same journey he'd done on way, way too many occasions. Only ten minutes and he'd be through those damned entrance gates yet again and past the sign, which read: '*You have now arrived at your happy place so SMILE!*' He wanted to stick pins in his eyes just thinking about it.

Another endless day at work was about to begin only today was worse. In fact it was one of the worst days of the year. Today he would have to pretend he was firmly in his happy place when it was the last place on earth he could possibly be happy in.

Today was audition day. And not only that, it was Halloween audition day. He knew as he followed the brown tourist signs to 'The Wonderland Theme Park and Resort' that even as he drew into the staff car park there would already be a few hopefuls lingering around, waiting for their chance to shine. The keen ones always came early and they were always the worst. Hope plastered across their faces as thickly as their caked-on foundation. All super-keen to tell him that they were super-talented and on the fast track to a superstar career. The kind that would drop into their laps as soon as they auditioned for next year's *X Factor*. They'd only failed this year because they'd been told they didn't have enough performing experience. So here they were, at a theme park, super-excited about looking grotesque as a zombie and frightening the living daylights out of the general public.

This was Tom's fourteenth Halloween at Wonderland. A truly horrifying thought. He'd joined at eighteen as a performer in the Wild 'n' Wacky Pirate Show as well as taking on the duties of the various costume characters that appeared around the park. Apart from the odd fluttering with a touring musical theatre company he'd never escaped. The day his boss had said to him that he wasn't far off being too old to perform but he would be a natural in entertainment management was possibly the worst day of his life. Laura on the other hand had been over the moon at the prospect of a permanent rather than a seasonal contract, relieved that it would give them more stability. And so he couldn't say no. He owed it to her. She had been the main breadwinner throughout their marriage up to that point so he couldn't turn it down to continue the pursuit of his dream of maybe one day making it big on stage or screen.

It was the hope and the innocence he saw on audition days that made his job pretty unbearable. They all reminded him so much of how he used to be. Keen and desperate. It was his job to smile and encourage when all he really wanted to say to them was to stop being so fucking deluded and go and work in KFC so that at least they would earn enough money to go and get wasted in Ibiza for two weeks a year and be happy.

To be perfectly honest he'd rather audition the weirdos that turned up at Halloween. They held no false dreams of future fame. They weren't there in the hope they were on a stepping stone to greater glory. They actually just wanted to dress up as a zombie and terrify people. An altogether much healthier aim in life.

He turned right and stuck his tongue out at the welcome sign at the staff gates. He waved at the security guard; the man never waved back. Tom found it oddly comforting that someone was even more miserable to be here than he was every day. Five hundred yards up a driveway and that was it, the day would have to start and there was nothing he could think of that could make it in any way the slightest bit enjoyable.

He glanced at the girl staggering halfway up the drive, dragging an enormous leopard-skin suitcase. Wannabe singer/dancer – he immediately recognised it. Long fit legs clad in shiny purple poking out underneath some kind of hairy purple coat that must be a fashion thing. As he indicated to overtake her, she glanced over her shoulder and rather than the cheery, hopeful 'I'm here' wave he expected he could see distress written all over her face and she immediately stumbled and fell to the ground.

He slammed on his brakes, put on his hazard warning lights, which struck him as depressingly sensible, and leapt out to see if she was all right.

'Are you OK?' he asked, offering his hand for her to pull herself up with. He felt long fake nails scratch at his palm as he clutched her hand and hauled her up. 'Talk about stopping traffic,' he said, smiling.

'I'm so sorry,' she gasped. 'I just tripped and there's no path and this stupid suitcase is so heavy and...'

She looked as though she was about to burst into tears.

'It's OK,' he said, noticing her beautiful blue eyes, fantastic figure and immediately felt ashamed. He pictured Velma out of *Scooby Doo*. Never failed.

'No it's not,' she said, shaking her head. 'I have an audition today and if they saw me arrive like this, in such a state, they'd never give me the job and I need this job. I *really* need it.'

Tom's heart sank but before he could speak she carried on.

'My boyfriend's thrown me out and I have nowhere to go and no work and ... and ... ' The tears started their full-on descent down her cheeks.

Tom's heart sank even further. Why was it that wherever there were dancers, singers and performers there was relationship drama? Sometimes he felt his team was more in need of an agony aunt than a boss.

'Anyway,' the girl said, sniffing loudly. 'Not your problem.' She forced out a smile. 'Thank you for having the decency to stop. I'll let you get on with your day. Goodbye.' She grabbed the handle of the suitcase and staggered off.

Tom was stunned. Most unusual in his line of work for someone to begin a drama and then stop, despite the fact they had an audience. He'd never seen that before.

'Let me give you a lift,' he said, running after her and grabbing the case. 'It's not far but I can't leave you struggling with this case.'

'Oh.' She turned back to face him. 'That's really kind.' She looked at him through watery eyes, blinked rapidly, laughed and then touched her hair.

Shit, thought Tom. She'd done that weird thing a lot of women do when they first meet him. It was Laura who first identified it. She even had a name for it. She called it Tom's Fondle Fondue look. Apparently, according to his wife, he was so good-looking that he had the power to reduce new female acquaintances to melted cheese and wish they were in a fondle with him. He couldn't see it himself.

When he looked in the mirror all he could see was something quite ordinary apart from the slightly wonky nose and the horrific dimples that formed on his cheeks when he smiled. The girl was still standing on front of him flicking her hair. He pictured Velma digging a garden.

He turned away and went to go and put the case into his boot. By the time he was back in the car she had settled herself into the passenger seat.

'You got rocks in that case or something?' he asked, putting the car into gear.

'Oh no,' she replied. 'I didn't take the diamonds. I didn't think that was fair.'

'Oh, I see.' Tom nodded. There was an awkward silence. 'So you were engaged then? That's tough.'

'No,' she replied. 'He just liked to buy me diamonds. Well, he used to.'

Tom could hear sniffing again and wondered what his exit strategy should be. He turned into the staff car park and headed towards his usual parking space, preparing his instructions of where she could go and get a coffee and sort herself out.

'Here we are,' he announced as they pulled up.

'I certainly hope so,' she replied. 'Or else you're a psycho who's secretly drugged and kidnapped me, then taken me to some weird other land where they numb your mind with wacky music constantly playing and freak you out with giant ladybirds lurking around every corner.'

'So you've been here before?' asked Tom.

'No, actually. Many like it. So can you give me any tips?' she asked, turning to face him and making no move to get out of the car.

'Well, let's see,' replied Tom. 'Don't go within a country mile of the hot dogs and if someone asks you if you want to win a pink teddy, run away very fast and whatever you do not look back; I repeat: do not look back. The Games Team are evil predators and they will hunt you down.'

She laughed at him and he liked it.

'No, silly, I mean about the audition. My friend auditioned last season and said the Entertainment Director is a right misery, never smiled once. Is he still here, do you know?'

Tom swallowed. 'I believe so.'

'Drat. I hate auditioning in front of someone who doesn't smile. I know it's probably all quite tedious, but come on, if you're in that job you're on the best side of the table really, aren't you? You're in work and the rest of us aren't. The least you can do is smile.'

'I suppose.' Tom shrugged, opening his door and getting out. He lifted her suitcase out of the boot, deciding he had better 'fess up that he was in fact the miserable Entertainment Director.

'Carly,' she said, sticking her hand out to shake as she grabbed her suitcase from him.

'Tom,' he responded, taking her hand.

'You have been an absolute star,' she gushed. 'Literally picked me up off the street *and* cheered me up.'

'I didn't really do anything,' he muttered.

'You made me laugh.' She grinned. 'On today of all days. Now if you could just point me in the direction of coffee I might become human again – unless you'd care to join me? Would you let me buy you a coffee?'

'No, oh no – no need,' he replied, backing off. 'Stuff to do, you know. Canteen's through that door over there.' He pointed towards the bottom of the car park.

'OK,' she said, touching her hair again and not moving. 'Wish me luck.'

'For the audition?'

'With the misery guts of an Entertainment Director.'

'He's really not that bad.'

'We'll see. Good to meet you,' she said with a little wave.

'Yes. Bye,' said Tom abruptly; then he turned away to go and hide somewhere.

'I'm late, I'm late for a very important date,' screamed Nathan from Cleethorpes as he jumped up and down in an approximate impression of a demented rabbit before stopping suddenly, leaping forward off the stage and running at speed towards Tom and growling angrily in his face.

Tom smiled inanely back at him from his aisle seat in the Celebration Theatre located in Back of Beyond World at Wonderland.

'Excellent,' he said through gritted teeth when Nathan eventually dropped out of character and took a step backwards.

'I did a lot of improv at college,' said Nathan. 'So this type of exercise is like a walk in the park for me.'

'So what do you think, Amy?' said Tom, turning to his assistant seated next to him.

'Utter shite,' she mouthed at him before addressing Nathan. 'Nathan,' she said, 'I think I need to see a bit more. I'd like you to get back on stage and improvise a bunny being boiled to death.'

Nathan nodded enthusiastically and dashed back down the aisle towards the stage.

'Amy, that's not fair,' hissed Tom.

'He asked for it,' replied Amy.

'So should I be the White Rabbit out of *Alice in Wonderland* or can I choose what type of bunny I am whilst I'm being boiled?' Nathan asked once he'd leapt up on stage.

'I don't care,' Amy shouted back.

'Right, OK, so just give me a minute.' He turned his back on his possible future employers.

'For fuck's sake,' muttered Amy. She tucked her lime-green Wonderland polo shirt further into her khaki polyester trousers. Tom had told her she didn't have to wear the park uniform any more now she worked for him but she insisted. As she had pointed out to him, it was free, easy to clean, didn't need ironing and had an elasticated waist, which was good for when you were having a fat day. Given that Amy was clearly overweight so likely to be having a fat day every day, and – although only twenty-two years old – capable of scaring the shit out of him on a frequent basis, he decided that he would never raise the issue of what she wore ever again.

'I can't watch,' Amy whispered in Tom's ear as Nathan turned around. His face was scrunched up and he had twisted his arms around his shoulders. He emitted an ear-piercing howl and began to spin around and around until he collapsed on the floor in a heap and lay there juddering for a few seconds before emitting one last ear-splitting scream. There was a moment's silence before he leapt to his feet and took a bow.

'Boiling water doesn't spin,' shouted Amy. '*Why* were you spinning?'

'Aah,' said Nathan, raising his finger to point at Amy. 'I was the White Rabbit, you see. Not any ordinary rabbit. I was in a *hurry* to be boiled to death.'

Amy stared back at him, then raised two fingers to her head and pretended to shoot herself.

Tom pushed Amy's hand down sharply.

'Thank you, Nathan,' he said. 'That was, er, very interesting.'

'Thank you.' Nathan nodded in agreement. 'And I'd just like to say, Tom – may I call you Tom?'

'Er, yes,' replied Tom.

'I'd just like to say that I think your theme for Halloween is genius. *Malice in Wonderland* is so clever.

It's like a gift to someone like me. Really something I can get my improv brain's teeth into.'

'Improv brain's teeth?' muttered Amy in amazement.

'And I know you have probably only thought of all the obvious interpretations so far but what I have learnt from all my experience in improv is that it's the unexpected that really works. Do you know what I mean?'

Tom and Amy nodded mutely.

'That's why I did the White Rabbit,' he continued. 'No one will think of the White Rabbit, and no one will think of turning him into an angry white rabbit, like I just did in my audition.'

Tom cast his mind over the thirty-plus Halloween interpretations of the White Rabbit out of *Alice in Wonderland* he'd already seen that day. He stood up and walked down towards the stage and grasped Nathan by the hand.

'Well, thank you, Nathan. We'll be in touch.' He smiled and nodded his head towards the exit to indicate his time was up.

'Mad Hatter,' Nathan suddenly shrieked, just as he was about to depart. 'I could do you one brilliant Mad Hatter. Bet you've not seen any of those today either, have you?'

Tom cast his mind over the fifty-plus Mad Hatters he'd seen that afternoon. 'Thanks, but you really have given us enough for now. Goodbye.'

Nathan reluctantly walked off the stage and Tom returned to his seat. 'What?' he asked when he noticed that Amy was glaring at him.

'You're weird today,' she announced.

'And your point is?' he said grumpily, picking up the list of applicants.

'What's with all the smiling and the handshaking bollocks?'

Tom just shrugged.

'You never smile or shake someone's hand during auditions. In fact it's the first rule you ever taught me. Don't look them in the eye, you said. Don't be nice, you said. You said you gave me the job because I excelled at being cold and dismissive.'

'Maybe I've remembered what it's like to audition. It's shit. So maybe we should actually try and make it a bit less shit.' He picked up his pen and put a cross through Nathan's name. 'I assume you agree Nathan's performance was utterly dire and we hope never to see him darken our door ever again.'

'Correct,' said Amy. 'I crossed him off before he even opened his mouth. He was wearing a Take That T-shirt. I can't bear all that retro crap.'

Tom groaned. Another downside of working at a theme park was that generally everyone was younger that him and he hated it when they so casually reminded him.

'So who have we got next?' he asked.

Amy flicked through some pages on her clipboard. 'Last but not least for today we are doing the female lead in the show,' she said. 'Are we marking out of ten for this one? What are today's criteria? Best Whitney Houston impression? Best Cher impersonation? Or the one who looks the most like a drag queen?'

'Let's not, eh?' muttered Tom, glancing down the list and spotting Carly's name.

Amy looked at him. 'All this smiling and hand-shaking has made you even more miserable than usual,' she told him.

'Just bring 'em in, Amy.'

'You're the boss,' she said, hauling herself up from her chair and heading out to the changing rooms to notify the next set of lambs to the slaughter.

Tom sat back in his chair feeling slightly sick. Somehow he hadn't managed to get Carly out of his head. He'd been dreading her audition and the moment she realised that not only had she been dumped but she'd also insulted the man who today held her fate in his hands.

Amy arrived back and told him not to get his hopes up. There were only five left in the running after Leon the choreographer had weeded out all the rubbish dancers in his audition that morning.

'There's really only one that's any good appar-ently,' said Amy, 'so if she can't sing we're screwed.'

A short girl who'd overdone it with the hair exten-sions, which made her resemble Captain Caveman, strode on to the stage.

'Hold on to your hats,' said Amy, blowing her rosy round cheeks out. 'This could be a bumpy ride.'

One by one they trooped up and, sure enough, Captain Caveman warbled like Cher and the next one broke down in tears at the end of 'I Will Always Love You', confessing, 'I still can't believe she's gone.'

'We are doomed to putting on a back-from-the-dead Whitney tribute act this Halloween,' muttered Amy.

'Bad taste,' Tom muttered back.

'Carly Stevenson next,' said Amy. 'I think Leon said this was the good one.'

Tom swallowed hard. Maybe she wouldn't see him because of the stage lights. Maybe she'd do her audition and not mention that they'd already met. Maybe if he smiled enough she'd assume he wasn't the grumpy Entertainment Director that her friend auditioned for a year ago. But what if she couldn't sing? What if he had to turn her down and she thought it was just because she'd insulted him earlier in the day? Today was turning out to be much worse than normal.

He watched her emerge from the wings shrouded by an enormous red cloak, a hood covering her head. She glided to the middle of the stage and positioned herself behind the microphone, her head bent low, waiting for her music to begin. Tom was holding his breath.

The opening chords of a familiar tune struck up and he watched Carly slowly raise her head and look him straight in the eye before she started to sing.

'I put a spell on you because you're mine
You better stop the things that you do
I ain't lyin', no, I ain't lyin'
I just can't stand it, babe
The way you're always runnin' 'round
I just can't stand it, the way you always put me down
I put a spell on you because you're mine...'

Tom was mesmerised and still didn't breathe. Her singing was strong, clear, full of expression and so haunting he felt chills running up and down his spine. They had never had anyone of this calibre audition before. Halfway through she shrugged off her cloak to reveal a racy sparkling red gown that showed off her figure to the max, causing him to take a sharp breath and Amy to dig him in the ribs. Carly moved out from behind the microphone and performed a mini dance routine with grace, elegance and style before returning to finish the song.

She came to the end of her performance and there was a stunned silence in the auditorium. Even Amy sat there speechless at what she had just seen in their humble little theatre in Back of Beyond World. She was the first to come back to her senses, however, and without thinking stood up and clapped her hands enthusiastically.

'Brilliant,' she roared. 'Eh, boss?' She glanced at Tom over her shoulder. 'That's more like it.'

Tom couldn't move. She was holding his gaze, not a shred of acknowledgement of their previous interaction on her face. She looked poised, professional and expectant.

'It's yours,' was all he could manage to blurt out. 'It's yours. Please say you'll take it. Please.'

'Aw,' interrupted Amy. 'Do you mean we won't be doing the dead transvestite Whitney Houston slash Cher tribute band after all?'

'On hold until next year,' said Tom. 'That is if Carly wants the job.' It was his turn to look expectant.

'Really?' she said into the microphone.

Tom nodded. 'Really.'

'Yes!' She leapt off the stage and ran straight at Tom to wrap him in a bear hug. 'Oh my God, what would I have done without you today?' she cried. 'When I saw it was you I nearly pissed my pants, seriously. I'm so sorry about earlier. I can't believe what I said to you.'

'Whoa there,' said Amy, looking confused. 'You two have met before?'

'No, not really.' Tom shook his head vigorously. 'I just helped with her suitcase this morning.'

'Suitcase?' asked Amy.

'My boyfriend's chucked me out,' babbled Carly. 'Today of all days, can you believe it? So I arrived with a suitcase and no job and now I have a job and just need somewhere for me and my suitcase. Actually, if you could direct me to the nearest Travelodge then the day will have turned out much better than expected.'

Neither Tom nor Amy responded. Tom was very conscious of Carly's arm still draped around him and of the evil glares that Amy was giving their new leading lady.

'The Cow will have a room,' muttered Amy eventually.

'She means the Red Cow,' added Tom. 'A pub nearby.'

'Perfect! I could do with a drink after the day I've had. Couldn't give me the number of a taxi firm, could you?' Carly asked, giving Tom the Fondle Fondue look again. 'You must think I'm such a pain expecting you to sort out all my problems. I'm not normally like this, I promise.'

'No problem, honestly,' replied Tom. 'Look, I can drop you off there if you like. I only live down the road.'

'Seriously?' cried Carly. 'I think you are the kindest man I have ever met.'

'No, I'll take her,' said Amy firmly, taking a step forward and putting her hand on Tom's free arm. Her face was grim and set and Tom had seen that look before. Normally it meant he had to let her have her own way even though he was the boss.

'Well, that's very kind of you,' he said, taking a step back so that neither lady was in possession of one of his limbs, 'but how exactly are you going to get Carly and her suitcase on the back of your moped, Amy?'

'I'll do it in relay. Suitcase first then her.' Amy stabbed a cursory finger in Carly's direction.

'Well, that does seem a bit ridiculous, doesn't it, when I'm already passing with a car that not only has a passenger seat but also a boot?'

'I think he's right,' agreed Carly. 'But thank you for offering, so kind... Sorry, I didn't catch your name?'

'Amy,' spat Amy.

'Amy. Well, I'm really looking forward to working with you.'

Amy didn't reply; she just turned to Tom. 'I think Nathan would work really well with her, don't you think? The perfect match in fact.' She turned and stomped out of the theatre.

'Well,' said Tom, turning to face Carly. 'Welcome to Wonderland. We hope your stay is a pleasant one.'

'Oh, I'm sure it will be,' replied Carly, going slightly Fondle Fondue on him again.

He coughed. 'I just need to grab my things; then let's get you installed in the Red Cow, shall we?'

'I'll go and take my stage clothes off,' she replied and turned to go. About halfway back to the stage she stopped and shouted to Tom: 'You will let me buy you a drink, won't you? I mean you must, after all you've done today?'

Oh fuck, thought Tom. A woman in a skintight red dress with a thigh-high split was asking him to go for a drink with her.

He nodded. 'Just one then.'

Couldn't hurt, could it? As long as he had Velma with him.

CHAPTER THREE
LAURA

Laura slammed the washed saucepan on to the drainer. Tom had been upstairs 'showing Carly her room' for the past fifteen minutes. The spare room wasn't even that big. Only nine by eight, in fact. She remembered feeling really posh because she owned a house with a spare room. She'd never lived in a house with a spare room before. She now realised there was a very good reason not to have a spare room: so your husband couldn't bring home every beautiful blonde waif and stray that he liked, to stay in it.

She stiffened as she heard the kitchen door open behind her. Tom came in and opened the overhead cupboard where the wine glasses lived. He was humming, for goodness' sake. What on earth was there to hum about? She felt him approach her and bristled, then melted slightly when he landed a kiss on the back of her neck. She waited for him to speak. To request forgiveness for his outrageous behaviour or at the very least to ask for misguided reassurance that it was OK to bring a stranger into their home.

But there was silence and then to her horror she heard him leave the kitchen to go into the dining room without saying anything. No apology, no nothing. She slammed another vigorously cleaned saucepan on to the drainer.

She was just drying her hands on a towel and preparing her tirade when Tom popped his head back around the kitchen door.

'You'd not put any glasses on the table,' he told her.

Her jaw dropped in reply.

'I've done it and I'll set an extra place for Carly, shall I?' He disappeared and she could hear the clanging of the cutlery drawer complemented by Tom whistling. If he made any more happy noises she thought she might actually kill him.

'I've lent Carly a towel,' he shouted from the dining room. 'That's OK, isn't it?'

Now you ask for permission, she thought. For a *towel*! When exactly were you planning to ask permission for a blonde bombshell to invade our home? She reached round to untie her apron. Some things needed to be made clear before this all got any further out of hand.

Bing-bong.

'That must be the others arriving,' shouted Tom.

No shit, Sherlock, thought Laura, pausing to find out whether his current mystery-solving powers would actually lead him to open the door to see if he was right. The clanking and jangling of cutlery continued as he evidently decided against greeting their guests personally. Laura chucked her apron on to the counter, strutted out into the hall and for the second time that evening threw open the door. Thankfully the sight that met her this time was no surprise. There was Jerry, Tom's best mate since forever, red-cheeked and jolly, standing next to his long-suffering and patience-of-a-saint wife, Hannah. Behind them hovered Will, Tom's older brother, casting a lopsided grin in Laura's direction.

'There she is,' cried Jerry, stepping inside with two bottles of wine swinging from his hands. 'The hostess with the mostest. Is that the Laura Mackintyre infamous king prawn curry I can smell?'

'No,' replied Laura briskly, stepping forward to give Hannah a hug. 'It's probably Anton Du Beke. He's dead and floating at the top of the fish tank.'

'Oh dear,' said Hannah.

'*The* Anton Du Beke?' asked Jerry.

'Of course not,' said Laura. How many more people did she have to explain Anton Du Beke to? 'The goldfish was called Anton Du Beke.'

Jerry screwed his face up. 'Why?' he asked.

'Because we can,' replied Laura.

'I worry about you two sometimes,' he said, shaking his head.

'Not half as much as we worry about you,' said Tom, strolling in and slapping Jerry on the back. 'Hi, everyone.'

31

'Tom, could you get Anton out of the tank and do something with him?' asked Laura as she hung up Hannah's coat. 'I think he's beginning to smell.'

'Erm, I...erm...' stuttered Tom, looking horrified. 'I'm not sure I actually could. Will?' he asked, turning to his brother with a hopeful look on his face.

'It's all right,' said Will, beginning to roll up the sleeves of his red-and-black-checked shirt. 'I'll do it. He might get his hands dirty,' he said, winking at Laura.

'It's not that,' said Tom. 'It's just, you know...it's dead.'

'Exactly,' replied Will. 'What's it going to do? Bite you?'

'It'll feel all funny,' Tom continued, screwing his face up.

'You big jessy,' declared Jerry.

'You do it then,' challenged Tom.

'Er, no, you're all right. Will asked first. He's good at that sort of stuff. Anyway, where have you been all day, Tom? Thought you were popping on to site for a cuppa,' he said, hastily changing the subject.

'In audition hell,' said Tom, rolling his eyes. 'Speaking of which, I hope you don't mind but we have an extra guest at dinner.'

So he asks his friends if it's OK, seethed Laura, but not me, his wife, the one who's cooked the sodding dinner.

'Will he be supplying beverages?' asked Jerry.

'It's not a he, it's a she,' replied Tom.

'Oooooooh,' Jerry said. 'A she? Details, quick. Young, old, fat, thin, blonde, brunette, legs ... Tell me she has legs, and most importantly of all ... the big question ... would you?'

'*Jerry*,' gasped Hannah. 'You've not even met the poor woman yet.'

Laura watched as Jerry studied Tom's reaction to his question. Tom's cheeks took on a rosy glow.

'Result,' cried Jerry. 'So where is she?'

'Having a shower,' replied Tom. 'We lent her a towel, didn't we, Laura?'

Laura couldn't take her eyes off him. He was still slightly pink from Jerry's interrogation and now he was passing on the responsibility for allowing Carly to rub her naked body with their towels. She blinked at him and tried the raised-eyebrows approach again to indicate that all was not well with this new situation but Tom looked away.

'Drink, anyone?' he asked.

'Do chickens cross the road?' replied Jerry, roaring with laughter at his own wit. 'Do you get it?'

'No,' Laura answered.

'It's a joke,' said Jerry. 'You know, why did the chicken cross the road?'

'I know the joke,' Laura said, not in the mood for Jerry's off-kilter humour. 'It just doesn't make sense in this context.'

'You know your problem?' said Jerry. 'You over-think things. It's a joke, that's all.'

'But it's not funny,' replied Laura.

'Why-did-the-chicken-cross-the-road jokes aren't funny?'

'Yes they are but you weren't telling that joke.'

'I was. Wasn't I?' he said, looking round. 'Didn't I just say: why did the chicken cross the road?'

'Because she wanted to lay it on the line,' came a voice from behind them.

Everyone turned to see Carly standing there in all her glory.

Jerry whistled under his breath. 'Bloody hell.'

Oh, hilarious, thought Laura, staring at Carly's beautiful sparkling red sequined strapless dress with a slit up to her…well, her crotch.

'I'm rubbish at jokes,' she said nervously when no one laughed, just stood staring at her. 'Did that come out right?'

'Did that come out right? Did that come out right? I have never seen anything come out so right in my life,' boomed Jerry, glancing rapidly between her face and her hemline.

'What a beautiful dress,' said Hannah politely. Laura looked daggers at her.

'Oh, I know it's over the top,' Carly answered, glancing at her audience dressed in their high-street best, 'but I didn't have anything else.' Her eyes hovered for a moment over Will and then snapped back to look innocently at Laura.

You really had nothing other than a dress more suited to a red carpet than their cheap Ikea hall runner? thought Laura.

'I didn't have time to pack properly so I just bought my work clothes really which are pretty much all Lycra and I didn't think you'd want to see me in those.'

'Don't know about that,' muttered Jerry.

'So this is Carly and she auditioned at work today – wearing this dress, I believe,' Tom announced by way of explanation.

'I was supposed to be like a girly devil,' added Carly. 'I had this big red cape over it and some little horns... I think I pulled it off,' she continued, looking at Tom.

'She blew us away,' Tom told them all. 'Best Halloween devil I've ever seen.'

The devil, mused Laura. How apt.

'So you're a singer?' asked Jerry.

'Well, a dancer really, but I can sing as well. Whatever I need to do to get work.'

'So you're taking in performers now?' Jerry asked Tom.

'It's just temporary,' he replied.

Jerry turned to Carly. 'You know we have a lot of spare rooms at ours. To be honest, our house is much bigger than this one. You could have your choice of any number of guest rooms complete with walk-in wardrobes and en-suite with the latest state-of-the-art rainforest-effect shower.'

'Jerry is a builder,' Tom told Carly, 'and very house-proud.'

'Not just a builder,' said Jerry. 'A very successful builder.'

'*Jerry*,' said Hannah in a pleading tone.

'And this is Hannah,' continued Tom. 'Jerry's much better half, and my little baby brother Will.'

'Oh,' said Carly, gazing up at Will's six-foot-tall frame, broad shoulders and well-cultivated facial hair.

Will bent to offer her a handshake. 'I'm actually older than Tom but he likes to keep me in my place,' he said. 'I'll go and sort out that dead fish problem for you now, shall I, my big brave brother?' He grinned at Tom and then headed for the kitchen, leaving an awkward silence behind him.

'So,' said Jerry eventually, slapping his hands and rubbing them together. 'What does a thirsty man have to do to get a drink around here?' he asked as he took Carly's arm and led her though to the dining room. 'Let's find out some more about this young lady, shall we?'

Laura was staring at Carly through narrowed eyes and a fog of red wine as she reached for another cheese biscuit. If she concentrated hard enough she could picture red horns coming out of her head and red flames leaping around in her eyes. Her tinkling laughter had punctuated the evening like daggers through Laura's heart as she winced over her simpering at Jerry's terrible jokes and thinly veiled flattery. Jerry had now pulled out the big guns and was in full throttle, telling Carly all about how he'd built his father-in-law's local building firm into a thriving company specialising in leisure developments across the country.

'I started as an apprentice and then married the boss's daughter.' He chuckled, winking at Hannah. 'We were just twenty-one, can you believe it? Mind you, she's the brains behind it all. She manages the office, deals with the suppliers, pays the wages, all that kind of stuff. I'm just the front man really, but I'm a bloody good front man. I just got a deal for two new hotels in the North-West. I won't tell you how much it's worth for fear of embarrassing you!' He laughed and punched Carly lightly on the shoulder.

'So you're married *and* work together,' said Carly. 'How ... amazing.'

'We're a really good team, aren't we, love?' Jerry smiled at his wife. 'I bring the punters in, then Hannah organises ... well, everything else really.'

'I'm a qualified accountant,' added Hannah. 'Comes in handy when Jerry gets his numbers wrong.'

'I don't get them wrong very often!' Jerry defended himself.

'You do sometimes,' said Hannah with a resigned smile.

'I can't help it if I bring in such enormous deals that it gets complicated,' replied Jerry. 'This woman is a goddess with a spreadsheet.' He pointed at Hannah. 'Smartest woman I know, seriously. As I said, we make a great team.' He leant forward and chinked his glass against Hannah's.

'Cheers,' they both said in a private toast.

'And what do you do?' asked Carly, turning to Will. 'I don't think you said.'

'Oh, I'm just an electrician,' said Will, scratching his beard. 'I work for Jerry and Hannah.'

'Not really *just* an electrician, are you, Will?' said Hannah. 'He plans everything to do with electrics for all of our builds and manages a big team of electricians,' she told Carly. 'I don't know what we'd do without him.'

'Well, I don't know about that,' replied Will, blushing slightly at Hannah's praise.

'It's true,' said Jerry, slapping him on the back. 'You're bloody brilliant. When I don't understand some of the technical building stuff,' he said to Carly, 'I can always rely on Will to explain it to me. He makes me sound like I actually know what I'm talking about.'

'Someone has to,' added Hannah.

'Exactly,' agreed Jerry.

'You just have to be really logical and then it all makes sense,' said Will, shuffling awkwardly in his chair. He obviously didn't enjoy being the subject of the conversation. 'I like solving problems. I like that there's a right answer. Not like what you and Tom do.' He shrugged, looking at Carly. 'You know, all that creative stuff. That needs real talent.'

'Well, that's really kind of you to say,' replied Carly.

'Very kind,' agreed Tom. 'But I think mine has long gone. Carly, however – now she really has got talent,' he gushed.

Laura got up abruptly to clear the dishes away, glaring at Tom in a silent request for help, so that she could get him into the kitchen for a bollocking. Tom ignored her, staying in his seat to silently replenish Carly's glass without her asking. Hannah of course leapt to her aid and followed her into the kitchen with an armful of empty plates. They glanced at each other over the kitchen table, neither knowing what to say first about how the evening was panning out.

'Seems like a nice girl,' offered Hannah.

Laura humphed and then turned to open the dishwasher. 'She probably is,' she replied, crashing forks into the cutlery holder. 'If she was in someone else's house.'

Hannah smiled. 'Not staying for long though, is she?'

'A month I believe,' said Laura, straightening up and slamming the dishwasher door shut. 'Although I haven't actually had the chance to discuss it with my husband yet. He's been slightly preoccupied since he got home.'

'She's just a girl,' said Hannah.

'Precisely. In my house, at my husband's request. Doesn't that strike you as just not right?'

'He's only being kind. She had nowhere to go, right?'

'Being kind?' exploded Laura. 'You offer kindness to people who are suffering, the poor, the needy, people who haven't got what you've got; you don't offer kindness to someone like that,' she raged,

pointing towards the dining room. 'You take imme-
diate dislike to them because they are prettier, thin-
ner, and younger than you are. And you ask them to
move away from you as far as possible. Not move into
your bloody spare room and watch as your husband
fawns all over them. It's wrong to be kind to someone
as beautiful as that. Just wrong.'

'Tom's not like that,' said Hannah.

'He's pouring her wine!'

'So?'

'Without her asking?' Laura exclaimed. 'You do
that for your wife, not a stranger.'

'I think you're being paranoid. It's just wine.'

Maybe she was. Maybe she was overreacting.
She looked at Hannah. Jerry was always like this.
He was forever openly flirting with whichever
female came to hand and yet it never seemed to
bother Hannah. His effusive flattery and sweet-
talking had knocked some much-needed confidence into her when she'd been a cripplingly shy
teenager. Now she didn't seem to mind that even
though they were married he didn't reserve his
compliments just for her.

'Don't rise to it,' advised Hannah. 'You'll create a
problem that doesn't even exist. She'll be gone soon
and that will be that. All back to normal.'

'I'm overthinking it, aren't I?' said Laura.

'Yes,' said Hannah. 'That analytical brain of
yours has added one plus one, and made forty-eight.'

'OK.' Laura tried to slow down her rapid breathing. 'I can do this; you're right. Just let it blow over. I'll put some more white in the fridge, shall I?'

'Good idea. I'll see you back in there, OK?' She gave Laura a reassuring smile and then headed back into the dining room.

Laura put two more bottles in the fridge, took a deep breath and returned to the next room where somehow the dynamic had totally changed since she'd left. Jerry and Hannah were moving glasses at speed across the table. Carly was shifting chairs out of the way and putting them to the side of the room. Will was sitting still, looking slightly concerned at the hive of activity going on around him, and Tom was nowhere to be seen, until he poked his head out from underneath the table.

'What are you doing under there?' asked Laura.

'I'm trying to drop the leaf, but it won't budge.'

'What are you doing that for?'

'Carly's going to show everyone how to do the cha-cha-cha.'

'Why?' demanded Laura, throwing Hannah a panicked look.

'Because Jerry's never done it.'

Laura dropped to her knees and put her head under the tablecloth out of sight of the others. 'Do you really think that's wise?' she hissed.

'It's OK,' replied Tom, still feeling his way round the bottom of the table, trying to find something that would move and cause collapse. 'I know what you're thinking. I know what Jerry's like. He'll be all over her. She's going to demonstrate with Will. There it is. Oops, sorry.'

'Ow,' exclaimed Laura as the table leaf dropped on her head. She crawled out backwards, rubbing the back of her head, to see Carly standing with Will in her arms. Or rather Carly standing with a worried-looking Will in her arms. He shot her a pleading look. How could Tom be such an idiot? This was Will's idea of hell. Will wasn't at all like Tom. At two years older he was an altogether quieter, more practical man, who liked to make things work with his hands, not create beautiful shapes across a dance floor with a vamp-like creature. If Will was ever a contestant on *Strictly Come Dancing* his partner would definitely be forced to make him do the comedy routines where lack of dancing talent was covered up by ridiculous costumes and crazy stunts.

'The first thing we need to do is get the posture right,' announced Carly, pulling Will's arms into position before leaving him stranded. The rolled-up sleeves of his checked shirt didn't suit the elegant, clean stance Carly was trying to achieve; neither did the beard and rugged boots. She walked all the way round him, studying his frame. 'Get that tush in,' she warned, tapping him lightly on the backside of his jeans, to Jerry's roar of approval. 'We need those buttocks high.'

'Friday nights are never going to be the same again, are they?' Jerry said to Laura, laughing.

'Possibly not,' replied Laura, looking at Will's horrified face. His right arm looked awkward, suspended high in mid-air as Carly returned to face him. She grabbed his left elbow, lifting it horizontal to his shoulder. 'You need to keep this arm up here,' she demanded.

'Too high,' Tom cried, having emerged from under the table. 'More like this. Let me show you.' He pushed Will to one side and effortlessly formed an elegant shape with his arms and upper body.

Carly smiled. 'Perfect.'

'My mum taught me,' Tom told her. 'She loved to dance, but Will was never interested. He was too busy taking stuff apart and putting it back together again.'

'Well, maybe I can get him interested now?' Carly searched over her shoulder to see where he was. But Will had spotted his escape route and darted to the other side of the room where he was sitting next to Hannah with his arms firmly crossed.

'Come on, mate,' said Tom, 'you might enjoy it!'

'No.' Will shook his head. 'It's not going to work. Dancing with me is no fun, believe me,' he told Carly. 'I leave all that to Tom. I'll put you a light fitting up or dispose of any dead fish you might have hanging around but don't ask me to dance. I *don't do* dancing.'

'Not even with me?' she asked, painting on a sugary smile.

'Not anyone,' he said firmly.

'Well' – she turned her head back to Tom – 'I shall just have to make do with you then, won't I? Shall we?'

'Don't mind if I do.' He paused to take in the beat of the music and then effortlessly began to twirl Carly around the makeshift, minute dance floor.

'Bravo, bravo. My turn next,' shouted Jerry as they spun again and again. Hannah was talking to Will, no doubt about some work thing; Laura couldn't catch her eye. Was she legitimately allowed to be paranoid yet? Her husband was now dancing with the lodger. Surely that meant this had gone far enough? She kept a fixed grin on her face as the twirling went on and on, trying to look as though she didn't have a care in the world. The song finished and Tom double-dipped Carly as their dance came to an end. Jerry was on his feet applauding wildly.

'I've got it,' he said as the dancing duo straightened up. 'I've just remembered who you remind me of, Carly.'

'You mean Ginger Rogers?' asked Carly coyly, fluffing her hair.

'No, Natalie. Doesn't she remind you of Natalie, Tom?'

Tom visibly froze and Hannah and Will stopped their quiet muttering. Laura stared open-mouthed at Jerry.

'She's got the mannerisms and everything,' continued Jerry. 'She's the image of her, don't you think?'

'Who's Natalie?' asked Carly.

'Tom's ex-fiancée,' replied Jerry.

CHAPTER FOUR
TOM

'Can I come in?' Tom whispered through the closed bathroom door.

No answer.

'Hannah said I should come up and see if you are all right?' He pressed his fingers against the frosted glass and it gave way. He pushed harder and peered inside. Laura was perched on the edge of the bath, her head bent low, hair falling in a curtain over her face. He looked at the toilet longingly. He was bursting to go. He'd not been all night and he'd drunk at least a bottle of wine.

'I'm really sorry, love,' he apologised. 'But I've really got to go.' As he walked over to the toilet he heard a sniff behind him. A big sniff, then another, then another. He glanced over his shoulder. Laura's head was still bent low but her shoulders were now rhythmically heaving and she was showing all the signs of being in full-on crying mode. Oh hell, thought Tom. Now what do I do? He had to go; he was beyond having a choice in the matter and would just have to get it over with as quickly as possible.

'Are you OK?' he shouted once he was in position and had his back turned to her.

No answer.

He looked over his shoulder. She was still crying.

'Please tell me why you are crying?' he asked. She shrugged, her head still bent low.

'Oh shit,' he exclaimed, his concentration having lapsed. He looked down; he'd forgotten to lift the loo seat. This was turning into a logistical nightmare. Now he had to finish his business and wipe the loo seat and then tend to his wife. Or should he finish and find out what was the matter with Laura straight away? No, Laura might shout at him for not raising the loo seat in the first place and would definitely have a go at him for not wiping it.

Put Laura first, he decided, tucking himself away. Deal with the loo seat later. He turned and walked over to Laura and perched beside her.

She sniffed. 'Don't forget to wipe the seat.'

'OK,' he said stiffly. He got up and grabbed some paper. He knew he'd get it wrong.

'So what's up?' he asked after all toilet duties had been taken care of. The hair curtain remained so he couldn't see her face. She shrugged.

'Come on,' he said, putting an arm around her. 'You need to tell me.'

She raised her head to look at him, her eyes rimmed red. 'It's just...it's just...' she began before breaking down again.

Tom felt his heart sink. It usually started with an 'it's just' which would rapidly morph into a recitation of his misdemeanours that she'd been brooding over for the last six months. Things he'd done which he didn't even remember, never mind recognise as something he should be apologising for at some unspecified date in the future. He wished that Laura would sometimes just say exactly what she was thinking there and then rather than using her brilliant analytical brain to over-examine every detail time and again. Unfortunately she tended towards storing her findings until she got to breaking point when the slightest thing would push her over the edge and months' worth of data on his failings would come out in a massive rush.

He racked his brains as to what might have tipped her over this time. Had there been a tense moment that he'd missed? Something he'd forgotten to do that she finally wanted to bring out into the open now she was fortified by copious amounts of red wine? She had been knocking them back tonight, he'd noticed. More so than normal. He stared at the overflowing washing basket opposite them, his Batman pants strewn on the floor. He really liked his Batman pants, he thought idly.

'Is it something I've done?' he asked, deciding to take the direct approach so they could return to the party downstairs before dawn arrived.

Laura shook her head. But he wasn't fooled. He knew at this point in the proceedings, before she managed to overcome her distress and spit out what the problem was, that she would go through the blaming-herself phase. Only after that would the path be clear to make way for the blaming him phase.

'It's not you,' she finally managed to mutter. 'I'm just being silly.'

'Silly about what?' he asked patiently.

She shrugged before the tears came again. He stayed quiet, putting his arm around her, waiting for the mandatory second lot of tears to fade.

He reached forward and got her some loo roll when she appeared to be calming down. She blew her nose and he held out his hand to take her snotty tissue. She smiled weakly at him. He tossed it towards the toilet and missed. He got up and picked it up and put it in the toilet. Even he knew discussion would not begin with a damp piece of toilet roll on the floor. He sat down again and took her hand and waited.

'It's just...' she said again. 'I'm sorry, I'm useless when I cry, aren't I? I just can't get my words out.'

True, he thought.

'It's OK,' he said. 'Take your time.'

'I'm just not very happy with Carly being here,' she finally managed to get out.

'But why?' he replied; he was amazed – in fact quite relieved. So he hadn't done anything wrong. It was Carly who had upset her. Yet he was confused:

'Has she said something to you?' he asked. She seemed so sweet. He was sure she couldn't say anything to upset anyone.

'No, no, of course not,' said Laura. 'It's just you never asked. You know, if she could stay.'

'Oh, I'm so sorry, I really am. I was going to tell you – I really was – when I had the idea but then I realised I'd forgotten my phone.'

'Forgotten your phone,' said Laura simultaneously.

'Yes, that's right, and I can never remember your mobile off the top of my head. I'm sorry, Laura. Really I am.'

'OK.' Laura nodded, tearfully.

'You don't mind though, do you?' he asked. 'We'd talked about getting a lodger for a bit again, hadn't we? I thought this would be perfect as it's not for long.'

Laura looked back at him with red glistening eyes.

'I should have asked first, I get that.' That had been his error, he realised. He should have made sure he called her before landing back on the doorstep and surprising her. She didn't like surprises. 'I'm really sorry,' he said. He took her in his arms and kissed the top of her head. He felt her relax against him and reach her arms around his neck.

'Come downstairs and dance with me,' he said pulling back slightly and giving her a smile. 'I think we're ready to go public with our tango, don't you?'

'No!' she exclaimed. 'No way.'

'Why not?'

'Not after ... I'm not as good as ... No, I just can't, not now.'

Tom sighed. Laura was a lot better than she thought she was and he liked dancing with her. It felt different to dancing with anyone else.

'She's very pretty,' he heard Laura mutter.

'Who is?'

'Carly.'

This was a trap; Tom instantly recognised it. He hadn't been married this long without learning that under no circumstances should you ever comment on another woman's appearance.

'Is she?' he replied. He shrugged. 'S'pose so. You coming?' He stood up and held out his hand.

'I'll just wash my face,' she replied. 'You go, I'll be down in a minute.'

'OK,' he said before reaching forward and hugging her again. He kissed her forehead. 'Don't be long.'

He closed the bathroom door behind him and skipped down the stairs two at a time.

Crisis averted.

CHAPTER FIVE
LAURA

'I'm very disappointed to find you here,' Laura said, peering around the plywood door.

Hannah looked up from the computer in surprise, and took off her glasses. 'I needed to get some paperwork done,' she replied with a shrug.

'But it's Saturday,' stated Laura. 'What are you doing at work on a Saturday? And where's Jerry? Is he here working as well?' She cast her eye around the empty office of Camberwells Construction Ltd.

'No, Jerry is grouse shooting,' replied Hannah.

'Grouse shooting?'

'Yes,' she sighed. 'I told him not to go. I can't stand the thought of all those poor birds dropping out of the sky but you know what he's like. John Pinkerton invited him. You know, the one we built that two-million-pound home for in Chesterton. He can't resist hanging out with that crowd even if it is a bloodbath they're going to.'

'Has he ever been grouse shooting before?'

'No.'

'Does he own a gun?'

'He does now. He went out and bought three, last week.'

'May I borrow one?'

'Of course not.'

'Why not?'

'Well, for a start he's not allowed to tell me where the key to the gun safe is.'

'Who says?'

'The police.'

'Why?'

'In case I decide I want to kill him. Apparently they specifically state that a husband should not allow a wife access to a gun.'

'Very sensible.'

'I agree,' replied Hannah. 'Having said that, Jerry can't be trusted to hide anything and not immediately forget where, so he's put the gun safe keys on a hook next to the corkscrew. What do you need a gun for anyway?'

'To shoot Tom with, of course,' said Laura, walking over and sitting down on the office chair next to Hannah.

'Oh, that bad eh? I sent him up to see if you were all right – I could tell you were upset. What did he say?'

'Well, for a start, he walked straight past me and went to the toilet.'

'Euurgh, gross.'

'And he didn't lift the seat.'

'Grosser still.'

'Then he apologised for not asking me first if it was all right for Carly to stay.'

'Good,' replied Hannah, nodding.

'And that was it,' said Laura.

'Right,' said Hannah.

'So what do I do?'

'About what exactly?'

'About Natalie.' Laura looked at Hannah expectantly. Hannah was her voice of calm, her voice of reason, who somehow managed to cope with the extremes of Jerry's personality and still stay married. Hannah would tell her what to do.

'What do you mean, Natalie?' asked Hannah, looking very confused.

'Natalie, living in my house. What do I do about her?'

'Erm...' Hannah hesitated, leaning forward and putting her hand on her friend's knee. 'Natalie isn't living in your house,' she said quietly. 'Carly is.'

Laura's hand flew up to her mouth in shock. She had no idea she'd said Natalie. Why had she said Natalie?

'Is that why all this is bothering you so much?' asked Hannah. 'You think that Carly is Natalie.'

'Noooo,' cried Laura. 'Of course not. Because that would make me some seriously screwed-up psycho bitch, wouldn't it?'

Hannah nodded. 'Possibly.'

Laura paused, studying Hannah's face.

'But she does remind you a lot of Natalie, doesn't she?' she blurted out, unable to stop herself.

'No,' replied Hannah.

'Really?' cried Laura. 'But she's young and blonde and beautiful and she can sing and she can dance and she's everything that Natalie was and everything that Tom was totally in love with and engaged to.'

'OK,' said Hannah calmly. 'Let's just take a breath, shall we?'

'OK,' gasped Laura, trying to control her breathing.

'They were twenty-one,' Hannah continued. 'It was eleven years ago. She left him for an extra on *Coronation Street.*'

'He was devastated,' breathed Laura.

'I know,' said Hannah. 'And who got him through it?'

'You never saw him at his worst.' Laura was close to tears now. 'You never had to sit there with your arm around him whilst he sobbed his heart out and told you that he'd never find another woman like Natalie,' she spat out.

'But he did, didn't he?'

'No he didn't,' replied Laura. 'He didn't find another woman like her. He settled for me, his buddy, his mate, his best girl friend, the one he felt comfortable with, the one he could have a laugh with, the one who made him feel better when the love of his life walked out on him.'

'Now you're just being dramatic,' said Hannah.

'Dramatic!'

'And stupid.'

'No I'm not,' said Laura, shaking her head. 'I always knew this would happen. Always. That one day someone more exciting would appear. A dancer or an actress or something. Someone in his profession. And then I'd be history. Who wants to be married to a market research analyst when you can have Britney bloody Spears?'

'He loves you, Laura,' said Hannah.

'Hah, that's what you think. But it's statistically irrelevant.'

'Please don't start giving me your statistics mumbo jumbo now. This is life we are talking about, not maths.'

'No,' stated Laura. 'Think about it. One hundred per cent of people say they are in love when they get married, right? Therefore love is not an indicator of whether a marriage survives. In theory everyone is in love on day one so there must be other factors that impact on whether a couple splits up or not. And do you want to know what one of the most significant factors is?'

'Not really.'

'Occupation,' said Laura. 'The stats clearly show that some professions are more likely to have a marriage end in divorce than others and guess which occupations are right at the top of the list?'

'Oh, please tell me,' replied Hannah.

'Dancers, singers, actors, entertainers, that's who. I totally married into the wrong profession. I should have married an engineer. Only 0.02 per cent of engineers ever get a divorce.'

'But Tom isn't an engineer,' Hannah said.

'Precisely,' answered Laura. 'That's what I've been saying. I've always known he was in a high-risk category and, with his track record, we are doomed.'

'What track record?'

'Of being in love with Natalie.'

Hannah looked back at her blankly.

'Who was a dancer,' said Laura, starting to feel slightly frustrated with her friend. 'We already know he really likes dancers. I struggle to get the Macarena right.'

'Have you got a headache?' asked Hannah.

'No.'

'Well, you're giving me one.'

'Sorry,' said Laura, dropping her head. 'I just have a really bad feeling about Nat— I mean Carly.'

'So you are assuming that just because there is a blonde performer who's kind of attractive, if you like that type of thing, living under your roof that your husband is automatically going to fall for her.'

'Yes. And don't forget he works in a high-risk occupation, like I said before.'

Hannah nodded silently. 'I think you're forgetting something actually,' she said.

'What?' gasped Laura. She didn't think she could have forgotten anything; it had been spinning round and round in her head all night as she lay awake reliving the last few hours. From the carefree smile plastered all over his face when she'd first opened the door and found them swaying gently on their doorstep, to the way he'd held her as they demonstrated an effortless cha-cha-cha. A very far cry from her desperate attempts to be an equal match during their clunky late-night tango efforts. Carly was gently tugging at his heart strings and she didn't feel as though she had a firm enough grip to hold on to him.

To be honest she'd always thought her grip was shaky. It was total chance they'd been thrown together at Wonderland when Laura had joined during her holidays from university. He was by far the best-looking bloke there and she couldn't believe her luck when she was assigned to protect him from over-excited kids when he strolled round the park dressed as Wonderbear, the theme-park mascot. He was a brilliant Wonderbear. He truly made the costume come to life with his animated nodding, pausing, stretching, jumping and listening, but it was a real shame to cover up such a handsome face, she thought. During breaks he would share his dreams of making it to the West End. He wanted to be a stage actor, he told her. That's all he'd ever wanted. He seemed so exciting to her, so driven, so talented, so different to her and her love of facts and figures and her ambition to get her maths degree with no clue as to what she would actually do with it.

He often talked about his girlfriend, Natalie, the lead singer/dancer in all the park's entertainment productions. They were the Posh and Becks of Wonderland, their perfect looks and talent glowing out of them whenever they were together. Laura wasn't jealous as such, she was just happy to be friends with Tom. She knew he was out of her league so friends was a massive bonus.

When Tom and Natalie got engaged, however, she did feel weird. She'd tried to look delighted when – giddy with excitement – he had shared his news with her. And she'd nodded politely, despite the fact she felt a bit sick, when he admitted they were too young but they both knew they would get married eventually, so why wait?

Then one day he didn't turn up. Laura was asked to be Wonderbear whilst Shirley from reception looked after her. Shirley failed to stop a toddler kicking her in the shins, leaving Laura praying for Tom's return the next day. But he didn't come back for three days, leaving Laura battered and bruised by the tiny terrorists running around park. He looked deathly when he eventually walked into the Costume Department, five o'clock shadow almost destroying his glamorous looks.

'What's happened?' she asked. His face immediately crumpled and he fell into her arms sobbing. They sat there for an hour on a bench shielded from the rest of the world by a five-foot-high polystyrene penguin patiently waiting for the Santa Spectacular to come around again in a few months' time. He poured out a sorry tale of a phone call from Natalie to say she was in Blackpool having taken a role at the Top of the Tower Show. She thought they should call their engagement off, as she didn't think she could cope with a long-distance relationship. He'd begged to go and see her, to sort it out and despite the fact she'd said no, he'd got on a train to go and find her and ask her to reconsider. He'd found her in a bedsit shacked up with Bobby who spent all day every day supping pints in the Rovers on the set of *Coronation Street*. She'd met him at an audition for extras in *Hollyoaks* five months ago. Tom had come back to Wonderland devastated, only to discover the rumour mill had already kicked into action that they'd split up, at which point both Captain Bill and Fisherman Ted from the Party Pirate Show confessed they'd been shagging her all along and he was well shot of her.

Laura patiently listened to his outpouring, saying sympathetic words when required whilst inside thinking what an utter bitch and how could she possibly do that to someone as wonderful as Tom. It didn't cross her mind once then that it left him wide open for her to move in. He was premiership and she was possibly, on a good day, league one.

'What have I forgotten?' Laura asked Hannah. 'Tell me what else could make it even more inevitable that Tom will fall for Carly?'

Hannah looked away; then she returned her gaze to Laura. 'He's a man.'

'Jesus,' breathed Laura. 'I'm totally screwed.'

'Talk to him,' advised Hannah.

'What do I say?' moaned Laura. 'I'd like the cheerleader to move out of my house because she's too damned beautiful and she looks a bit like your ex-fiancée and I can't hack it. How would that sound?'

'Totally paranoid and extremely insecure.'

'Precisely.'

'You know the problem with being totally paranoid and completely insecure?'

'What?'

'You can't do anything about it.'

'Excellent, Hannah. Really, really helpful.'

'You're welcome. Look, Tom isn't like that. He's married to you. Just don't make her feel too welcome. She's only stopping for a month, isn't she? She can't do that much harm in a month, surely?'

'I keep having vivid nightmares that I'll come home and they'll be doing the paso doble all over the kitchen table.'

'Like I said, not a lot you can do about paranoia and insecurity,' replied Hannah, looking up at the clock on the wall.

'Oh, I'm sorry,' said Laura, getting up. 'I'm distracting you from your work. It's bad enough being in work on a Saturday without me coming in and pestering you.'

'It's OK.' Hannah smiled. 'I ... ' But she didn't get the chance to continue as the office door opened and someone shouted a cheery 'hello'.

'Will!' cried Laura when he came into view. 'Jerry hasn't got you working on a Saturday as well, has he?'

'We're going through the electricians' wages spreadsheet,' interrupted Hannah, throwing a resigned smile in Will's direction. 'It's easier to do when no one's around and we don't get interrupted.'

'Oh,' said Laura. 'Well, I'd better get out of your way then or else *I'll* be interrupting you.'

'No, no,' said Hannah, waving at Laura to sit down again.

'No, it's fine,' added Will easily.

'No, I'll let you get on,' Laura said, grabbing her bag. 'I should be off anyway. I've bent your ear for long enough. Hannah and I were just catching up about last night,' she told Will.

'What about last night?' he asked, sitting down at his desk next to Hannah's.

'Well,' Laura began, wondering what to share. 'It was different, wasn't it? Having an added guest at our usual Friday-night gathering.'

Will shrugged his shoulders. He was a functional speaker. He mostly used words to make useful things happen, not to express emotions or – heaven forbid – for idle tittle-tattle.

'What did you think of Carly?' she asked when he made no further comment.

Will looked at her in confusion as if it was ridiculous to be asking his opinion on such a thing.

'She was all right, I suppose,' he said eventually, 'if you like that sort of thing.'

Laura nodded, her brow furrowed as though he had imparted some strange wisdom. 'So you didn't like her?' she pressed.

'No, I didn't say that,' said Will. He glanced at Hannah as if seeking guidance. But Hannah chose to make matters worse.

'So you do like her then?' she asked.

'No, no,' replied Will, looking trapped as he glanced between both women. 'She seemed perfectly nice but... but... not really my cup of tea. You know, a bit young and, er, too *dancey* for me.'

'You see,' said Laura to Hannah. 'Should have married an electrician.'

CHAPTER SIX
HANNAH

'Coffee?' Hannah asked Will a few minutes later when Laura had finally gone.

'Sure.' He looked away, tapping into his computer.

'Sorry about the inquisition,' said Hannah. 'It's just that Laura has got herself into a bit of a tizz about Carly. Thinks Tom's going to end up running off with her or something. I was trying to get her to see that just because she's a dancer that doesn't mean all men will instantly fall at her feet.'

'Fine.' He shrugged, without looking at her.

Hannah studied his stony face. She was worried they may have upset him somehow. Will wasn't really one for displaying his emotions so when he did you knew it was serious.

'I didn't mean to embarrass you,' she continued. 'Who you might or might not be attracted to is really none of my business.'

'It's fine, seriously,' he replied, turning to look at her.

He didn't look fine. He looked troubled. He looked like he was about to say something. She waited. Perhaps he needed to get something off his chest.

'There is s...someone,' he finally stuttered.

'Well, that's brilliant,' said Hannah, feeling relieved. To be honest they'd all been wondering about him. He didn't seem to have had a girlfriend for ages. 'Why didn't you say? But you don't have to tell me. I understand if you want to keep her to yourself.'

'But it's never going to happen,' he continued, shaking his head and looking away.

'Why?' Hannah asked. Will was a good-looking, likable man. She'd never understood why someone hadn't snapped him up long ago.

He swallowed hard. 'It just won't,' he said.

'Have you said anything to her?' she asked, puzzled.

'I can't.'

'But you should. Have some confidence. What have you got to lose?'

Will didn't say anything, just stared back at her. Clearly whatever he was thinking he felt he couldn't share with her.

'Just tell her,' she urged. 'Go on, go home and give her a call or text her or whatever you do these days. But not until we've sorted this spreadsheet, mind. You don't get off that easily.'

He gave her one last lingering look and then laughed. She was relieved to see his troubled expression disappear. Whoever this girl was she must be something special.

CHAPTER SEVEN

LAURA

'Are you coming? It's starting,' Laura bellowed from her seat on the sofa in the lounge. She caught sight of the pink carnations on the mantelpiece that Tom had greeted her with after she'd been to see Hannah that morning. She sighed and for the first time since last night's arrival she felt herself relax.

'I should have rung and asked you first,' he'd said, thrusting the flowers into her hand. 'I'm so sorry.'

Carnations were her least favourite flower but she knew it was the thought that counted.

'Thanks,' she said, forcing a smile.

'I took Carly to the station,' he said gravely. 'Rehearsals start on Tuesday so I told her we'd see her on Monday. She insisted on paying the rent in advance.' He handed over a wad of notes from his back pocket.

She swallowed, taken aback at how much money there appeared to be.

'I'll put it in the baby fund,' she said, looking at the cash in her hand.

'Good idea,' he enthused. 'Maybe by the time Carly has gone, we might be able to start thinking about what we need to buy with that fund?'

She looked back up at him. His smile was utterly devastating. 'I really hope so,' she said, gazing at him.

'So do I,' he replied, softly.

'Really?' she asked.

'Of course,' he said, putting his arms around her and pulling her in close. 'I can't wait,' he said into her hair. 'I really can't. But in the meantime I'm very happy to keep practising.'

She grinned and some of the tension that had built up over the last twenty-four hours drained out of her. Maybe it was going to be all right. Maybe she was worrying about nothing. She breathed in his warm familiar smell and then pulled away.

'Chinese tonight?' she asked.

He laughed. 'You read my mind,' he replied.

By early evening, the two of them were crammed on the sofa eating off plates on their knees as the usual ritual of watching Saturday night telly with a takeway unfolded. The familiar theme tune struck up and she glanced over at Tom feeling content, something she would not have predicted a few hours earlier.

'Do we have everything to hand?' asked Tom glancing around. 'Food, wine, my favourite lady beside me and dancing on the telly.'

'I believe everything is in place.' Laura grinned happily. 'Can't believe we are in week four already,' she added, waving a chopstick at the TV as all the stars of *Strictly Come Dancing* popped up on the screen during the opening credits. 'I really feel for Chris Whatshisname, don't you? You'd be gutted if you went out in week one. Everyone's forgotten him already.'

'I'd be ashamed,' replied Tom. 'He deserves to be forgotten. And as for Patrick – he'd better be in the dance-off this week. His jive was just embarrassing. I want to see him gone before the Halloween show starts.'

'Oh no,' cried Laura. 'I'd forgotten your show clashes with *Strictly*.'

'It's only two weekends but you will record it, won't you, and promise not to watch it without me?'

'Will you miss my hugely insightful commentary if I don't watch it with you?' she asked.

'You mean your opinions on the outfits and who's had Botox?'

'Exactly.'

'Of course I would. Now shhh, Darcey Bussell is speaking.'

Laura listened to Darcey's expectations for the evening before looking down to help herself to more food.

'Damn,' she exclaimed. She'd dropped sweet and sour sauce on her lap. 'That's going to stain. Did you bring the kitchen roll in?'

'Sorry, no,' replied Tom, without taking his eyes off the screen.

'Won't be a sec,' she muttered, easing herself off the sofa to go and find a cloth.

By the time she had come back the first couple were already dancing. She picked up her plate and wedged herself back on to the sofa.

'Can you pass me the wine?' asked Laura, noticing her empty glass.

'Just a minute,' said Tom, mesmerised by the dancers on screen.

Laura shooed away the memory of Tom topping up Carly's glass without being asked to the night before. She leant forward to grab some more prawn crackers before Tom absent-mindedly polished them off.

'She let her top line fall halfway through,' said Tom, shaking his head as the couple on screen took their bows. 'And she forgot all about her heel leads, don't you think?' He looked over as Laura held up her wine glass expectantly.

'Sorry,' he said, reaching down his side of the sofa and handing her the bottle, forcing her to precariously balance her plate on her knee whilst pouring wine into her glass.

'Did *you* notice her heel leads?' he asked again.

She nodded, taking a gulp of wine. She hadn't noticed the heel leads but she'd had time to note that, in her opinion, the split up the thigh of the woman's dress was perhaps inappropriate for someone of her age.

They both shouted out their scores as the judges gave their verdict. Laura awarded a safe seven, which seemed to be in line with the critics on screen as well as the one sitting next to her in her living room.

'Yeah, it's Selina next,' said Tom, as the ex-Olympic athlete posed on the dance floor with the very handsome professional dancer, Besnik from Albania. 'I reckon Selina should nail a tango. She's a natural.'

'Just like me, eh?' muttered Laura, taking another glug of wine.

'Just like you,' agreed Tom, flashing her his dimples.

Laura glowed and picked up a spare rib as they both fell into silence watching the pair go through their routine. To Laura's untrained eye they looked spectacular as they proudly strutted around the dance floor, changing direction with quick clean steps; she marvelled at how anyone could make their bodies move together that way. In a final impassioned movement Besnik flung Selina across the floor and she slid to a halt in front of the judges, casting them a victorious glare.

'Wow,' said Tom, putting his plate on the floor and standing up to applaud the couple. 'That was close to perfection.'

Laura watched as Besnik stalked across the floor to take Selina's hand and pull her to feet. They maintained their dance faces to take a bow and then broke into rapturous beams in response to the standing ovation erupting around them in the studio.

'They are so sleeping together,' said Laura, wiping her sticky fingers on a piece of kitchen towel.

Tom sat down and picked up his food. 'Do you think so? You always say that. They're just doing a job.'

'A job that requires them to touch each other all the time,' replied Laura raising her eyebrows.

'You don't *have* to be shagging to dance like that. It's just part of the performance.'

Laura turned back to the screen to watch Selina and Besnik as they embraced, kissing and hugging, twirling round and round, never taking their eyes or their hands off each other. If you'd seen a newly-wed bride and groom look as happy or as in love you would have done well.

'So you don't think they have feelings for one another?' asked Laura.

'Probably not.'

'Probably?'

'Well, I can't be sure, can I, but just because you dance together doesn't mean it's going to lead to anything.'

'But it does though, doesn't it, quite often?'

'Occasionally, I guess.'

'How often is occasionally?' asked Laura. 'Let's take your department, for example. How many of your performers arrive single and then end up dating a fellow performer. I bet it's high, right? Like over fifty per cent?'

'I don't know.' Tom shrugged. 'They're all at it as far as I can tell, to be honest.'

'All at it?'

He shrugged again, digging his chopsticks into some chow mein. 'They're all young and good-looking, aren't they? Bound to happen.'

'And they get to spend all day every day touching each other's bodies,' added Laura.

Tom looked baffled. 'It's not like some orgy down there every day.'

'So how many times did it happen to you?' she asked.

'What?'

'You falling for someone you danced with?'

He stuffed some chow mein in his mouth half-way through her question. Laura kept looking at him until his mouth was empty and he could give a response.

'A few times,' he said, reaching forward to grab his wine and taking a big gulp.

'A few?'

He shrugged. 'Yeah.'

She looked away. She'd only ever been aware of Natalie in his past. It had never crossed her mind that of course he must have had girlfriends before her.

'In fact all my girlfriends have been dancers apart from you. You saved me!' He grinned. 'Thank the

Lord,' he said, raising his eyes to the ceiling. Then he caught sight of the TV screen again. 'Oh my God, Patrick's on. Let's see how much he can screw it up this week.'

Laura stared at him for a moment before putting her plate down on the coffee table, no longer hungry.

CHAPTER EIGHT
TOM

Tom leant forward and banged his head on the boardroom table.

'Tom!' exclaimed Hazel. 'What is the matter?'

Tom slowly raised his head and gazed into Hazel Gough's eyes. She was wearing eye shadow. He should have known their fifty-five-year-old, people-hating, undiplomatic, indiscreet and yet head of Human Resources only ever wore eye shadow when she knew she had a presenting slot during the regular Monday-morning management meeting. He thought enduring the usual pointless debate about the state of the previous week's visitor numbers (including a twenty-minute discussion about why the north-west coach market was in decline) was bad enough. But a meeting when HR was given licence to blind the entire management team with a slew of unnecessary paperwork they had dreamt up to prevent anyone from being able to get on with their real jobs was sheer torture.

Hazel's eyes were still boring into him and he realised he had to respond.

He looked around the room for a glimmer of revolt, a sense of camaraderie, or just any sign of support that it would be acceptable to tell Hazel exactly what the problem was. But the General Manager was also giving him a disapproving glare. Head of Operations was flicking through some paperwork mentally rehearsing his response to whatever complaints might have been caused by his team that week. The Head of Food and Beverages was tapping her pen on the table keen to get it over with so she could go and work out how on earth she was going to open all her units given the huge amount of absences that had called in that morning. Only his mate Sam, Head of Technical Services, was grinning at him whilst fiddling with his radio, itching to get a call that he was urgently needed on park so he could escape the tedium of Hazel.

'Do you need some air?' asked Hazel tersely.

'Yeeeees,' exclaimed Tom, just stopping short of doing a fist pump.

'Bastard,' he heard Sam mutter under his breath.

'Yes, I do need some air,' Tom said, leaping up and gathering his papers at rapid speed. 'Been feeling a bit odd all morning, to be honest. Thank you, Hazel. You are so right. I need fresh air.' He was already walking to the door as fast as he could when she called after him.

'I'll drop by your office later and take you through the Y2H Health Benefits Rights Form and the Casual

Dress Awareness Review Away Day that you need to prepare for,' she shouted.

'Thanks, Haze.' He waved over his shoulder. 'If I'm not there then talk Amy through it.'

He shut the heavy door behind him and leant against it, heaving a sigh of relief. He turned round and peered though a small glass pane three-quarters of the way up. Hazel was already in full flow, undeterred by the blank looks being directed her way. Sam was waving two fingers at Tom out of Hazel's eyeline whilst trying to look as though he was listening. Tom gave him a thumbs up and dashed back to his office.

'Good meeting?' asked Amy, when he banged his notepad on the desk and reached for his coat.

Tom grinned. 'Excellent. Hazel gave me a pass-out.'

'What!' exclaimed Amy. 'Doesn't sound like the old bat.'

'She thought I might pass out so she gave me a pass-out. Best meeting ever.'

'Oh,' Amy grunted, before looking back at her computer. She looked different today but Tom couldn't work out why. 'Louise rang,' she added. 'She's refusing to use fishnet stockings for the female sexy zombie costumes. She says it's sexist and against her feminist principles. And that we as a market leader should be making a stand and not succumbing to traditional stereotypes.'

Tom stared at Amy, at a loss at what to say. Amy blinked back at him expectantly. When he didn't reply she put the words in his mouth as she quite often did.

'I told her to put the male zombies in fishnets as well.'

'Genius,' exclaimed Tom. 'What did she say?'

'She said that wasn't the point she was making.'

'What did you say?'

'I said if she had a problem with costume design then perhaps she shouldn't work in costume?'

Tom nodded. 'Again, genius.'

'And perhaps she should therefore consider herself more suited to a position serving hamburgers since there is nothing remotely sexy or sexist about a polo shirt, elasticated trousers and a hairnet.'

Tom gasped. 'What did she say to that?'

'She put the phone down on me.'

'Amy,' declared Tom, putting his hand on her shoulder, 'an excellent morning's work.'

Amy blushed slightly and shrugged, pretending to scrutinise something on her screen.

'Right, seeing as you've got it all under control here, I'm going on park,' Tom told her, grabbing a litter-picker. 'To, er, go and check out how the Halloween set build is coming along.'

'Say hello to Jerry,' said Amy, turning to face him.

'How do you know I'm going to see Jerry?'

'Because you only take a litter-picker if you are skiving off somewhere but want to look like you are busy and still willing to muck in with everyone and pick up litter. If you're really going out to do something you don't bother.'

Tom looked down at the metal extended claw in his hand. How come he was so transparent? He carefully put it back in the corner.

'I'm going out to see how the building of the Halloween set is coming along,' he repeated.

'Say hello to Jerry,' replied Amy.

'I will,' he said and left at speed for the second time that morning.

It took Tom fifteen minutes to walk across the park to a wooded area located next to the Wonderland Hotel. There was six-foot-high hoarding surrounding the area and an intimidating number of men walking around in hard hats and yellow high-visibility jackets. There had been much cause for celebration when Jerry's firm had secured the contract to build twenty-five woodland lodges for guests who wished to extend their stay on park. Tom was delighted that he suddenly had a bolt-hole he could disappear to when his work got too depressing and Jerry was very happy to have a project so close to home. He was taking full advantage of being able to legitimately escape the office on the edge of town and avoid any administrative duties that Hannah tried to put in his path.

As Tom walked through the site-access gate he bent his head low, trying to avoid all eye contact with the hard-hat men scattered everywhere. However many times he visited, he never stopped feeling less of a man when he stepped into the macho environment of the building site. He was so intimidated by those who could do the manly things he couldn't – like drive an enormous beast of a digger when he could barely work a domestic drill. As they strutted around in their steel-toecapped boots and neon jackets he knew what they were thinking: that you're not a real man if your job doesn't require you to wear a hi-vis vest.

Tom tiptoed around the huge muddy tracks in his immaculately polished, on-trend brown brogues and prayed that he wouldn't fall over. The humiliation, surrounded by so much testosterone, would be too much to bear. Breathing a sigh of relief, he reached the Portakabin which acted as the site office and hoped that it would be empty apart from Jerry and he wouldn't get the an-alien-has-landed looks from the real workers.

Thankfully Jerry was sitting there alone with his steel toecaps up on an untidy makeshift desk, his red hard hat set at a jaunty angle and a mobile phone glued to his ear.

He motioned Tom to take a seat and stood up, hauling his canvas trousers up over his protruding belly. Somehow, despite his outfit, Jerry never intimidated Tom. Probably because Tom knew that Jerry never really got out there and dirtied his hands doing the real work. Jerry was definitely the outward face of the company; his skills lay in schmoozing prospective clients rather than any of the actual heavy lifting.

'You are an utter dog,' cackled Jerry into the phone. 'And a dirty dog at that. If I'd been Kempy I'd have left you there, I can tell you. At least until you'd dried out...

'No way was I as bad, you lying fucker,' he continued down the line after a comment. 'I was completely sober...

'Fuck off. I never did that, did I?' Jerry collapsed in hysterics. 'Pair of dirty dogs, you're right. Now, I can't waste any more of my extremely valuable time chatting with you, my next appointment's just arrived.' He winked at Tom.

'Yes, it's someone way more important than you. Now piss off and I'll get the office to send those contracts out today. See you. Bye.'

'Who was that?' asked Tom, wandering over to a site plan on the wall.

'Richard Marsh. Ops Director for Horncliffe Hotels. I think I hooked him for another new build during that shooting thing I went to at the weekend.'

'Good.' Tom nodded. 'When do you reckon our chalets will be done then?'

'Chalets!' exclaimed Jerry. 'We don't build chalets, Tom, these are dreams. This development is fulfilling every middle-class family's desire to shell out a fortune to stay in a wooden shed.'

Tom smiled.

'Honestly, this project is the most bonkers thing I have worked on,' Jerry said in amazement. 'All our conversations are about de-speccing to fit in with this so called "Rustic Theme". We've downgraded the toilets three times and your bosses still aren't happy. But it's hard to source a rustic toilet. Where would you go for a rustic toilet?'

'The loos in the Celebration Theatre could be described as rustic, if not decrepit. Take one of them out and show them. Put new loos in the theatre.'

'Do you know what? I might,' said Jerry, getting up. 'Rustic toilets – I ask you. Tea?'

'Yeah, decaf please.' The minute he said it he knew he'd made a mistake.

'For fuck's sake, Tom, decaf?'

'I know, I'm sorry, I wasn't thinking.' He looked around the empty room nervously in case anyone else had overheard his error. 'I'll have whatever you're having.'

'Obviously,' replied Jerry, sloshing hot water out of a filthy kettle over two teabags in enormous mugs. 'So did you get my text?' he asked.

'Which one?'

'The one I sent you on Saturday morning.'

Tom cast his mind back. Jerry was a prolific texter. If his ear wasn't glued to his phone his finger was. 'Doesn't really narrow it down,' he said.

'Why do you never reply to my texts?' asked Jerry.

'Because I need time to eat and sleep and have a life.'

Jerry threw him a confused look, picked up his phone and started to scroll through it.

'It said: *What a night. How the bloody hell have you got away with that you sly dog?*'

'And what is *that* referring to?' asked Tom. This was exactly why Tom chose to ignore most of Jerry's texts: they often came with no explanation for whatever was going through Jerry's mind.

'Carly, of course,' he said, slamming down Tom's tea in front of him. 'I have to say I'm seriously impressed, mate. Takes some balls, that does.'

'What does?'

'Are you serious? Moving a hot piece of stuff in like that. Under your wife's nose. Fucking awesome. I told all the guys at the shoot about it; they literally took their deerstalkers off to you. You are a fucking legend.' Jerry raised his mug to chink against Tom's. Tom stared back at him.

'She had nowhere to stay.' He picked up his mug and instantly scalded his lips. 'We're just helping her out, that's all.'

'Well, helping her out of something is what I'd like to do.'

'Jerry. Do you have to?'

'Oh come on, Tom, you can't say it hasn't crossed your mind, seriously? She's a babe.'

Tom shrugged, blowing on his tea. 'OK, she's pretty, I guess.'

'Are you real?' replied Jerry. 'She's stunning, and … and her moves when she was dancing – oh my

God – in your dining room, I thought I'd died and gone to heaven for a minute there.'

'Well, I guess I'm around dancers all the time so you kind of get used to all that.'

'What, the near-nakedness, the perfect bodies, the sheer… *bendiness* – you can't get used to that, surely? That decaf shit must be doing something to your manhood.'

Tom couldn't deny that the odd exciting thought did pop into his brain every now and then but he thought he'd learnt to shove them to one side and get on with the job.

'They're just people like you and me.'

'If I had a body like that I'd love myself even more than I do now.'

'Not possible,' said Tom, shaking his head.

'But fair play to you, mate, for getting her in the door past Laura. Oh my God, what I would have given to see her face when you arrived home with that.'

'She's totally fine about it. Sure, she was a bit upset that I didn't ask her first but apart from that she's chuffed to bits with the extra money and it's not for long anyway.'

'She really thinks that?' asked Jerry.

'Yes. She's absolutely fine. No problem with it at all.'

'Not even the fact that Carly looks frighteningly like Natalie?'

'She doesn't look a bit like Natalie.'

'Oh come on, Tom, she's the image of her. Must be freaking Laura out that you've brought a younger version of your ex-fiancée into the marital home.'

'She doesn't look anything like her and so what if she did. Natalie's history: you know that; Laura knows that. Don't know why you're even bringing her up.'

'She still sending you Christmas cards?'

'Yeah.' Tom shrugged again. 'It's just a Christmas card.'

'Does Laura know she still sends you a Christmas card?'

'No. I don't see the point in having to raise the subject of Natalie every flipping year for no reason. The card comes to work, I open it, read what she's been up to then put it in the bin.'

'Right.' Jerry nodded. 'Mmmmm.'

'Why are you looking at me like that?' asked Tom. 'I'm not doing anything wrong. I'm helping someone out and you're acting as if I've invited the leaders of al-Qaeda to move in.'

Jerry shook his head and drew his breath in through his teeth. 'This is women we're talking about,' he said. 'A known terrorist moving in may have been preferable to a beautiful woman.'

'You're worrying about nothing,' said Tom. 'Besides, I have other hopes for Carly.'

Jerry's eyes flew wide open.

'Will,' declared Tom.

'Will!'

'Yes, Will,' replied Tom.

'...and Carly?'

'Yeah.' Tom nodded vigorously. 'He needs a woman. I'm worried about him.'

'He needs a shag is what he needs.'

'Has he mentioned a girlfriend at all?' asked Tom.

Jerry shook his head. 'Four-eyes Chloe was all over him for a while. You know, who does the accounts in the office?'

'You've mentioned her in a derogatory manner before, I believe.'

'She's such a nag and she looks over her specs at me in a weird way when I don't have the paperwork she wants.'

'So she's just trying to do her job?'

'Well, yes, but I'm paying her and I certainly don't pay her to nag me. Anyway, when I got Will a desk in the office so he had somewhere to do his paperwork, Chloe looked like all her Christmases had come at once. She was all over him. It was great, got her off my back for a bit. I told him he should take advantage and he looked at me like I'd told him to stick his hands in a cement mixer.'

Tom shook his head. 'Perhaps he's got one on the go and not told me. I wouldn't put it past him. He's can be very secretive. I don't know half of what he's up to at times. Mum rings me if she wants to know what he's doing – not that I'm much help.'

'Well, I've not spotted him making a fuss of anyone at work,' said Jerry.

'Unlike you, you mean,' said Tom. 'Fussing up to anything on two legs despite the fact you're married. You were a bit full on with Carly on Friday night if I'm honest, even for your standards.'

'Blah.' Jerry threw his hands up. 'That's just me, isn't it? I don't mean anything by it. Hannah knows what she signed up for.'

'Yes, well, I'd prefer it if it was Will giving her the eye and not you. I think she's just what Will needs. If she can't get him interested then no one can.'

Jerry raised his eyebrows at Tom. 'Whatever it is you're trying to achieve with this apparently innocent move – inviting a beautiful stranger into your house – it's got trouble written all over it. Major trouble.' Jerry stood and picked up the empty mugs. 'But you clearly know what you're doing,' he added with a grin. 'And I will personally enjoy the company of the gorgeous Carly until it all blows up in your face. Friday night at ours as usual then?'

Tom nodded mutely, his brow furrowed.

'Be sure to bring Carly too and let's see if Will takes the bait. Even if he doesn't, it's sure to be an entertaining evening.'

CHAPTER NINE
LAURA

Somebody had left the landing light on. She'd left first that morning so it must have been Tom. She sighed, rifling through her large handbag for her key, past plasters, an opened packet of tissues, expenses receipts and her laptop, which she'd bought home so she could fine-tune a presentation she was doing to a Marketing Director from a large retail chain the following day. She'd left work early and was looking forward to putting the kettle on away from the hustle and bustle of the open-plan office and concentrating her mind on distilling exactly which major points would be most useful to her client. Key located, she plunged it into the lock, her ears pricking up as she pushed her way into the hall. Now that really does take the biscuit, she thought. Tom must have left the TV on as well – or worse the Xbox as she could hear electronic noises coming from the living room. What on earth was he thinking, sneaking a quick go on the Xbox before work? That was addict behaviour – or in his case a way of avoiding going to work until the last possible moment. She dumped her bag in the hall, took off her coat and went into the lounge to go and sort out the chatty Xbox.

'Oh my God,' she said, leaping in surprise when she entered the room.

'Hiya.' Carly waved. She was stretched out languidly on the sofa, eyes glued to the TV screen, Xbox handset glued in her fists. 'Be with you in a sec, just about to get utterly trashed by Atlético Madrid.'

Laura stood awkwardly in her own living room, not knowing what to do or what to think as uncooperative footballers dashed about the screen, looking as though they didn't have a clue what was going on either. She'd been expecting Carly to turn up later that evening, Tom having told her that she could move in on Monday ready for rehearsals on Tuesday. She'd hoped to have the afternoon to go through her presentation as well as mentally prepare herself for Carly's arrival. The last thing she had imagined was arriving home to find her already installed and enjoying the facilities.

'Aaaaaaah,' cried Carly, as a box flashed up on screen announcing defeat. 'I really don't get it. I'll have to ask Tom to tell me what I'm doing wrong. Can I make you a cup of tea?' she asked, leaping up and leaving the controller carelessly behind her on the sofa, just like Tom. 'How do you take it?' Carly stopped in the doorway so that they were standing nose to nose. She was minus the layer of audition make-up she'd been wearing on Friday night. Sadly she still looked flawless.

'White, no sugar,' Laura replied as calmly as she could.

'OK.' Carly smiled. 'Coming right up.'

Laura followed her into the kitchen and stood helplessly next to the table as Carly nonchalantly flicked the switch on the stainless-steel Russell Hobbs kettle that had been Laura and Tom's first purchase when they moved in together. The kettle that Laura prayed every day would break so she could buy a purple one to match the toaster. She watched as Carly grabbed two mugs off the mug tree and threw in two teabags. Laura sat down in the chair opposite the sink, oven and fridge. She didn't think she'd ever sat on that side of the kitchen table for the entire four years they'd lived there and now she noticed with horror that in this light, even at a distance, the oven splashback was filthy.

Carly turned and handed Laura one of the Cath Kidston flowery mugs that had looked cool three years ago when she'd bought them in an over-priced gift shop but now just looked old-fashioned and chintzy, especially in the hands of the twenty-something opposite her.

'So how was work?' asked Carly, settling herself down.

'Fine,' replied Laura, picking up the mug and taking a gulp of scolding hot tea.

'I'm so sorry,' Carly continued, 'but on Friday I don't think I asked you what you actually do. It was such a lovely evening I got a bit carried away, I'm afraid.' She laughed. 'So nice, you know, to spend time with *normal p*eople.'

'Normal?' said Laura, unable to stop her eyebrows shooting up.

'Yeah, you know. Not theatrical types. They can be just so…theatrical. It can be totally exhausting.'

'Yes, well, as you've no doubt noticed I don't have a theatrical bone in my body.'

'Oh absolutely,' replied Carly. 'You are clearly very normal.'

Laura's eyebrows shot up further.

'Which is great,' Carly went on. 'Refreshing.'

Laura chose not to reply.

'So what do you do then?' asked Carly. 'That allows you to be so refreshingly normal?'

Laura swallowed. 'I'm a market research analyst.'

Carly nodded but clearly was none the wiser as to Laura's occupation.

'I review data and make sense of it,' continued Laura.

'Brilliant,' said Carly cheerfully.

'It could be existing data: the internet has transformed the availability of information so we now spend a lot of our time collating and analysing information for our clients online,' Laura informed Carly. 'But that usually leads to more specific research requests at which point we come up with detailed plans and methodologies that give our clients answers to the questions that will help drive their business forward.'

Carly stared back at her blankly.

'We find the answers to the questions that drive our clients' businesses forward and allow them to grow and flourish,' said Laura. 'That's our mission statement.'

'Wow,' replied Carly. 'Sounds super important.'

'I actually think it is,' replied Laura, feeling her shoulders rise.

'You must think what I do is kind of pointless?'

'No,' Laura responded immediately. 'Of course not.' Damn that politeness gene, she thought. 'You entertain. That's important.'

'Do you really think so?' asked Carly.

'Well, yes,' said Laura. 'Tom obviously works in entertainment, so of course I think it's important.'

Carly nodded. 'He's a really good dancer,' she added distractedly.

'Well, he used to do what you do,' said Laura. 'He did perform, before he got promoted.'

'Oh, really? That makes sense now. So does he ever perform any more?'

'No.' Laura shook her head. 'He was lucky. He got offered a management position. It worked out really well because it meant he had a permanent contract and because, well...' She paused, wondering if she should proceed. '...we knew we wanted a family at some point and he might have had to start looking for work elsewhere, which is hard when you have kids, isn't it?'

'I understand,' replied Carly, having nodded throughout. 'Married men don't stay married long in entertainment.'

Laura gasped. She hadn't expected Carly to spell out her worst fear quite so bluntly. 'Yes, well,' she stumbled. 'Statistically that is actually true.'

'You see it all the time,' continued Carly, clearly oblivious to Laura's pale face. 'In particular married men working away from home for long stints – a recipe for disaster.'

'Exactly,' agreed Laura.

'They come on to me all the time,' added Carly, shaking her head. 'Occupational hazard, I guess.' She shrugged, getting up and putting her mug in the sink.

Could you not just put it in the dishwasher? thought Laura. Who's going to do that for you? The washing-up fairy? Carly turned back to face her.

'You're right,' she went on.

'About what?'

'You're very lucky,' she said, casting her eyes around the kitchen. 'Mind if I wash my hair?'

'No,' replied Laura and watched her leave the room, the mug still in the sink.

'Where've you been?' cried Laura the minute Tom walked through the door. She was running around the hall like a whirlwind, trying to gather her things whilst also avoiding acknowledging the hideous occurrence that was somehow taking place in her kitchen.

'Work, sadly.' Tom shrugged, taking his coat off. 'Got a bit held up getting everything ready for rehearsals tomorrow.'

Bloody Halloween, thought Laura. If it weren't for that, Carly would never have entered their lives and she wouldn't be hiding in the hall whilst Carly played domestic bloody goddess in her kitchen.

'You remember I'm out tonight,' said Laura.

'Really? Going anywhere nice?'

'It's Zumba,' spat out Laura. 'Remember, I go every Monday night?'

'Oh yeah,' said Tom vacantly. 'Zumba, cool. What's for tea?'

There might just be a Halloween bloodbath right here in their hall, thought Laura, ignoring his question. Tom glanced over at her when she didn't respond.

'I mean what's for tea so I can make it, of course,' he added quickly. He smiled at her innocently.

'There's no need,' replied Laura, through gritted teeth.

'Oh, why's that?' He looked confused at her tone.

Laura stared at him. She could have quite happily burst into tears. 'Because Carly's already made it.'

Tom's eyes widened. 'Wow,' he said. 'She's an angel. See, I told you it would be really helpful to have her around.' He brushed past Laura to go into the kitchen.

'Hiya,' she heard him announce cheerily. 'Wow, that looks delicious. We didn't expect you to cook on your first night, did we, Laura?' he shouted through the door.

'It's no bother,' she heard Carly say. 'I love cooking. Take a seat. I bet you're starving.'

Laura turned round and strode into the kitchen.

'How cool is this, eh?' said Tom, having settled himself at the table. 'Having your tea cooked for you in your own home. Just brilliant.'

Laura didn't know how to point out to him that actually he had his tea cooked for him almost every night in his own home ... by *her*, apart from on the odd night when she went out at which point she always got all the ingredients out for him and laid them on the kitchen counter so that even a chimpanzee could cook it. As could Carly, as it had turned out, much to Laura's surprise, when she'd come downstairs having changed into her exercise clothes to discover Carly cooking the shepherd's pie that had been left for Tom to prepare.

'Delicious,' announced Tom after a plateful of steaming pie was put in front of him.

'I've got to go,' said Laura, unable to stand the scene a second longer.

'Don't worry about us. We'll be fine,' she heard Tom shout as she pulled the hall door to behind her.

Chapter Ten
Tom

'She's not a morning person,' said Tom as Carly secured her seatbelt in Tom's car early the next day. They'd just had the most awkward breakfast in the history of the universe. Carly had sat down chatting away happily, bubbling over with excitement about the imminent start of rehearsals, until it had been made clear by Laura's monosyllabic answers and thumping down of cereal bowls and cartons of milk that she wasn't in the slightest bit interested in engaging in early-morning banter with their new lodger. Carly had cast Tom a nervous glance and then stalled her chat to a stop as they all chewed cereal in silence.

'Right.' Carly nodded. 'That's perfectly fine. I'm an all-dayer. Always have been. Gordon used to tell me not to speak until he'd had at least one cup of coffee. If I did start he'd simply hold his hand up and I knew I was driving him nuts already.'

Tom laughed. 'She'll be back to normal tonight. If she's quiet later on then it won't be you, it'll be something I've done and I'll have to deploy interrogation tactics worthy of MI5 to get out of her what's wrong.'

'Gosh,' said Carly, flipping down the visor and carefully applying lipstick whilst looking in the mirror. 'Weird.'

'It's what I call marriage. You'll find out one day.'

'You're not making it sound very tempting.'

'No,' said Tom, shaking his head, suddenly feeling guilty. 'Marriage is great. When it's good it's the best thing in the world, but sometimes there's other crap you seem to have to wade through to get to the good bits.'

He bent to turn the radio on, unwilling to continue with the conversation. He quickly flicked from his usual Radio Two to Radio One to avoid embarrassment in front of his younger passenger.

'So,' said Carly, flipping the visor back up and dropping her lipstick into her bag. 'Less than two weeks to get this show ready. That's kind of scary, hey? I assume you're in this first rehearsal?'

'Unfortunately yes,' he replied.

'Unfortunately?'

'You'll see.' Tom swallowed. He knew he shouldn't share his feelings on first rehearsals. He knew exactly how it would pan out. Having Carly around had distracted him from his usual early-morning despair at the prospect of going into work. Being reminded that it was first-rehearsal day plunged him back into gloom.

'So have you thought about whether we'll tell them or not?' Carly asked after a few minutes of claustrophobic quiet.

Tom glanced sharply at her. 'Tell who what?'

'That we're living together.'

'We're not though really, are we? You're just staying whilst the show is on.'

'I know, but it might seem a bit weird if it gets out and we haven't told anyone.'

Tom knew she was right. If the others in the show got hold of that information there was sure to be drama: he'd be accused of preferential treatment at some stage and it would all end in tears.

'Let's just keep it to ourselves for a while, shall we?' he said. 'Let's not complicate things.'

She shrugged. 'OK.'

'But I'll tell Amy,' Tom said.

'Is she the scary one from the audition?'

'Wasn't I the scary one?' asked Tom, shooting another brief glance at her.

'Oh no,' said Carly. 'You were a pussy cat. She was a horror story.'

'Well, I will need to tell the horror story.'

'You're the boss,' Carly replied leaning down to turn the music up to full blast.

'I've just got something to tell you,' announced Tom as he entered the Celebration Theatre in Back of Beyond World ready for the first rehearsal of *Malice in Wonderland*. Amy was sitting at a table she'd set up in front of the stage and was laying out photographs of the entertainers coming in for the first time that day. Next to her on the table stood a coffee and a bacon bap ready and waiting for Tom.

'What would I do without you,' he said, seizing his mug and sitting down. 'Christ, it's bloody freezing in here.'

'I've switched the heating off to acclimatise everyone for when it breaks down,' said Amy. 'So what do you need to tell me?'

'Right, well, do you remember Carly from last week? The one who blew us away and who we picked for Malice Alice?'

Amy nodded mutely.

'Well,' said Tom, taking a huge bite out of his bacon bap. 'She brooved in wid us. Beeded bumware do fray por a pit.'

Amy didn't reply, just looked at him expectantly.

'Borry,' he said, chewing laboriously until his mouth was empty.

'I said,' he said, wiping brown sauce off his lips. 'She's moved in with us, just so you know. The Cow was full on Friday and she had nowhere to go so I said she could have our spare room and then it seemed to make sense to let her stay until the show is finished; it's only a month.'

Amy said nothing, just stared back at him.

'Thought you should be aware of the situation, that's all,' he continued. 'We're not planning to make it common knowledge, you know what people are like, but we thought you should know.'

Amy nodded again slowly and then stood up, picked up the paper plate with the half-eaten bacon sandwich on it, turned round and, as Tom watched, walked over to the bin and disposed of it. She returned to the table and sat down silently.

'I hadn't finished that,' he said.

'Sorry,' replied Amy, writing something down in her notepad.

That was the second time this morning a woman had stolen his half-eaten breakfast and chucked it away. Laura had snatched his bowl from under his nose before he had finished. Women! He coughed and cleared his throat, looking up to check the array of dropouts he had to attempt to get into shape ready for performing in just twelve days followed by two weeks of live performances every day. He stood up with a sinking feeling in his belly. Here we go again, he thought. Where my dreams fail to become reality.

He stood up, banging his mug on the table, spilling half his coffee in the process. Amy leapt to his aid, miraculously producing copious amount of thin white serviettes to mop up the mess. He smiled gratefully at her and then turned to address his expectant audience. He took a deep breath. Might as well give it his all at this stage, he thought as he surveyed a sea of over thirty faces. Most of them were new but there was also a handful of old faithfuls who were employed throughout the season to deliver entertainments and events; most of them had minimal talent but he didn't have the heart to let them go.

'Welcome, everyone,' he announced, 'to our annual Halloween Extravaganza.' The newbies looked at each other excitedly. Everyone else already looked bored.

'So we have a very exciting show planned for this year which will be staged in this very theatre we are sitting in now.'

'Great,' muttered someone in the front row. 'So we are going to freeze our tits off again to an empty house because no one can be bothered to walk this far.'

Tom chose to ignore this comment. Amy chose to get up and seat herself heavily alongside the heckler, who paled significantly.

'We've got a full schedule planned for today,' continued Tom. 'For the benefit of those of you who have never worked at Wonderland before, Amy here will take you through some general housekeeping basics shortly. For those of you who are part of our more permanent staff it won't hurt to hear it all again.'

There was an audible groan from the room. Amy leant into her neighbour, which halted the noise immediately.

'I will then take you through the concept of *Malice In Wonderland* in detail and after lunch we'll do some improv work around the story to allow us to bond as a company,' Tom ploughed on. 'If we have time we'll start to walk through the show at the end of the day before we begin rehearsals for the main numbers tomorrow. Any questions?'

A man in his twenties on the front row shot up his arm.

'Can I be the Mad Hatter?' he gasped. 'I know I did the rabbit for my audition but I can do a really good Mad Hatter now – let me show you.' The man started to get up.

'No, no, nooo,' said Tom, waving at him to sit down again. 'Nathan, isn't it? Take a seat, mate, hey.' Nathan beamed at him for the recognition and obediently sat down again. Tom glanced over at Amy, confused. Nathan had been in their definite rejects list, he was sure. She shrugged.

'We had a last-minute dropout who'd had his hands cast in an advert for toilet cleaner. Nathan was the only person I could get hold of who could make it today,' she muttered.

Tom turned back to face Nathan. He was too ugly even to be a zombie. 'Parts will be discussed later today,' he said dejectedly. 'I'll hand you over to Amy.' He sat down with a thump and then couldn't help but glance over at Carly. She gave him a cheerful thumbs up; then she slapped her hand as though telling herself off for fraternising with the boss.

'Right,' said Amy, getting up and turning to face the group. 'Listen up. This is important. Nathan, will you hand these out for me?' She waved a thick sheaf of A4 paper at him and he leapt to his feet, keen to be teacher's pet.

'There are three sheets of paper you need to collect. I repeat three,' she announced, holding up three fingers as further confirmation. 'I have photocopied exactly the right amount so if you don't have three different sheets in your hand then someone else has yours and I suggest you find them and ask for it back. I will *not* be copying any more. It is your responsibility to make sure you have these documents. Do I make myself clear?'

'Hell yeah,' squawked Carly with a grin. Amy glared at her.

'Sheet one, on pink paper,' she continued, holding it aloft, 'is your rehearsal schedule. Do not lose it. You will be expected to be at rehearsal at least ten minutes before it is due to start, and stay until Tom says you can go. We operate a zero-tolerance policy on this. Understood?'

'Hell yeah,' repeated Carly. Tom tried hard not to laugh.

'Sheet two, on blue paper,' said Amy, ignoring Carly this time. 'This is the show schedule. You will be expected to be in full costume and make-up at least thirty minutes before curtain-up, understood?'

'Hell yeah,' came back the cry as some of the others decided to be brave enough to join Carly in the response. Amy glared at Carly again, pausing for a few seconds to ensure her displeasure was obvious.

'Do not lose the blue sheet,' she demanded. 'Finally, on the white paper, are the mission and values of the company,' she announced. 'Any questions?' She sat down abruptly before Carly could steal her thunder any more. However, Carly was the first to stick her hand up. Amy nodded tersely to indicate that she was allowed to speak.

'You didn't mention that we couldn't lose the white sheet?' she asked. 'Does that mean it is permissible to lose the sheet with the company mission and values?'

'Correct,' replied Amy, without missing a beat. 'Knowledge of the company mission and values is not essential to your role here; however, it is apparently a requirement of my role that I give them to you. In fact I would go so far as to say that you might find the mission and values more of a hindrance to you in your job than a help. I would suggest that you discreetly place them in one of the recycling bins on your way out today.'

'Thank you.' Carly nodded. 'Very helpful.'

Amy nodded curtly back.

Tom raised his eyebrows; he'd long since given up trying to persuade Amy not to be quite so obvious in her disdain of certain company protocols in front of cast members. But – as she regularly pointed out – they just got in the way, which was something he could not disagree with.

'Right,' he said, getting up. 'Thank you, Amy. Now I am going to take you through the show concept. Are you all sitting comfortably?'

'Hell yeah,' cried Carly, followed by a few enthusiastic shrieks by others. He smiled at her gratefully.

'...and so hopefully you can see in your heads the amazing, terrifying, wonderful world of *Malice in*

Wonderland,' said Tom over half an hour later as his audience sat spellbound. They'd been entranced from the moment Tom began to describe the opening number: a seventies-inspired dance routine involving a troupe of crazed technicolour disco-dancing rabbits on a stage crammed with swirling, whirling multicoloured lights. Having performed a spectacular acrobatic routine they lead Alice down the rabbit hole where things quickly turn dark and sinister when she's confronted by her trick-or-treat challenge. She falls for the charms of the delicious-looking cupcake with 'EAT ME' iced on it but little does she expect that the tasty treat will turn her, Alice, into Malice. From cute and innocent she turns monstrous and transforms an all-star dancing troupe of grinning Cheshire Cats into a fleet of terrifying zombies. She then creates havoc at the Mad Hatter's Tea Party, taking an instant dislike to the sleeping dormouse, forcing the Mad Hatter and March Hare to desperately try and hide him until the inevitable happens and Malice chops off his head. Tom had slammed the table in front of him at that point, making the entire room jump in surprise.

'The Queen of Hearts and her card soldiers don't fare much better,' he'd continued. 'Malice turns the playing cards into tarot cards who hound the Queen out of the kingdom during a ghoulish, spooky tribal dance. But then the cards turn on Malice herself and hustle her into court where she stands trial for crimes against Halloween and so we end with a rousing finale.

An all-singing, all-dancing show-stopper involving the entire cast along with all the special effects you can shake a stick at as Malice pleads her innocence to a jury made up of all the cutest costume characters you have ever seen. On stage you will see a *Pitch Perfect*-style dancing and singing battle as scary Halloween characters led by Malice attack the cutesy, cuddly characters led by the White Rabbit. All comes to a close when Malice is unable to resist stealing a treat from behind the White Rabbit's back with an 'EAT ME' sign on it. All of a sudden everything goes dark. We see a puff of smoke and gradually the lights are raised and there is Alice alone on the stage, back to her normal self, scratching her head, wondering what had happened to her. Wondering if it was all a dream…' Tom paused to check he was still holding their rapt attention.

'The lights go off again,' he continued, nodding at Amy, who had walked over to the other side of the auditorium. She flicked a switch and the entire room went pitch black. Everyone gasped. Two people screamed. Tom flicked a switch on a torch underneath his chin so the only thing illuminated in the whole room was his face. A face he had covered with a horrifying Malice mask.

'So, children,' he said in a deep, spooky voice. "What do you dare ask for this Halloween, a trick, or… treat… ha ha ha?'

He flicked the off switch on the torch plunging everyone into darkness again. Three seconds passed then Amy put the lights back on as instructed.

To his utter amazement there was spontaneous applause as soon as the lights went on. Again he glanced over at Carly, unable to help himself. She was clapping and whistling and stamping her feet. Tom blushed and looked away. This was unusual. Normally all he heard at this point was a clamour of people trying to bagsy themselves the best parts.

'Thanks,' he muttered, feeling bizarrely shy.

'It's just genius,' said Nathan, shaking his head. 'That trick you described that the Mad Hatter's going to do with the levitating cut-off heads just blows my mind.'

'That dance-off at the end is going to be amazing,' a girl sitting next to him said excitedly. 'I love the idea of cute, fluffy bunnies dancing against zombies. Epic.'

'It's a proper show,' said another excitedly. 'With like a beginning, a middle and an end, and with lots of different sets and special effects and pyros...you did say pyros, didn't you?'

Tom looked back into her excited eyes. He glanced over at Amy, who seemed to be oblivious to the hype the story had caused as she sat writing notes in her notebook. He felt his shoulders sag slightly; his confidence of a moment ago had evaporated.

'Well, that's the story of the show,' he said quickly. 'The vision, if you will, but we have a lot of challenges to overcome in order to achieve it.' He swallowed. 'I feel it's only fair to warn you that due to budget restraints, time and resources that it is highly likely we will have to cut some elements of the show. It may not end up being exactly how I just described it.'

Everyone stared back at him in silence. Carly raised her hand. Amy glared.

'Yes, Carly,' said Tom, eager for someone to fill the awkward silence.

'Where did the idea for the show come from?' she asked.

'What do you mean?' replied Tom.

'I mean, where has it been done before? Maybe it would be good for us to see how other people have performed it, get some ideas?'

'Oh no,' he said. 'You don't understand. It's my idea. I wrote the show. It's never been done before.'

'Wow,' she said, slightly taken aback. 'Well then, we'll make it our own, won't we, guys?' she said, looking around.

'Hell yeah,' shouted Nathan.

'I think that will be lunchtime,' Amy announced, standing up and planting herself firmly next to Tom. 'You all know where the canteen is, don't you? But for those of you planning a successful career on the stage you'll find the toilets in the hallway outside. Thank you, off you go.'

'Amy!' said Tom. 'You can't say things like that. You'll get yourself fired.'

'You going to fire me?'

'No, of course not.'

'Well then, I've got nothing to worry about, have I? Now, after the morning I've had I think I'm going to go and give Costume a bollocking. Cheer myself up. See you later.'

Tom nodded and didn't move. He felt too depressed to eat. He watched the cast troop out of the room with the same feeling he had when they started to rehearse every show: that despite his grand ideas, the end result would be anything but grand. He knew it could be fabulous, if only he had the resources to make it happen. As always it would be half the show he had described once the money ran out and his cast proved to be lacking somewhat in the talent department.

Carly, the last to leave, came up to punch him on the arm. 'Seriously brilliant concept,' she said, her eyes shining. 'You're like some kind of genius.'

'Thanks,' he replied, barely able to raise a smile. 'Go and get your lunch before people start talking,' he said, waving her away.

'Sure.' She grinned. He watched her walk away; then she turned and shouted back to him: 'This is going to be brilliant. You wait and see. We'll make it brilliant.'

'Aye aye,' came a low voice behind him after Tom had sat with his head in his hands for five minutes.

'What are you doing here?' he gasped, watching Jerry stroll in. 'And what are you wearing?'

'Can't a builder look smart every so often?'

'A builder, yes. You, no.'

'Thanks a bunch.'

'You're welcome.'

'So what are you doing here?'

'Oh, I've just been up to see the big boss man to give him an update and thought I'd come and see you in your natural habitat for a change. Just seen Carly outside actually. I mentioned Friday to her; sounds like she's up for it.'

'Right,' said Tom, nodding slowly.

'So why have you got a face like a donkey's arse that's been slapped because someone died?'

Tom assumed Jerry must mean he looked miserable. He shrugged. 'Just the usual work crap,' he said. 'Knowing there is likely to be failure around every corner.'

'Aah, but it's what you do with that failure that can lead to success,' replied Jerry.

Tom stared at him for a moment.

'Jerry?' he said.

'Yes, my friend,' answered Jerry.

'Just fuck off, will you?'

'Absolutely,' replied Jerry. 'I annoy myself sometimes. See you Friday night.' He turned and walked out, leaving Tom to wonder if he dare get the cold bacon sandwich out of the bin.

CHAPTER ELEVEN
JERRY

Jerry looked down at the bowl of green salad Hannah had just placed in front of him. 'Is there any food to go with this salad?' he asked. She was fiddling with something on the enormous central island in their enormous kitchen. He prayed it was a big juicy steak or a plate of chicken wings. She turned round and approached him with a tin of sardines.

'Sardines?' he questioned.

'Yes. You know what the doctor said. You have to reduce your cholesterol. Sardines are good for that.'

He looked at the sad-looking greasy fish now beached on a piece of iceberg lettuce. Possibly the most unappetising thing he'd ever seen. He looked up at Hannah for some kind of explanation as to why she would torture him in this way but she just smiled and sat down. He sometimes wondered if she took joy in denying him the things he loved. Good food, great wines, foreign travel: all the trappings their wealth should bring them. Hannah wasn't really interested in any of that. She was proud of what they'd achieved together, he was sure, but she'd seemed happier in the two-up two-down they'd started married life in. Polished granite and Italian porcelain floor tiles seemed to make her uncomfortable, miserable even, and despite the fact they'd lived in what Jerry believed to be their dream house for over two years she'd never truly seemed at home surrounded by such glamour and opulence.

He looked down at the sardines still waiting patiently to be consumed. Perhaps Hannah was relieved his cholesterol level meant they mostly dined in on simple food rather than took advantage of a wealth of fancy restaurants in their area. He sighed and picked up his fork and stabbed at the pathetic fish before biting its head off. He stared at Hannah, chewing steadily, trying hard not to spit it out.

'Reminds me of being a kid,' he said, reaching for a glass of water to wash it down.

Hannah nodded. 'That's nice.'

'Of when we had no money and had tinned sardines about three times a week because Mum did the night shift down the shop and got a discount.'

'Well, these were two for one in Aldi. I couldn't believe it – and they're good for your cholesterol. I bought a dozen tins.'

Jerry stared at Hannah and then cast his eyes around their state-of-the art kitchen with four ovens including a steam oven he'd had flown in from Germany and an LED lighting system that cost more than one of the entire lodges he was building up at Wonderland. And yet his wife was excited about a cheap deal on sardines at Aldi.

He scraped his chair back and got up. 'Well, I think these bargain-basement tiddlers at least deserve to be accompanied by a decent glass of Sauvignon,' he announced, striding over to the full-height wine chiller. He pulled open the door, having already decided what he needed to add some excitement to his meal.

'Let's have a drop of this, shall we?' he said, sitting down again and unscrewing the top. 'Pretend we're in Oz with Charlie.'

'We can't drink that,' protested Hannah.

'Why not?' asked Jerry. 'Don't you like my brother's wine any more?'

'Of course I do. It just costs so much to get it here, doesn't it? Makes it so expensive.'

'Well, if Charlie got off his arse and sorted a UK distributor, like I keep telling him to, then it would be cheap, wouldn't it? Save me a fortune shipping it over just for us to drink. I keep telling him he would make a killing over here but will he listen?'

'He's not over there to get rich. He just likes the lifestyle.'

'Lazy more like.'

'He's happy.'

'I dare say he is,' replied Jerry, defiantly raising his glass and necking half of it. He put his glass down and topped it up, then proceeded to eat more salad in silence.

'We finished the footings for all the lodges at Wonderland today,' he eventually said.

Hannah nodded. 'We really need to chase them for the second payment.'

'Well, that's your department. I did go up and see Phillip though – you know, to give him an update.'

'Had he asked to see you?'

'No.'

'So what did you go and see him for?'

'Reassurance. That it's all going to be ready in time. Keep him off our backs.'

'You didn't promise anything, did you?'

'No, I'm not stupid. I kept it vague.'

Hannah nodded again. 'Good.'

'I'm not an idiot.'

'I know you're not,' said Hannah. 'It just causes all sorts of problems in the office if you over-promise.'

'I know,' sighed Jerry, taking another slug of wine. 'Oh, by the way, I dropped in on Tom whilst I was up in the admin building. Checked he and Laura are OK for Friday. And I saw Carly too so I invited her. That's all right, isn't it?' He shrugged; then he filled his face with sardine so he could say no more.

Hannah looked up from her own salad. 'What did you do that for?'

Jerry was forced to leave the question hanging in the air as he emptied his mouth. 'What do you mean? I was just being nice.'

'I don't think Laura will be too pleased to hear you've invited Carly.'

'Why? Doesn't she like her?'

'What do you think?' replied Hannah. 'Her husband brings home a glamorous woman and moves her in. Laura's all over the place. She's already been to see me about it. She's really upset with Tom.'

'I knew it,' Jerry exclaimed. 'Tom thinks she's cool with it. Says she's delighted to have another woman around the house. I told him he was deluded but he wouldn't hear any of it.'

'Yeah, well, perhaps he needs to listen properly to his wife. She's petrified something's going to happen – especially after you dragged up Natalie of all people. That really wasn't the right thing to say. What were you thinking?'

'Oh, I didn't think. It just popped in my head and I'd said it before I could stop myself. Anyway, you can tell Laura she has nothing to worry about, Tom has a plan for Carly.'

'What do you mean a plan?'

He chuckled. 'He wants to try and fix her up with Will.'

'What!' exclaimed Hannah, dropping her fork on the floor. She made no attempt to retrieve it. 'Why would he want to do that?'

'Why not?' Jerry shrugged again. 'Will could do with a shag and if Carly can't switch him on then I don't know who can.

Hannah visibly flinched.

'I know, I know,' continued Jerry, seeing that Hannah was not impressed with his language. 'I did point out to Tom that inviting a girl to stay and lining her up to have sex with his brother isn't exactly PC but Tom's worried about him. Thinks Carly might be able to bring him out of his shell.'

'You are a pair of idiots,' said Hannah, getting up and walking across the kitchen to throw her half-eaten salad into the stainless-steel bin. 'Will doesn't even like her and you can't... you can't force him on to someone just because you think that's what he needs.'

'How do you know he doesn't like her?'

'Because he said so.'

'When?'

'When we met to do the wages on Saturday. Laura was there and asked him point blank.'

'Aah, rubbish,' said Jerry dismissively. 'He's a man. No man would turn a girl like that down.'

Hannah turned to glare at him. She considered telling him that Will was preoccupied with another woman to the point that he was blind to the attractions of anyone else but decided that the last thing Will needed was for Jerry to trample all over this piece of news.

'Besides, he's been on his own for far too long,' declared Jerry, knocking back another slug of wine. 'He needs to have some fun. He shouldn't be living the celibate life now. There's plenty of time for that when you're married.'

Hannah gasped. Their eyes locked. He'd gone too far. He gave her a sad smile and then looked away, unable to face the tears starting to brim at the corner of her eyes.

'I'm going to take the dog out,' she said after another moment's silence. She crossed the floor to the boot room, which was the size of most people's kitchens. He heard the clank of the dog lead and Sherlock, her treasured bloodhound, brushed past him instantly, clearly as eager to escape the confines of the house as Hannah was. He heard words of affection directed at the dog, which made him sad. Words he never heard directed at him any more. The back door banged without a word of goodbye or promise of return.

CHAPTER TWELVE
LAURA

'Hello, Harvest Research, Laura speaking,' said Laura, picking up the phone whilst checking her watch to see how much time she had before her group started.

'It's me, Hannah.'

'What's wrong?' asked Laura. 'You never call me at work.'

'Oh, nothing in particular,' said Hannah. 'It's nothing really, I just thought I should probably warn you that Jerry's invited Carly to dinner on Friday night.'

'What!'

'I know. I said you wouldn't be pleased.'

'What did you say that for?'

'Well, because you're not pleased, are you?'

'No, but you don't need to tell Jerry that.'

'Why not?'

'Because he'll tell Tom.'

'And that is bad because ...?'

'I don't know,' proclaimed Laura. 'I don't know anything any more. She's playing with my head, Hannah, I tell you. She's doing really nice stuff like cooking the dinner and cleaning the bathroom and she even took the bin out without being asked.'

'And you hate her for it?'

'Exactly,' breathed Laura.

'It's because she's pretty,' stated Hannah. 'One of the few advantages of being ordinary-looking is that people are always grateful when you do something nice, never suspicious.'

'But that's not fair really, is it?'

'No. But maybe the world shouldn't be fair to beautiful people.'

'I was so looking forward to a Carly-free night,' sighed Laura. 'What on earth possessed Jerry to invite her?'

'I haven't a clue. I told him it was a bad idea, but you've not heard the worst of it.'

'There's more?'

'Yes. Tom and Jerry are cooking up a plan to get Carly and Will together.

'Oh,' said Laura.

'I know – it's a terrible idea, isn't it?'

'Well…' Laura did a quick assessment. 'Not really. At least it keeps her out of Tom's way.'

'But he said he wasn't attracted to her.'

'I know,' replied Laura. 'But he hasn't been out with anyone in ages. It's a bit weird. Do you think he's got some secret woman on the go or something?'

'What makes you say that?' asked Hannah quickly.

'Well, it's a bit odd, isn't it? He seems to have totally lost interest. Tom's quite worried about him.'

'Well, he did kind of mention something after you left on Saturday, but I'm not sure if I should say anything.'

'Mention what? What did he say? Come on, tell me?' Laura heard Hannah sigh, clearly weighing up whether to spill the beans.

'It was nothing really,' she said eventually. 'Just that there was someone he liked but it was never going to happen.'

'Ooh,' said Laura. 'Wonder who that is then? Have you any idea? Can Jerry think of anyone?'

'There's no way I'm mentioning it to Jerry,' spat Hannah. 'You know what he's like. He'll blunder in with his size tens and ruin whatever's going on as he usually does.'

'Are you OK?' asked Laura. 'You seem a bit tetchy.'

'Oh, it's nothing. I'm fine. Jerry just wound me up more than usual last night, that's all. I took the dog for a walk to get out of his way. By the time I got back he was asleep on the sofa with *Real Housewives of New York City* blaring in the background.' She paused. 'I think that's the kind of wife he'd like really, you know.'

'What, plastic?'

'Yeah.' Hannah sighed. 'Or maybe rubber.'

'Ueeergh, too much information,' said Laura. 'Look, I gotta go. I've got half a dozen women in their menopause waiting to tell me about how they think the middle-aged are portrayed in advertising.'

'Well, rather you than me.'

'Thanks. See you Friday then. Ooh, what are you wearing?'

'When?'

'On Friday.'

'I've no idea. Why are you asking? It's just dinner; we never normally dress up.'

'I know but Carly will. Look at what she wore last time.'

'I don't care what Carly will be wearing,' said Hannah. 'I'll be wearing what I normally wear. The clothes I've been in all day probably.'

'OK,' replied Laura. 'I hear you. See you Friday.'

Maybe I'll get the chance to pop into town at lunchtime, she thought as she put the phone down. Treat myself to something new.

'OK then, ladies,' said Laura, settling herself down in the purpose-built research suite on the ground floor of their office building. There were six women sitting on low chairs grouped around a coffee table, all sipping cups of tea and gingerly eyeing each other up. Six total strangers, all aged between forty-five and fifty-five, plucked from the high street by a recruiter that morning and who were hopefully going to give her some quality insight on how to market to their age group.

'Thank you so much for taking time out today to sit and talk to us. It really is appreciated,' Laura began. 'I really hope you enjoy what should be a very relaxed, open chat. There's nothing to be worried about; anything you say is of course treated as anonymous. We are going to start with a very general chat about how you feel you are treated as a consumer group and then I'll introduce later the specific product my client would love to hear your views on. Does that sound OK? Does anyone have any questions?'

'Will we get any freebies?' asked a lady who had leant back in her chair and put her feet up on the table.

'Er, no, Karen. No, there won't be, I'm afraid,' said Laura, leaning forward to read her name label.

'Oh,' replied Karen. 'When I did a panel for Pumpkin Paradise we got a shedload of soup to take home.'

'Right, well, not in this instance. The products we are testing are not always suitable to give away and obviously we wouldn't want your feedback skewed by the fact you are getting freebies.' Laura wrote a note to have a stern word with her recruiter. People who had previously taken part in focus groups were supposed to be filtered out. They quickly got wise to what they thought the researcher wanted to hear. Also people prone to agreeing to take part in market research often turned out to be big talkers who actually never said anything useful at all.

'Right,' said Karen, rubbing her hands together. 'So is it a really expensive product then – that's why you can't give it away?'

'Not necessarily,' replied Laura, shuffling her notes to indicate that Karen should just pipe down.

'Bet it's Apple or someone.' Karen looked conspiratorially around the room. 'They must do mega research. Maybe she's going to tell us what the next new Apple gadget is, see if we like it. Maybe we'll get to try it.'

Laura smiled a tight smile. So Karen was the derailer. Every group had one. Someone determined to distract the entire conversation to something they wanted to talk about.

'Why don't we start with something easy?' she said, beaming at the other five women in the room. Some of them would warm to Karen, she knew, start playing to her tune, enjoying her rebelliousness. Others would go quiet with embarrassment whilst the rest would choose to simply ignore her and focus on responding to Laura. She hoped the majority were that way inclined.

'So can you tell me who you admire in the media, who are your role models? And I'm talking specifically people within your age group.'

Everyone looked blank. Laura beamed at them encouragingly; some turned their eyes away.

'Come on,' she said. 'There must be someone on the television or in films who you aspire to.'

'Our age, you say,' asked another lady wearing a label with 'Helen' written on it. She looked around shiftily, trying to judge exactly what age group Laura was referring to.

'Yes,' nodded Laura, still smiling. 'Anyone roughly between forty-five to fifty-five.' She watched as everyone glanced sideways to assess who in the group was wearing well and who had clearly had a tough paper round.

'My mind has gone blank,' declared Karen.

'Mine too,' said Helen.

'I really love Judi Dench,' said a lady called Beth, 'but I think she's over eighty now.'

'Oh, oh, oh,' said Karen, 'what about Helen Mirren? She's amazing.'

'I'm sure she was seventy this year,' replied Helen.

'Seriously,' said Karen. 'I need to have whatever she's having.'

'Julie...You know, Julie...' Suddenly Carol, in the corner, came to life. 'You know who I mean – dead funny, in *Acorn Antiques* but then she went a bit highbrow.'

'Julie Walters?' offered Beth.

'Yes, her,' replied Carol.

'Mid-sixties, I reckon,' said Beth.

'Is it definitely fifties you're after?' said Karen, turning to Laura.

'Well, yes really.' Laura swallowed. 'Over sixty isn't really the target customer.'

'OK,' said Karen. 'Come on, girls, we must be able to think of someone famous in their fifties who we'd like to be?'

The room went quiet for the second time.

'What TV shows do you like to watch?' asked Laura. 'Are there any actors your age in those that you think are good role models?'

'I love a good crime drama,' said Beth, 'but I guess women of that age are always either murdered or kind of in the background. Nobody in a lead part comes to mind.'

Carol shrugged. 'I only ever watch *Strictly*. The rest of the telly is rubbish.'

'*Strictly*!' said Laura in relief. 'Great one. Now, whose shoes would you have liked to have filled on there? There's all ages on there, isn't there?'

'Oh, don't,' said Beth, shaking her head. She looked around the room. 'I don't know about you, I love *Strictly*, I really do, but I wish they wouldn't have the older women on.'

'Why not?' asked Laura. 'Isn't it great to see women of your age represented in this way?'

'No,' replied Beth.

'What do you mean?'

'Because they're crap at it?' added Karen helpfully.

'They're mostly like the stooges, aren't they? There for laughs or for people to feel sorry for.'

'And a big fat reminder that you can do most things better when you're younger.'

'Right,' said Laura. 'That's really very interesting that you feel that way.'

'To be honest,' added Karen with a chuckle, 'me and my husband mostly watch *Strictly* to see who's going to fall for one another.'

'Ooh, I know.' Carol nodded. 'You can tell a mile off, can't you? It's like watching a love story unfold. Me and my mate have bets on which male celebrity will fall first!'

Laura sighed. She could really do without this conversation right now.

'Well, it is foreplay, after all, isn't it?' said Beth.

'What is?' asked Carol.

'Dancing,' replied Beth.

Laura looked down at her notes. She needed to move the conversation on quickly.

'Well, at least it used to be,' continued Beth. 'You must all remember those end-of-the-night dances down at Paradise, that nightclub on the edge of town?'

'Way hey!' exclaimed Karen, throwing her hands in the air. 'I can remember rubbing up to some pieces of work in there years back.'

'Exactly,' Beth agreed. 'Come the early hours we were all on that dance floor, weren't we? Hoping to fall into the arms of some random bloke we'd been eyeing up all night and gyrate away to a soppy love song. Proper turn-on that was. Back then dancing with a man nearly always came before sex.'

'It's not like that now,' sighed Carol before Laura could interject. 'You don't need to go dancing to pull any more because it's all online, isn't it? Believe me, I know. I've been divorced three years.'

'Oh, I'm sorry to hear that,' replied Beth.

'It's OK. I'm getting used to it. But it's all so dif-ferent trying to date these days. Sexting is the new foreplay now, not dancing. I keep getting messages late at night from pissed-up blokes via dating websites sending me pictures of their you-know-what. What I'd give for a man who just asked me to dance. So much sexier.'

'You're right,' agreed Beth. 'Who can resist a man who wants to dance with them? Sexiest thing on earth. Me and Terry still dance. We go to festivals and are the daft pair at the back twirling each other round. I reckon couples who dance together stay together.'

'Aah, that's really nice,' said Carol, looking as though she might burst into tears there and then.

'And it's exactly why the celebrities end up having it off with their partners on *Strictly*,' cut in Karen. 'They should be at home dancing with their wives, not with someone who can do things with their body that shouldn't be legal.'

'I tell you what, ladies,' said Laura, having heard more than enough and feeling utterly depressed. 'Shall I introduce the product we're discussing today?'

'Oh yes,' said Karen, cheering up again. 'Brilliant, I love this part.'

'Well, it's a well-known brand that you will all have heard of and who want to branch out and move into a related product category for your age group. It is quite a sensitive area, I must warn you—'

'Condoms,' shrieked Karen. 'It's geriatric condoms, isn't it? They've finally developed one for the older man that keeps him up longer.'

'That's a good idea,' said Helen excitedly. 'A really good idea. Like adding Viagra to the actual condom rather than having to take it as a pill or something.'

'Are you sure you've got no free samples?' Karen asked Laura again. 'We're willing to test them, aren't we, ladies? In the interests of science, of course.'

Four of the women nodded vigorously; the other two turned bright red and looked at their shoes.

'That isn't actually the product,' replied Laura, surreptitiously writing it down as a good idea to give another one of her clients. She looked up and took a deep breath. This wasn't going to be easy.

'Actually,' she said, clearing her throat and trying hard to remain composed, 'the product we are discussing today is designer incontinence pants.'

'Jesus,' said Karen. 'Shoot me now.'

CHAPTER THIRTEEN
LAURA

Laura looked up at Tom as they stood on the door-step of Jerry and Hannah's house. They could hear the deep chime reverberating inside as the motion-sensor lights illuminated their warm breath. He was holding her hand but was grinning at Carly. Laura lifted her other hand to wipe off some of the lip-gloss she'd carefully applied half an hour earlier. It had seemed like a good idea at the time, to dress up a bit. She'd bought a new top with a daring plunging neckline and she'd spent ages carefully straighten-ing her hair to a smooth and silky finish that looked almost as good as when the hairdresser did it. The lip-gloss had been an impulse purchase that lunch-time. Why not? she'd thought. Why shouldn't I wear lip-gloss? She wore 'Matt Rose' every day to work and so lip-gloss for the evening seemed entirely reason-able. Well, it did until she raced downstairs in some leg-breaking high heels she'd found in the depths of her wardrobe at just after seven to find Tom and Carly waiting to head out to Jerry and Hannah's for dinner. As soon as she saw Carly she lunged for her coat to cover up her extra special efforts that evening. Her exposed cleavage was soon engulfed in a faithful full-length black wool coat and she discreetly kicked off her heels and plunged her feet into some handy Ugg boots standing by the door.

'You look nice,' said Carly.

'Not really,' said Laura, buttoning her coat up quickly whilst trying not to notice how good Carly looked in sweatpants, a hoody, no make-up and a high scraped-back ponytail.

'Jerry said casual when he invited me,' said Carly, 'and I was so overdressed last time compared to everyone else. Am I all right like this – should I change?'

'No,' said Tom and Laura in unison.

'Right,' said Carly. 'If you're sure.'

'You look great,' Tom reassured her. 'No need to change, is there, Laura?'

Laura felt her lip-gloss smear over her teeth as she forced a smile. 'You're fine. Shall we go?'

'Welcome, welcome, welcome,' declared Jerry, throwing open his front door. 'You are so very welcome.'

'Waistcoat, Jerry?' said Tom, pushing past him. 'What's the occasion? You didn't tell the rest of us it was fancy dress.'

Laura took off her overcoat and tugged her top up to cover more of her chest.

'No occasion – well, unless you count the fact I've done a bit of a revamp of the bar downstairs, which I'm hoping we'll well and truly christen tonight.'

'The bar?' asked Carly.

'Jerry has a den downstairs in the basement,' explained Tom.

'The den of iniquity,' announced Jerry with a smirk.

'It's where all of Jerry's bad taste is stored out of Hannah's way,' continued Tom. 'Oak-panelled bar, pool table, fifty-inch plasma, that kind of thing.'

'Aah, but just you wait,' announced Jerry. 'Your brother's already here putting me some finishing touches up. I'm so excited I cannot tell you. Cocktails downstairs before dinner, anyone?' He held out his arm towards Carly.

'Well, I don't mind if I do.' She grinned, tucking her hand into his elbow. 'Lead me to your den of iniquity, kind sir.'

'It would be my utmost pleasure,' he replied. 'Come on, troops,' he said over his shoulder to Tom and Laura. 'This is going to blow your mind.'

Laura and Tom looked at each other.

'What do you think he's done?' Laura whispered to Tom as they walked towards the basement door.

'Knowing Jerry, it could be anything. He has mentioned an underground hot tub in the past. But he was pissed and installing a wax figure of Cameron Diaz was also discussed at the time.'

'Perhaps we'll get down there and find Will in a hot tub with Diaz,' said Laura.

'Wouldn't that be a sight to behold!' Tom grinned, reaching round to squeeze her shoulders. She grabbed his hand tight and didn't let go as they began their descent of the basement stairs.

'Oh my God,' they heard Carly scream when they were halfway down. 'This is amazing.'

They arrived at the bottom of the steps and turned the corner to enter the large basement area. Laura's jaw dropped.

'So what do you think?' asked Jerry. 'Looks good, hey?'

Laura and Tom took a few more tentative steps into the room. The pool table had disappeared; the enormous couch had been pushed to the back leaving the vast open space of wooden floor to be lit by tiny little flecks of coloured light that bounced off the enormous glitter ball slowly rotating from the middle of the ceiling. The fifty-inch plasma on the back wall was playing the black-and-white classic movie, *Singing in the Rain*. Will was balanced on the top of a stepladder to the side of the room screwing something into a lighting track, a workman's tool belt slung around his waist. As they ventured further into the room he leapt down from his perch and hurriedly started to collapse the ladder.

'There you go, Jerry,' he said. 'They should all be working now.'

'One word,' said Tom to Jerry. 'Why?'

'Why the hell not?' said Jerry.

Tom and Laura stared back at him.

'Come on,' he cried. 'How much fun was it dancing at your house last week?'

Laura winced at the memory of Tom and Carly gliding around together.

'It was great,' agreed Tom, 'but not many people learn a few steps of the salsa and immediately build their own dance floor in their basement. And where is the damn Xbox Jerry?'

'Gone, mate.'

'What?'

'Gone.'

'But I was beating you,' replied Tom, looking genuinely angry.

'I thought you'd be pleased,' said Jerry. 'We can have parties, we can dance, *you* can dance. You never dance any more. You always used to dance.'

'You used to call me a pink poofter for dancing when I was a kid,' replied Tom.

'You so had no sense of humour when you were young,' replied Jerry.

'Yes I did.'

'No you didn't.'

'You were a bully.'

'No I wasn't.'

'Oh, don't start,' sighed Laura. She didn't know what to say about Jerry's creation. She wanted to say it was brilliant. Pre-Carly turning up she would have said it was amazing and she would have shoved her husband straight on to the middle of the floor and danced with him just for the hell of it. She might even have risked showing off their tango, given that Jerry and Will were never going to be the harshest of critics. But she couldn't do it now – despite what the ladies at the focus group had said the other day. Dancing with her husband when there was a professional in the room somehow sucked all the fun out of it.

'I don't think I've ever been in your house this long without being offered a drink,' she announced.

'Coming right up,' said Jerry, dashing across the dance floor and positioning himself behind his bar. 'How about we start with a little Kir Royale?' he suggested, reaching into a fridge behind him and pulling out a bottle of Prosecco.

Carly went bounding up and sat on a tall stool. 'This is seriously cool, Jerry,' she cried. 'Gordon didn't have a bar, or a dance floor.'

'And who is Gordon?' asked Jerry, pouring their drinks.

'My ex,' said Carly. 'The bastard who dumped me last week.'

'Well, cry no more, my friend, you may not have a Gordon, but you now have friends with dance floors and cocktails.' He handed out the tall glasses. 'To friends with dance floors and cocktails,' he said, raising his glass high with an enormous grin.

'Hell yeah,' cried Carly, 'the best kind of friends.'

We are not friends, thought Laura. We will never be friends. She downed half her drink. These are my friends. This is my life, not yours.

'Where's Hannah?' she asked once the warmth of the drink had calmed her.

'She's running late. Had to do something at the office. She'll be here any minute.'

'And what does she think of your latest addition to the home?' asked Laura.

Jerry paused before he answered.

He shrugged. 'She's not seen it yet.'

'I thought you said you were going to ask her first,' said Will as he arrived at the bar having put the stepladder away. 'I'll have that pint now, if it's still on offer, Jerry.' He nodded at the fully functioning beer pump.

'I was going to ask her,' said Jerry, turning to grab a glass off a shelf behind him, 'but I thought she'd prefer the surprise.'

'She's going to love it, right?' said Carly. 'Who wouldn't love coming home to a husband who'd installed an enormous glitter ball in the basement?'

Laura, Tom and Will raised their eyebrows at each other.

'You'll have another go at the cha-cha-cha with me now, won't you, Will?' asked Carly.

Will spluttered his first gulp of his pint back out.

'Now there is all this room and a proper dance floor? You can't look at that and not want to dance,' she went on, casting her arm around the vast wooden floor.

'Yeah,' said Jerry encouragingly. 'How can you say no to that?' He pointed at the dance floor. 'And that,' he continued, pointing at Carly whilst giving Will a wink.

Will took a long draw on his drink. 'Like I said last week,' he announced, putting his pint down firmly, 'Tom's the dancer, not me.'

Laura felt herself deflate at Will's response. Why couldn't Will behave like any other normal single man and let Carly do whatever she wanted him to do on that dance floor? If he did the dancing foreplay thing with her then she wouldn't have to watch her husband do it.

'What on earth...?' came a voice from behind them. They all swivelled to see Hannah at the bottom of the stairs, pointing at the enormous glitter ball and looking accusingly at Jerry. Laura couldn't help but notice that Jerry took another gulp of his drink without replying.

'Why?' Hannah asked, looking directly at Jerry. 'How much?' she added.

'It's all right, love,' said Jerry, coming out from behind the bar and walking over to her. 'We're installing one in a hotel ballroom in Somerset. I got it at cost. What do you reckon? Isn't it great? You gonna boogie with me later?' He grabbed both her hands and attempted a shimmy but she stood stock-still and stared right at him. No one dared speak.

'I...I...' she began, glancing over at the bar where the rest of them were poised waiting for her verdict. She looked back at Jerry and let her breath tumble out of her mouth and her shoulders drop. She looked weary. 'I'll go and check on dinner,' she finally replied, pulling her hands away from Jerry's. She turned and disappeared back up the stairs.

There was silence apart from the sound of Gene Kelly splashing through some puddles and singing about the rain. Jerry turned round to face them, his signature big grin plastered on his face.

'We'll give her a drink and she'll be giving it some Travolta before you know it,' he said, strutting back across the floor to his bartender post. 'She's working too hard,' he continued, shaking his head. 'I keep telling her she doesn't need to spend every bloody hour of the day in that office. What's the point in running your own business if you can't play hooky every so often?'

'I think her putting all those hours in means *you* can play hooky,' said Laura

'Laura Mackintyre!' exclaimed Jerry. 'Who gave you too much Prosecco and let you speak your mind so early in the evening? It's not even eight o'clock.'

'Well,' replied Laura, blushing slightly, 'she does seem to work really hard and you do seem to er... er... '

'Swan about a lot,' finished Tom.

'Fuck off,' said Jerry at Tom. 'That *swanning* about, as you call it, secured us a contract for two spanking new developments today. If I hadn't *swanned* around the muddy fields of Hertfordshire on Saturday, shooting with the great and good of the leisure industry, then we wouldn't have got it. I work very hard at my swanning around, I'll have you know, and it is very lucrative swanning around at that. Anyway, you're one to talk, you swan around all day telling young girls to writhe around semi-naked and dance in front of you.'

Will coughed and put his empty pint glass down on the bar. 'I think I'll go and put my stuff away,' he said. He turned and strode off up the basement stairs, his tools jangling around his waist on his belt.

'It's not like that, and you know it,' said Tom, turning on Jerry. 'Is it, Carly?' he asked.

'No,' said Carly firmly. 'No, it isn't. Tom is a complete professional.'

'Oh, stop getting your knickers in a twist,' said Jerry, leaning forward to top up everyone's glasses with Prosecco. 'I was only joking. I know you're not like that but I do remember you telling me about your old boss getting the entire Halloween cast to run around the lake in their underwear because he said they had to get used to performing in the cold. Tremendous.'

'Really?' cried Carly. 'No way!'

'I have to say there is nothing like running around in your undies in five degrees to bond a company,' said Tom. 'That was the year I was Count Dracustein. The most evil man in the whole of Wonderland. I based my character on the old Entertainments Manager actually as he was a proper devil to work for.'

'Count Dracustein?' said Carly. 'I would have liked to have seen that.'

'It was a brilliant show that year, even though I do say so myself,' he replied. 'But it was back in the days when we used to do them on a special stage outside after dark. It was so much better than in a theatre. The atmosphere was incredible.'

'Why don't they do them outside any more?' asked Carly.

Tom shrugged. 'Budgets. Some finance twerp looked at the cost of building the stage and putting in all the special lighting and decided it was a waste of money and we could achieve the same thing in the Celebration Theatre. But he was so wrong. No one can be bothered to walk all the way out to Back of Beyond World. And now of course the boss says not enough people watch it so he's not giving us any more money to spend.'

'Oh,' said Carly, looking crestfallen.

'I keep telling him that if we moved it back to the main plaza at the exit to the park then the entire day's attendance will see it,' continued Tom. 'But no, it's not worth the money apparently. Instead we'll end up with some shitty show in a falling-down theatre that hardly anyone bothers to go and see.'

'They're not shitty,' said Laura, suddenly feeling very sorry for her husband. 'Last year's *Pumpkin Plotters* was hilarious.'

'Thanks,' said Tom with a sigh. 'Sorry, Carly,' he said. 'Not what you need to hear.'

'But…but you made it sound so amazing when you described the show to us all,' she said.

'It could be. But the lighting in the theatre is past it and the stage is really too small for those big dance numbers so we will have to tone them down and limit the scale of the costumes.'

'It can't cost that much to build a stage, can it?' asked Jerry.

'Probably not, but the number-crunchers don't see it as money well spent so it ain't going to happen.'

'But everyone is so excited about the show,' said Carly. 'We can make it work, can't we?' She looked pleadingly into Tom's eyes. 'If we all pull together and work really hard? It's such a brilliant idea; we can't let it be rubbish. We just need to be positive. Make it happen. Come on, Tom, you can make it happen, can't you?'

'No I can't,' snapped Tom. 'I've tried before, believe me, and failed. You don't understand. It's too hard without the necessary resources.'

Carly shrank back on to her stool looking visibly stung. Laura could feel the tension flow out of her body and the guilt flood in. Oh, the relief that Tom had got frustrated with Carly's youthful naivety and that they wouldn't be having the tremendous time building a fabulous show together. And the guilt that she felt good about that.

'We'll build it,' said Jerry.

'What?' said Tom.

'What?' said Laura.

'What?' said Carly.

'We can build it,' he told Tom. 'We can build a stage, piece of piss. My boys could knock one of those up in a couple of days.'

'You're not listening,' said Tom. 'There's no budget for it.'

'Aah, don't worry about that,' said Jerry, reaching round for another bottle of Prosecco. 'We'll sponsor it or something. Tell you what, we'll build it if Phillip will let us put a billboard at the gates with our name on saying we're building the lodges' development. All sorts of people come through those gates from all over. Wouldn't do us any harm to get our name out there.'

'Are you serious?' asked Tom.

'Why not? Probably find we can write it off as a marketing cost or something. I'm sure Hannah can work out how to put it on the books.'

'Oh my God,' Carly cried, jumping off her stool. 'That's just brilliant, isn't it, Tom? You can do your show how you want to.'

Tom was staring at Jerry, speechless.

'But what do we do about lighting?' he asked when he'd finally found a use for his mouth. 'It's very generous Jerry, but a stage without lighting is useless. And Phillip will never stump up for lighting now. I'm so sorry, Carly.'

Laura grabbed the bottle off Jerry and poured herself another glass of Prosecco. What's he apologising to her for? It's his show.

'Can't you get someone to move the lights out from the theatre?' continued Carly, looking desperately between Tom and Jerry.

'Hang on a minute,' said Jerry, walking over to the bottom of the stairs. 'Will,' he shouted. There was no answer. 'Will,' he shouted even louder. Next minute there was a thumping down the stairs and Will, quickly followed by Hannah, reappeared.

'You're not at work now, you know,' said Hannah crossly. 'You can't go ordering people around like you do there.'

'I just wanted to ask Will a question, that's all,' said Jerry. 'Are the sparkies on schedule at the log cabins' build at Wonderland?'

'Is this a trick question?' asked Will, casting a worried look over at his brother.

'Why are you asking him that?' demanded Hannah.

'Just answer the question, please,' Jerry asked politely.

'We're ahead actually,' he replied. 'We're having to slow down because we're catching up with the builders. We will have run out of lodges to put electrics in any minute. I was going send a couple to another site on Monday before they're sitting doing nothing.'

'And there is your answer,' said Jerry with an elaborate bow directed at Tom and Carly. 'Will here will be able to solve all your electrical woes.'

'Oh my God, you are brilliant,' cried Carly, throwing herself at Will. 'This is going to be brilliant, isn't it, Tom? Just brilliant. I can't believe it. It's going to be the best Halloween show ever.'

'What is she talking about?' asked Hannah, looking confused and cross.

'Jerry's going to build us a mega Halloween stage so we can do Tom's dream show,' she said breathlessly, having released Will from her grasp. 'And we thought that the lights would be a problem but not any more now Will is in on it. Oh I could kiss you.' She stepped forward and kissed him on the cheek before he could do anything about it. Looking slightly dazed he reached up to wipe the lipstick off.

'There won't be enough lights,' interrupted Tom, shaking his head. 'Some of them will do but we'd need to buy special ones for outdoor.'

'What do you mean you're going to build a stage?' asked Hannah, still not understanding what was going on.

'We could ask Ferns if they have any lights,' said Will, looking furtively between Jerry and Hannah. 'They supply conference centres now who often use stage-grade lighting. We could ask if they'd lend us some. They screwed up a delivery the other week, so they owe us a favour at the moment.'

'Perfect,' said Jerry, grinning at Will. 'I'll ring old man Fern and tell him we'll put his name in lights if he'll give us a hand and we won't start looking for a new supplier just yet. And you'll be able to fit stage lighting, do you think?' he asked Will.

Will shrugged. 'Can't be hard,' he replied. 'I'm sure me and the other lads can work it out between us.'

'What a man,' said Jerry, winking at Carly. 'He's got it up here' – he pointed at Will's head – 'and he's got it here,' he continued, indicating his bicep, '...and he really has it here.' Jerry finished by banging his fist against Will's chest.

'Give over, Jerry,' said Will, pushing him away gently. 'Just doing my job.'

'That is where you are wrong!' Jerry threw his arms wide in amazement. 'What we are going to do with this stage is make dreams come alive,' he declared. 'Isn't that right, Carly? Isn't that right, Tom?'

'Oh God yes, Jerry, that's exactly right,' Carly replied, flinging herself at Jerry and Tom and jumping up and down.

'Can someone please tell me what is going on?' interrupted Hannah, now looking totally bewildered. 'Laura?'

Laura looked back at Hannah panic-stricken. We're doomed, she wanted to shout. Tom and Carly are going to create the most spectacular show together and they are going to have so much fun and achieve things together that I could never achieve with him and so when the moment comes, when the joy of success engulfs them and they feel happier than they have felt in ages, that's when they will kiss, that very moment. They won't be able to help themselves, it will feel like the most natural thing in the world and then ... and then my life will be over.

'Tell me, Laura,' repeated Hannah, glancing between Laura's distress and everyone else's joy. 'What has Jerry done?'

Laura opened and closed her mouth, not knowing how to communicate her inner turmoil in front of this hyped-up crowd.

The rest were now talking excitedly about where and when and how, leaving just Hannah and Laura staring at each other. Laura stepped around the back of Carly and went to whisper in Hannah's ear.

'*Strictly* Curse,' she breathed.

'What?' Hannah cried, turning to face her. 'I can't hear you.'

'*Strictly* Curse,' she repeated just a little louder in her ear. 'It's happening.'

'What's happening? I only went upstairs for ten minutes. Why are you in such a state?' Hannah hissed.

Laura couldn't answer; she felt close to tears. She shook her head, biting her lip.

'Why don't you come upstairs and help me check on the food again?' Hannah asked, taking her hand.

Laura nodded mutely back and gulped.

'We're going upstairs,' Hannah said over her shoulder to no one in particular.

'Sit down,' said Hannah gently once they'd arrived back in the calm sleekness of the kitchen. She opened a cupboard door and grabbed two crystal tumblers off the shelf and put them down in front of Laura. Next a bottle of brandy appeared and she sloshed two generous measures in them and shoved one into Laura's hand.

'Thank you,' muttered Laura, before downing it in one.

'So do you think you can tell me what just happened down there?' Hannah asked again. 'How come Carly is draped over every man we know?'

Laura swallowed. 'Well, it all started with Tom saying Wonderland won't let him do the Halloween show he wants to and this was news to Carly so she got quite upset because she was all excited to do it and Tom basically told her she was going to be in a crap show.'

Hannah nodded. 'I see. Carry on.'

'So Jerry offered to be fairy godmother and sort it all out for them.'

'I knew it,' said Hannah. 'He can't be trusted to be left alone for five minutes. He promises things left, right and centre before really knowing if it's possible.'

'Tom reckons the only way to do the show properly is to build an outdoor stage but there's no money to pay for it so Jerry said he'd get his lads to do it for free if he could get some advertising on park.'

'Mmmm,' said Hannah, rocking her head from side to side as if weighing up Jerry's offer. 'That's quite a good idea actually.'

'But then Tom said that they needed lights and stuff and Will said the electricians are ahead of themselves fitting out the lodges so he could do the lights and that's when they all started hugging and dancing about and acting as if they'd won the bid to host the World Cup or something.'

'Including Will?'

'Yeah,' said Laura, 'which I guess is good because Tom thinks Carly and Will should get it together so if Will is helping with the show then that might help and then that will mean Tom and Carly won't have their moment, Will and Carly will, which actually is fine, so why am I worrying?' She knew she was babbling but she couldn't stop herself.

'What moment? What are you talking about?' demanded Hannah.

'The moment, you know, the *Strictly* moment.'

'What on earth is the *Strictly* moment?'

'Well, we were on about the *Strictly* Curse at work today – you know, when the celebrities end up getting off with their professional partners and I was trying to work out why it's so common.'

'Isn't it obvious?'

'Well, yes, they are all very attractive, of course, and feel each other's bodies all day long, but I think there's more to it than that.'

'You've spent time thinking about this?'

'Yes,' gasped Laura, looking at Hannah as though she were the ridiculous one. 'Of course. I've concluded it's about shared success. Such an aphrodisiac, you see. You achieve something great with a member of the opposite sex and you celebrate ... '

'By having sex?'

'Well, yes. That's it. By having sex. So don't you see how dangerous this situation is? All the inputs are there. Tom is in a high-risk job...'

'Not this again,' sighed Hannah. 'The army is a high-risk job, bomb disposal is a high-risk job—'

'For divorce,' interrupted Laura. 'I've told you this before. Don't you listen?'

'Not when you come out with your statistics mumbo jumbo.'

'He's in a high-risk job for divorce and now, because of your husband, he is going to have a successful show on his hands, and be so happy, whilst spending a lot of time in close proximity to Carly.'

'So he'll end up having sex with her?'

'Correct,' said Laura, trying to hold back the tears. 'Totally and utterly inevitable... unless,' she said, pausing for a moment, 'unless it becomes Will's and Carly's success so they can have the success aphrodisiac moment.'

'Will doesn't even fancy Carly,' said Hannah, pouring herself another drink. 'We've been through this before.'

'All I can say is he looked like he was enjoying having her draped all over him downstairs.'

'He was probably just being polite.'

'We *have to* get him to like her,' said Laura.

'Why?'

'It's my only hope. Will has to get in the way of the impending moment that will inevitably happen between my husband and Carly.'

'You can't force Will to like her,' said Hannah.

'Why not?' replied Laura. 'Why's he being so fussy anyway? He can't afford to be fussy at his age or when he's been single for that long. Let's get him pissed. That's it,' she cried. 'Let's get him drunk tonight, then leave him downstairs with Carly, and stick some Barry White on. That should do it.'

'That's like entrapment or something,' said Hannah. 'And what about this other woman he mentioned?'

Laura shrugged. 'You said he knew it wasn't going to happen. She could be married for all we know.'

'Married? Do you think so?' gasped Hannah.

'It's possible,' said Laura. 'It would explain why he thinks it's a no go. Will certainly isn't a home-wrecker, so he wouldn't do anything about it.'

'I guess not,' said Hannah.

'In which case even more reason to distract him by putting him between my at-risk husband and Carly. Will could be my only chance of coming out of all this still married.'

Chapter Fourteen
Tom

Tom stared at Phillip, trying to read his response to their over-excited babble. He sat behind the large oak desk with a grim frown on his face, his elbows on the arms of his chair and fingertips pressed tightly together as he surveyed the four eager faces in front of him.

I should have come on my own, thought Tom, looking across at Jerry, Amy and Carly. We've overwhelmed him with our excitement of what we want to do and now he's going to say no and put an end to it.

Carly turned her head and winked at him. Shouldn't have bought Carly in for sure, he thought. Phillip certainly didn't know how to deal with a cropped vest top and a bare midriff at nine in the morning. And she seemed to have somehow upset Amy as well, who looked daggers at her whenever she opened her mouth. He'd thought it would be a good idea to bring one of the performers in so Phillip could see how passionate the cast were about putting on a good show and how a stage in the main plaza could make all the difference. But Phillip had just blinked rapidly at Carly's excitable spiel whilst trying very hard not to stare at her bare belly.

Jerry looked over at him and shrugged, looking confused. Welcome to my world, thought Tom. In Jerry's world, when you are your own boss, and someone offers you something for free, then you snap their hand off. But in the corporate-leisure industry things were very different. Who knew what conversations were going on between Phillip and his bosses at head office? What new-fangled thinking was evolving, what added complications were going to be thrown at them all in the name of progress? What should be a simple decision was always made complicated in the context of a large corporation.

'Well,' said Phillip, having sat there in silence and contemplated for quite some time. 'You have put me in a very difficult position.'

'Excuse me?' said Jerry, aghast. 'I really don't see how offering you free stuff can do that.'

Shut up, thought Tom, casting Jerry a warning glance. You're not the boss in this room. Just listen. Play the game, you idiot.

Carly cast Tom a nervous, confused glance. He'd tried to warn her that it wouldn't be straightforward and to be prepared for disappointment. He knew she hadn't listened.

'You see, the thing is,' continued Phillip, 'the group is currently reviewing our entertainment offering across all attractions to see how much value we think it's really adding.'

Tom swallowed. He didn't like the sound of where this might be going.

'So, as Tom is very well aware, there is currently a freeze on any additional investment in entertainment.'

'But we are offering you this for free!' said Jerry, starting to go red in the face with frustration.

Phillip glanced over at Jerry and then turned to address Tom. 'But it won't be, will it, as you well know, Tom. Any change will have unforeseen knock-on costs,' he said. 'What about on-park Halloween leaflets, for example – they'll all have to be reprinted, won't they?'

'Marketing haven't signed them off yet,' said Amy flatly. 'They can be changed before they go to print.'

'They're not already done?' exclaimed Phillip. 'But they must be?'

'No, they're not,' replied Amy. 'Marketing are a fly-by-the-seat of their pants department who seem to find panic exhilarating.'

'I see.' Phillip nodded, writing something in the notepad in front of him. 'But there will be other things,' he said, looking up again. 'signage, for example, will need to be changed.'

'Marketing are responsible for Halloween signage,' replied Amy. 'I would bet my end-of-year bonus they will not have done the signage yet. That is if I were ever to get an end-of-year bonus since you refuse to sign off upgrading my job to a band C even though I consistently exceed my key performance indicators, making a mockery of the appraisal system when in the employee handbook it clearly states that pay grades will be reassessed should you display a high level of performance.'

'Shall we take that up with Phillip another time, Amy?' said Tom gently. 'Let's focus on one thing at a time, shall we?'

Amy said nothing, just glared at Phillip.

Phillip coughed and gathered himself up in his chair. 'Look, it's a very generous offer but we are just not in the right climate politically at the moment to be able to accept it. I'm sorry.'

Jerry looked at him, startled. 'What do you mean?' he gasped. 'That we need a change of government before you can accept a freebie? Is this a tax issue or something?'

'But it's going to be amazing,' cried out Carly. 'Like the best show ever! How can we not do it?' She looked at Tom again in bewilderment.

Tom reached over and put a reassuring hand on hers. She clearly wasn't used to this type of corporate rejection.

Amy moved her glare from Phillip to him.

'What I mean is,' said Phillip, looking uncomfortable, 'that entertainment is a bit of a hot potato at the moment. There are those who believe that today's tech-obsessed public doesn't want the kind of low-tech old-fashioned entertainment we offer. They want futuristic rides and experiences and I'm afraid singing and dancing shows don't fit into that.'

'Rubbish,' said Tom, standing up. 'Look at the West End. It's thriving and there have never been so many musicals around.'

'But we are not the West End, are we?' said Phillip.

Tom sat back down again. 'Because we are never given the chance,' he said quietly.

'You only have to look at the satisfaction scores,' said Phillip. 'Entertainment barely ever rates above a six and most other attractions – even the kiddie ones – get over seven point five. And only ten per cent of our guests bother to go and see a show.'

'What are satisfaction scores?' asked a bewildered Carly.

'Guests get asked every day to mark out of ten how they rate our attractions,' said Amy scathingly, as if Carly was an idiot for having to ask.

'But we never get the opportunity to put on a decent show,' said Tom. 'And we are stuck out in no man's land – who's going to troll all the way over there? It's not fair.'

'Like I said, it's a hot potato,' said Phillip.

'What is it with these fucking hot potatoes,' muttered Jerry under his breath.

'Investing in entertainment is not an option at the moment.'

'But it's not going to cost you anything,' said Jerry, now bright red with frustration.

'They won't see it that way,' said Phillip.

'Who won't see it that way?'

'Head Office. All they'll see is a show and they'll ask me why I'm wasting valuable resources in an area that is considered poor value for money.'

'But it's not costing you anything!' repeated Jerry. The room went silent.

'Sadly, I understand,' said Tom. 'They've got an agenda and anything that distracts from that is seen as a bad thing, even if it's not costing anything.'

'Precisely,' said Phillip, standing up. He reached over to shake Jerry by the hand. 'Thank you for your very generous offer, Jerry. I hope you understand that it just doesn't fit in with the corporate objectives at the moment so we will have to decline.'

Jerry stared at Phillip's hand and eventually took it whilst shaking his head. 'I tell you, Phillip,' he said. 'The bigger the company is that we deal with, the less what they do makes any sense whatsoever.'

'I have absolutely no doubt that that is true,' replied Phillip, giving him a sad smile.

'Can I make a suggestion?' piped up Amy.

'Let's talk about your pay grade another day, shall we?' said Tom firmly.

'It's nothing to do with my pay grade,' said Amy curtly. 'I had this idea about how we could increase the food and beverage spend for the Halloween period.'

'Which department do you work in?' asked Tom.

'Let her speak,' interrupted Phillip. 'I've got a meeting later today with Gillian to discuss how we run our stocks down before the park shuts. So far the commercial team haven't come up with any brilliant ideas.'

'Well,' continued Amy, 'I was thinking if there was a way we could make people hang around for thirty minutes extra at the end of their day in the cold with nothing to do but buy hot food. That would make them spend more, wouldn't it?'

'Yes it would, Amy,' said Phillip, sitting down again, deflated. 'We'll just lock the gates shall we and stop them leaving to go and buy McDonald's cheaper down the road?'

'Don't be ridiculous,' said Amy. 'But there is another way we could stop them leaving.'

'How?' said Phillip, clearly stunned by Amy's retort and now starting to lose patience.

'We could put on a show to watch, like a Halloween Show, at the exit, next to all the food outlets. Just a thought.'

There was a moment's silence.

'Oh my God,' cried Tom, leaping up. 'That's it. She's right. We're putting on a show to stop people leaving so they spend more *money*!' He looked excitedly over at Phillip. Phillip was thinking. Thinking very hard. He hadn't said no. This had to be a good sign. He slowly started to nod his head.

'I don't understand,' said Jerry, looking around. 'Are we putting on a show or not?'

'Be quiet,' hissed Amy, staring at Phillip.

'And we can measure it,' added Amy. 'How successful it is. They like to measure, don't they?'

Phillip nodded. 'We could compare the spend per head to last year. I'm sure we can extract those numbers,' he said to himself.

'So the show could actually make money,' said Tom, trying to spell it out for Phillip.

'And we could measure the show,' added Amy. 'Ask the guests to score it. Prove we can get as good a score with entertainment as we can with rides?'

Phillip slowly raised his head. 'Like a test. A test the whole group could learn from?'

'That's it.' Tom nodded vigorously. 'Amy's right. We could provide some invaluable feedback to the rest of the group. That shows can actually make money and they can be experienced by lots of people and that they can get just as good satisfaction scores as the rides.'

'That's right,' agreed Phillip, looking straight at Tom. 'If we can measure it we can justify it.' He paused. 'Shall we say you have a target of over sixty-five per cent of park guests must see the show, that the average satisfaction score must be over eight and we increase food and beverage spend by ... let's say five per cent. Reasonable?'

Tom swallowed. 'Are you saying we can do it?' he asked.

'I'm saying that it would be in your interests to make sure you achieve those scores,' replied Phillip.

Tom nodded. He understood perfectly. He wasn't just fighting for this show, he was fighting for the future of the Entertainment Department.

'Will someone tell me what we've just agreed here,' demanded Jerry, still looking confused.

'We have agreed to leave Phillip as he is a very busy man, right now,' said Tom, bundling Jerry, Amy and Carly out of the office before Phillip could change his mind.

CHAPTER FIFTEEN
LAURA

Laura lay semi-comatose on the sofa. There was donut sugar all down her front, a red-wine stain on her top lip and for some reason she was only wearing one sock.

She stared blankly at the TV; she had downloaded the earlier edition of *It Takes Two* thinking that its dissection of the dances on *Strictly* over the weekend would somehow distract her. She knew she really should go to bed but she had two major obstacles in her way. The first was a half-drunk bottle of wine glaring at her from the coffee table. It was begging her not to be relegated to the kitchen counter where it would fester for a long time, rejected again and again in favour of a fresh bottle. Eventually of course it would be downgraded to a possible ingredient for a casserole – or worse a gravy – but by then it was inevitable that it would meet its putrid end down the plughole, the morning after a night before when any trace of opened alcohol had to be banished immediately before it made someone want to heave.

The second obstacle was her mobile phone. A device which she often thought constricted just as much as it liberated her movements. The need to be in plain sight of that small digital screen, our window on the world, could stop her doing a multitude of things, like having a life for example. It was the last text she had received that had confined her to her sick-bed sofa as her mind had slid into darkness, helped along by alcohol and donuts.

Great news. Phillip said yes. Staying late to finalise plan of stage and revise show with Carly. Don't wait up. Xx

He may just as well have written: **With Carly. Don't wait up. Xx**. How many times was she going to have to hear that over the next week? No doubt the increased scale of the production would bring more opportunities to spend lots of time together. What a bonus, thought Laura dully.

She heard the key in the door and hastily brushed the settled sugar off her shirt and hurriedly took her odd sock off and stuffed it under a cushion. She had some standards. After hearing soft laughter in the hallway she grabbed the remote control and banished Zoë Ball, who was now interviewing the previous night's rejected couple, as she was in no mood to encourage a relaxed post-mortem of the dance-off with her husband. A middle-aged man in a grey suit popped up on screen and Laura did her best to look interested in *News at Ten*.

She could see that the newsreader was speaking but couldn't take anything in. Her ears were straining to hear the muffled conversation that was still going on in the hallway. What were they talking about? Why hadn't they come in?

Eventually the door swung open and in strolled Tom followed by Carly, who said hello and then plopped herself down on the armchair and swung her legs over the arm in an all-too-familiar way. She kicked off her shoes, letting them drop with a clunk to the floor. Laura wished she'd kept her odd sock on.

'Sorry we're late, love,' said Tom, bending to kiss her and then dropping down on the sofa beside her. 'It's been one hell of a day. Did you get my text?'

'Yes,' replied Laura, trying to sound upbeat. 'Really pleased for you.'

'Great news, isn't it?' he said. 'Just to have the opportunity to put on the show I want to. Really exciting.'

Laura looked at him. He was grinning from ear to ear despite his tiredness. He hadn't looked as excited by a show since he used to perform, before he went into management.

'It's going to be great,' she managed to say.

'We've got so much to do, haven't we?' said Tom, shaking his head at Carly.

'Unbelievable,' said Carly, hauling herself back up in her chair. 'You have no idea, Laura. I had no idea. To get this show on the road in a matter of days?

It's like the most exciting and terrifying thing I have ever done.'

'I'm throwing everything in,' Tom told Laura. 'All the ideas I've always wanted to do but never had the chance. We're really going for it. Carly's been so helpful today. Don't know what I would have done without her.'

Laura watched as her husband cast a smile in Carly's direction. Carly beamed back.

'I've loved every minute of it,' she replied. 'I'm learning so much being involved in amping up some of the choreography. The Twisted Tango number at the end could be epic, I know it. I just need to teach everyone a decent tango.'

'Maybe you should tone down the choreography just a touch at this stage. Give people a chance to feel confident. Add in the more complicated stuff in a couple of days.'

'Do you think?'

'I do.'

'OK.' Carly nodded. 'I'm worried about Theo though. The chances of him getting it right are pretty non-existent.'

'I did notice his top line was all over the place,' said Tom. 'The man must stand like this.' He leapt up, going into hold with an invisible partner. 'But he stands like this.' He dropped his shoulder and let his tongue sag out of the side of his mouth.

Carly laughed.

Laura leant to peer round Tom's obstructing body so she could continue to watch a news story she had no interest in whatsoever.

'Oops, sorry,' said Tom, shuffling to one side so she could see.

'I know,' said Carly, leaping up out of her chair and inserting herself into Tom's arms. 'He gets it right when I place his arms for him, but as soon as we start dancing he goes like a wet lettuce and dribbles all over the place.'

Tom laughed.

'Seriously,' said Carly. 'We go into hold and he can barely keep his eyes off my chest and he dribbles. I mean actually dribbles. I don't think he's ever danced with a woman – no, strike that, I don't think he's ever touched a woman before.

Tom and Carly collapsed into laughter.

'Mmmm,' muttered Laura.

'What was that?' asked Tom, turning round.

Laura looked up. 'What?'

'You said something?'

They are still in fucking hold, Laura screamed inside. My husband is standing in front of me holding a girl in his arms in my living room. Can they not see that I'm interested in this news story and I do not wish to see my husband holding another woman in his arms, in my face!

'I said,' replied Laura, 'that David Cameron has had a really rough time in the Commons today. Look, they're all jeering at him.'

Tom and Carly turned to look at the screen.

Still in hold! Laura wanted at scream at them. How can you watch Prime Minister's Question Time poised to embark on a tango?

'Wow,' said Carly. 'Politicians are like crazy.'

'Shall we show Laura what we are thinking for the finale?' Tom asked Carly, ignoring the Prime Minister's struggle in parliament.

I don't want to see it, thought Laura. I'm not sure I can give them praise. Not while they are still in fucking hold!

'It's not like perfect yet' – Carly glanced over her shoulder to Laura – 'but I suddenly had this idea, didn't I?' she said, gazing back up at Tom.

Don't look at him like that, Laura wanted to sob.

'Thank goodness you did,' agreed Tom. 'When you said why not do it as a group tango, I was like: genius, utter genius. Don't you think it's a great idea, Laura? Can you image two sets of cards? One a set of evil tarot cards and the other happy families characters. They all pair up in a group tango so when they turn you only see either the evil tarots or the friendly happy families cards. Visually brilliant.'

'I can't quite picture it,' replied Laura feebly.

'We'll show you. Imagine on my back is a large tarot card with the devil on it and on Carly's back is – I don't know – cute little old Granny Smith. And there are ten other couples on the stage with similar cards. So we'll do the dance like this...'

Tom and Carly began to dance the tango in the confined space of Laura's hearth rug, strutting up and down until they did an about-turn just before they banged into the telly and suddenly Carly's back was facing her and Tom was grinning over her shoulder.

'Do you see? The stage would appear to be full of little devils and now, with just one synchronised turn, all you can see is sweet little old ladies.'

Laura blew her cheeks out. She didn't know what to say and the happy couple was now completely obliterating the TV so she couldn't even be distracted by the unlikely welcome sight of David Cameron.

'Do you get it?' urged Tom. 'Do you see what we're trying to do?'

'Yes.' Laura nodded. 'I get it. I can visualise it really clearly. It will have a massive impact. Now I need to go to bed. I find politics late at night so unsettling.'

'Oh, me too,' agreed Carly, finally dropping out of hold with Tom. 'Another big today tomorrow. Goodnight, guys.' She squeezed Tom's shoulder and wandered out of the room.

She's left her shoes where she dropped them on the floor, was Laura's first thought. She couldn't look at Tom. She busied herself looking on the floor for the elusive remote control that she'd used only moments earlier.

'I'll tidy up and lock up,' said Tom. 'You go to bed, you look as tired as I feel.'

'OK,' she said, glancing at him. She gave him a weak smile and turned her back. Perhaps she would pretend to be asleep by the time he came upstairs.

'Archie from Customer Experience might be calling you,' announced Tom as he crashed down into bed ten minutes later. Laura had got distracted by all the fake happiness on Facebook on her tablet so had forgotten to fake sleep.

'Why?' she asked, putting her tablet down and turning to face him.

'Well, Phillip said that this show has to score an average of eight out of ten for enjoyment. You know what he's like for measuring everything.'

'So he wants an on-park survey doing?' asked Laura. 'Does he want it integrating into the satisfaction survey or will this be a bespoke project?'

'I don't know,' said Tom, his eyes glazing over. 'He just said we have to achieve that score so – since Harvest Research do all that other survey stuff on park – I just wanted to warn you that you might be getting a call. Do you think you can fix the survey so we definitely score over eight?'

'No!' exclaimed Laura. 'You can't ask that.'

'I know,' said Tom, closing his eyes momentarily. 'It's just I got the feeling from Phillip that if we don't make a success of the show then he might be reviewing whether they continue to have an Entertainment Department at all. And you've told me before that you can manipulate research to make it come out with the answer you want it to ... '

'Shhhhhhh,' said Laura, putting her hand over his mouth. 'You're not supposed to tell anyone that. That's secret insider information.'

Tom was smiling when she took her hand away. 'I know,' he said, sliding his arm under her and pulling her close. 'I'm just scared, that's all.'

'Why?' asked Laura, settling her head into his chest, warmed by his smile and by his bare skin.

'That I'm going to let everyone down. That the show won't be brilliant and it will be all my fault and then everyone will get made redundant.'

Laura tilted her head up to look at him, her frustration at his obsession with all things related to the damn show – including Carly – ebbing away. Tom had always had the potential to put on really good shows, he was so amazingly creative, but he had a habit of letting the slightest obstacle get in his way and then giving up.'

'It will be brilliant,' she said, kissing him lightly on the lips. 'You've been working on *Malice* for months, it's really good. You *know* you can do it.'

'But can I?' he said, frowning. 'I've not really managed it before. I've never really had this opportunity. I've never been able to make it how I really want to. It's been so frustrating. What if I screw it up?'

'You won't,' said Laura, stroking his forehead. 'I know you can do it.'

'Do you?' he asked.

'I do,' she said, nodding firmly. 'I really do.'

Tom still looked concerned. She reached up and kissed him again. It was nice to be this close to him and have his full attention for a change. She reached up and wove her hand round his neck, pulling his mouth more urgently into hers. She liked the way he tasted; it seemed too long since they had kissed like this. She wanted to be closer. She snaked her other hand around his side, over his back and then down inside his pyjama shorts. What had she been worrying about? This was what she wanted. This was what she needed. She just needed him to be hers. She pushed her hand further down his shorts, feeling for his buttocks.

'Not tonight, eh?' said Tom, putting his hand over hers to stop her going any further. 'I'm shattered, I'm sorry. It's been a hell of a day; I really just need to go to sleep. Another big day tomorrow too.' He bent and kissed her on the nose; then he disengaged himself until he could turn around and switch off his bedside lamp, plunging them into darkness.

Laura lay absolutely still, staring into the darkness. She could just about make out the outline of his head crushed deep into his pillow, perfectly still, waiting for the relief of sleep.

She leant her head back on her own pillow and stared upwards into nothing, her heart pounding, her fists clenched tight. She wanted to scream in anger, in frustration, in self-pity, in utter confusion.

CHAPTER SIXTEEN
HANNAH

'Have you any idea what time it is?' Hannah hissed down her phone. She didn't really know why as she was trying to be quiet since she was all alone in her bedroom, but it was after ten thirty and loud telephone conversations seemed inappropriate. She stopped and all she could hear was sobbing. She knew it was Laura calling because it had said so on her screen but she hadn't actually said anything yet so it might be someone who'd stolen Laura's phone and chosen to call her to have a good cry about it.

'Is that you, Laura?'

'Yes,' came a snuffled reply.

'What on earth's wrong?' she asked. 'Shall I come over?'

'No,' came the firm answer. 'I'll be all right in a minute, I just needed to talk to someone.'

Hannah patiently listened to a few more deep sniffs.

'It's OK, take your time,' she said, looking at her watch. She could really do with going to sleep herself so she would be dead to the world before Jerry got back from the pub. 'Can you speak now?' she asked.

Laura sniffed. 'I think so.'

'So what's happened?' she asked. 'Where are you?'

'I'm at home,' came the reply. 'In the utility room.'

'What are you doing in there? Was there a major laundry crisis or something?'

She heard a faint laugh.

'No,' said Laura. 'I just didn't want to wake anyone.'

'Apart from me?'

'Oh, you weren't asleep, were you?'

'No, no. I'm in bed. You just caught me before I turned the light off.'

'I'm so sorry,' faltered Laura. 'I'll go, call you tomorrow.'

'No, no, don't go,' said Hannah. 'You can't call me in the middle of the night from behind the tumble dryer and not tell me what's going on.'

'OK. It's just... it's just...'

'Laura, it's clearly not an "it's just" anything if you are calling me this late.'

'Tom wouldn't have sex with me,' Laura blurted out.

Hannah heaved a sigh of relief. No life-threatening disaster had occurred then. 'And your problem is what exactly?' she asked. 'I dream of a

169

husband who doesn't come home and want to have sex with me.'

'Hannah!' exclaimed Laura.

'Let's just say the dog will be sleeping in our room tonight.'

'What's the dog got to do with it?'

'Oh, Jerry's bound to come home pissed from the pub thinking he's God's gift to women as he drools lager down his chin. Sherlock barks the minute he comes near me. Best guard dog ever.'

'Well, there was no need for Sherlock in our bedroom tonight,' muttered Laura.

'So what happened then?'

'Well, for a moment we were back to normal, you know, cuddling up in bed, talking about stuff. I was just thinking that this thing with Carly is in my imagination and then he said he was too tired. He needed his energy for tomorrow when he's with bloody Carly, rehearsing for that bloody show.'

'She'll be gone soon and then you'll have him back to yourself again,' said Hannah, yawning.

'But I want him back now. He's my husband. Why does she get to have him all day every day and most of the night as well? I bet he's bloody dreaming about her now.' Laura had raised her voice.

'Shush. You'll wake the washing machine up.'

'I don't care about the bloody washing machine. I just want my husband back.'

'How can you want him back? He never went anywhere.'

'He's not here, Hannah. I'm telling you he's so not here.'

Hannah sighed. What was she supposed to say? How do you give advice to someone whose husband hasn't quite cheated on them just yet?

'I don't know what to say,' Hannah finally settled on.

'Thanks for that. So helpful.'

'Hey, who's the one talking to you at goodness knows what time about an imaginary affair? I'm doing as much as I can, given the circumstances. Are you drinking?'

'There was half a bottle of wine left that was going to waste,' said Laura.

'You're drinking wine ... in the utility room?'

'Yes,' replied Laura as Hannah heard her draw breath and clearly take another sip.

'That's not good,' pointed out Hannah.

'I know,' said Laura.

'You're on the phone, in the middle of the night, whilst drinking alone in the utility room, because your husband might, I repeat might, have an affair with the lodger. That's not normal behaviour, Laura.'

'I admit it's quite irrational.'

'Hello – yes.'

'But I've made a list of reasons why he will sleep with her and reasons why he won't and the reasons why he will outweigh the reasons why he won't by two to one. That's not good odds, is it?'

'No,' said Hannah, now praying for Jerry to come home so she could get off the phone and stop trying to reassure her friend that her concerns were unfounded. It was too late for this and it was giving her brain-ache.

'Admittedly I haven't weighted it yet,' said Laura.

'Haven't what?'

'Weighted it. The responses ideally should be weighted in order to give a true outcome but I'm finding it hard to put a value on them. I mean how much do you weight the response... hang on a minute...'

There was a pause and Hannah could hear rustling. 'What are you doing?'

'Just getting my list out.'

'You carry the list with you?'

'I only made it tonight. I had to shove it in my pocket quick when Tom and Carly got back. Hang on a minute, I'll have to put the light on.'

Hannah waited patiently for Laura to come back on the line.

'So for example in the column under reasons why they won't have an affair is the response: "Because he is married to me." How would you weight that against a response in the other column which reads: "Because she is beautiful and reminds him of his ex-fiancée."'

Hannah sighed. 'Do you know what I think you should do?' she said.

'What? Please tell me.'

'Go upstairs and have sex with your husband so I can go to sleep.'

There was a moment's silence at the end of the line.

'You're right,' came the response.

Thank goodness for that, thought Hannah.

'I should just go upstairs and have sex.'

'Yes, do.'

'But what if he's asleep?'

'Then wake him up,' hissed Hannah, 'please, and then we can all get some sleep.'

'Great, good, thanks, Hannah.'

'You're welcome. Don't leave the wine in the utility room, hey? Too sad if anyone sees it. They'll think you've lost it.'

'OK, will do. Wish me luck.'

'Good luck having sex with your husband,' said Hannah wearily.

'Bye.'

'Bye.'

Damn, thought Hannah as she clicked the phone off and heard Jerry stumble into the hall below. He'd know she's awake. He'd have seen the bedroom light from the driveway. No time to pretend she was already in the land of Nod.

Two seconds later the bedroom door opened so forcefully that it ricocheted off the wall. Hannah winced and then her eyes grew wide as she struggled to comprehend what was coming through the doorway.

'G'day, Sharon,' came Jerry's voice from somewhere behind a seven-foot-long inflatable crocodile. He was struggling to get it through the door. All she could see was the belly of a croc pounding backwards and forwards trying to break into her bedroom. The dog was going mental, barking its head off.

'G'day, Sharon,' cried Jerry again.

'I think you'll find it's Sheila,' Hannah said under her breath.

'It's your ole mate Bruce back from the watering hole, home to his Sharon,' he declared, grinning over the croc's shoulder, having momentarily given up his battle with the doorpost and the amphibian.

'It's Sheila,' said Hannah. 'Not Sharon, Sheila. Come here, Sherlock. Ignore the weird scary man at the door trying to break in with a man-eating reptile.' Sherlock immediately jumped up on to the bed and calmed down.

'Why?' she asked, trying to remain calm as she took in Jerry's ruddy grinning face, panting from the excursion of walking home with an awkward companion and getting him up the stairs.

'Hang on a minute,' he replied before disappearing for a second. The next thing Hannah knew Jerry gave a battle cry as he took a run-up and threw his full weight at the beast. They landed in a heap just inside the door as Jerry pretended to fight off the tricky predator.

'Just give me a moment,' he gasped, rolling around on the floor. 'I'll soon have this critter in hand and then I will come and sweep my fair maiden off her feet.'

'No rush,' replied Hannah, reaching to turn off her bedside light. She watched as he scrambled to stand up. He picked up his new friend and tried to lean it against the wall. After five attempts, which all resulted in it slithering to the floor, Hannah felt she should step in.

'I can't sleep next to that,' she said. 'Please put it outside.'

'But he'll be lonely,' replied Jerry.

'Outside!' exclaimed Hannah. She was starting to lose it.

'OK, OK,' mumbled Jerry, grabbing hold of the inflatable and walking towards the door. 'Off you go, matey, and find some other friends to sleep with.' He swung the croc backwards before throwing it through the door with all his might. There was no sound for a few seconds and then a distant, gentle thud.

'Oh my God. I've killed him,' shouted Jerry, dashing outside. 'I threw him over the bannister. Are you OK down there?' Hannah heard him holler. The crocodile didn't reply. Jerry ambled back in and bellyflopped on to the bed, grinning beer fumes in Hannah's face.

'No croc bones were broken during the course of this performance,' he announced.

'So glad to hear it,' replied Hannah. 'You stink. Why don't you have a shower?'

'Don't you want to know why I've bought a seven-foot-long inflatable crocodile home with me?' he asked, frowning.

'Not really.'

'Oh.' Jerry buried his face in the duvet. Sherlock looked up and nuzzled his nose in Hannah's arm.

'It's all right, Sherlock,' she said, patting his head. 'He's just got drunk at the pub and bought, borrowed or stolen some random item from someone because he thought it might be funny. Yes I know, it doesn't feel that funny at this time of night, does it? But maybe one day he might grow up.'

'I bought it from the toy shop next to the travel agent's, this afternoon,' declared Jerry, rearing his head up. Then he let his face splat on to the duvet again, either because he thought he'd fully explained the new arrival or because he had room spin.

Hannah sighed. What had he been up to now?

'I wanted to surprise you,' he said, his face surfacing briefly.

Hannah swallowed. She didn't like Jerry's surprises. They typically involved a large amount of money having been spent on something that Jerry thought was a good idea but Hannah didn't.

'So tell me what you've bought then?' she asked.

His face reappeared and he propped his chin in his hands. 'Guess where we are going?' he said, a huge grin now spread across his face.

Hannah wished with all her body she was asleep.

'I can't believe you've not guessed,' he continued excitedly. 'We can take him with us. We can take Choppers home,' he declared, pointing out of the bedroom door.

'Aren't we too old for the zoo?' she asked, her eyebrows raised.

'Not the zoo!' He sprang off the bed. 'Look – here's another clue.'

Hannah watched as Jerry leapt around the bedroom, his hands clenched in front of his chest.

'Boing, boing, boing,' he shouted happily.

'No,' said Hannah, shaking her head. 'Not getting it. A rabbit sanctuary? Please can you stop? You're making me feel sick.'

He halted right next to her head and leant down to whisper in her ear. The beer fumes nearly made her pass out. 'Australia,' he hissed loudly

'What?' she said, sitting bolt upright up in the bed.

He stood up and threw his arms wide. 'Australia,' he roared. 'How about that? We're going to see Charlie for Christmas – well, eventually. Round-the-world ticket, Hannah. That's what I've bought. Six weeks seeing whatever we want to see with a week in the middle with my dear brother on his winery. Thank you, thank you, thank you,' he said, bowing repeatedly. 'No need for the applause, really. It was nothing.'

Hannah was wide-awake now.

'When?' It was all she could think to say.

'First of December we leave from the almighty Heathrow,' he replied.

'Six weeks?' she asked.

'Oh yes, baby. Six whole weeks. And before you ask, I've lined your dad up to look after the business. He's well up for it. It's quiet anyway.'

'Six weeks,' repeated Hannah.

'I know!' exclaimed Jerry. 'Fucking brilliant, eh? What a way to end the year.'

Hannah had gone white. She felt physically sick.

'It's all right, no need to thank me. I know it's you who always organises our holidays and Christmas – which you always moan about, what with the relatives and the ball-ache of presents and whatnot, so I thought I'd take it all off your hands and plan us a trip which will get us away from our nearest and dearest at Crimbo. Including my mother. Am I a genius or what?'

Hannah raised her gaze from the floral print of the duvet as a million different thoughts and emotions washed over her. Feelings she hadn't known she had engulfed her in response to what Jerry was proposing: six weeks alone with her husband, away from here. She knew she just couldn't stomach it. She looked at her husband, praying that the right reaction to his announcement lay somewhere inside her. She scrutinised his face, searching for the trigger that would spark a sense of joy in this moment. But it didn't come. She felt nothing but the slow cold realisation that by booking this trip Jerry had inadvertently prompted in Hannah the knowledge that the prospect of six weeks on holiday with her husband depressed her to the bone – and that was something she couldn't ignore.

CHAPTER SEVENTEEN
TOM

'Utter carnage back there,' declared Amy, plopping herself down next to Tom on the newly built outdoor stage. She pulled her scarf more tightly around her neck and blew on her hands.

Tom glanced up from where he was attempting to make notes on his script whilst a small army of builders clattered around him, desperately trying to add the finishing touches before the first dress rehearsal was due to start in an hour. Tom couldn't feel the ends of his fingers owing to the chilly October air but he didn't care. They were going to do an outdoor show and the cold was something they would all have to get used to.

'What's up with them?' Tom asked Amy. 'When I used to perform in the Halloween show we'd have been grateful for a dressing room at all. I remember I had a peg with my name Sellotaped on it in the gents toilets...and I appreciated it.'

'I think some of them would rather have the gents than the kitchen of an old burger-bar unit. The girls are moaning it stinks of chip fat and it's making them feel sick, whilst the blokes are saying it makes them hungry and can they send someone for McDonald's.'

'The youth of today,' said Tom, shaking his head. 'Never happy. You look different,' he added, squinting at her.

'It's the make-up,' she replied.

'Right.' He could see it now: the almost child-like application of blue/green eye shadow and pink lipstick. 'Unlike you?' he said and then broke out into a broad grin. 'You fancy someone?' he asked, nudging her.

'Fuck off,' she replied, going instantly pink.

'You do, don't you?' he continued, his eyes wide.

Amy went pinker and looked away.

'Who is it?' he demanded.

'No one,' she replied.

'It's Nathan, isn't it? I've noticed that he looks at you funny.'

'Fuck off. He looks at everyone funny, he's got a lazy eye.'

'Has he?'

'Of course he has. Don't you notice anything?' she shrieked at him.

'Ooh,' said Tom, shrinking back. He'd made Amy mad. She was more tetchy than usual today. 'Calm down. Can't say I've ever looked into his eyes. But clearly you have.'

Amy blinked back at him and if he didn't know her better he'd have said she was borderline teary. Amy never got emotional. She must have it really bad with this Nathan. She looked away and sniffed loudly.

'Look,' he said, regretting taking the piss. 'If I can help at all to get you two guys together, then you only have to ask. What if I tell him he's got to come in for extra rehearsal and then leave you to it? To rehearse him. Or whatever you want to do to him.'

Amy was staring back at him looking grim. This was not good. He needed Amy on side. She was his right-hand man and he couldn't function without her.

'I bet Carly would help you with your make-up,' he continued. 'She can put it on in the car at the same time as rehearsing her solos at the top of her voice whilst we're driving down the main road. It's true, I've seen her do it. I bet she'd give you some tips. I'll ask her if you want?'

'You really are an utter twat,' declared Amy. She wiped the back of her hand across her mouth and smeared the pink gloss across her face.

Tom reached into his pocket and offered her a handkerchief.

She grabbed at it, rubbing furiously around her lips and chin. 'Has it gone?' she demanded.

He nodded, not daring to speak.

She stuffed the hanky back into her coat pocket. Tom daren't point out that the handkerchief was in fact his.

They sat in silence for a moment.

'We're screwed, aren't we, if this show doesn't work?' Amy eventually said.

'What do you mean?'

'Entertainments will be no more. I'll be back selling candy floss and you' – she turned to look at him – 'they'll offer you a job in recruitment or training or something. Ask you to do your best to make the numpties who operate the rides and the losers who sell the burgers to be "entertainers" in everything they do. And they won't say they're getting rid of the Entertainment Department, they'll say they are expanding it to encompass every single employee because everyone who works at a theme park should be an entertainer whilst making everyone who actually *is* an entertainer redundant.'

Tom didn't know what to say.

'Am I right?' demanded Amy.

'I'm not sure but the prospects are not good,' said Tom.

She frowned. 'I want you to know you were the best boss I ever had,' she said.

'Whoa,' said Tom. 'We're not sunk yet. Phillip said if we get great satisfaction scores and enough people watching then we survive.'

Amy looked at him, and then glanced over her shoulder towards the makeshift changing room behind them.

'Like I said,' she said. 'Utter carnage. That's not a cast, it's a crèche.'

As if on cue a young lad dressed in the bottom half of a dormouse costume came running out on stage.

'Tom,' he screamed. 'Wayne is pretending to shag the Queen of Hearts whilst wearing my mouse-head, and I need to get into character. How am I supposed to find my inner dormouse if all I can picture is my character shagging an old queen?'

Tom glanced over to Amy. 'I think we'd both better get back there,' he said.

'And sort this pile of shit out,' said Amy with a massive sigh, heaving herself up.

Carnage actually didn't do justice to the scene that greeted Tom as he thrust open the door to the men's makeshift dressing room in one half of the restaurant kitchen. A tarot card and a happy families card were rehearsing their dance steps on top of a stainless-steel prep table, making the most hideous din with their shoes. The beheaded dormouse was screaming at the top of his voice whilst chasing Tweedledum around the table.

'Stop shagging in my mouse-head!'

Men in various states of dress were crowded around the one mirror that had been provided by the Costume Department. They were all trying to apply make-up in the way that a small child would paint a picture, with massive over-confidence but little skill. There was much pushing and shoving and contortion of bodies with one poor chap resorting to lying on the floor to procure a small area of mirror right at the bottom.

The worst sight of all, however, was the two young lads still in their civvies and smoking roll-ups, sniggering as they took it in turns to peep though a tiny slit in the dust sheet that had been draped across in the room in a desperate attempt to achieve separation between the male and female members of the cast.

Amy plucked a giant saucepan off one of the shelves and banged it hard down on the stainless-steel counter, causing the two rehearsing cards to leap off in fright and the rest of the males to turn in silent shock.

Amy nodded to Tom.

'Oh, right, yes,' he said, coughing to give himself time to gather his thoughts.

'You are a shambles,' shouted Amy at the top of her voice.

Tom stared at her in awe.

'Go on,' she said, nudging him.

'Amy's right,' he declared. Amy put the large saucepan upturned at his feet and nodded at it. He stepped on to it and surveyed his audience. By now faces from next door in the girls' dressing room were appearing through the gaps in the curtains.

'Call yourselves professionals?' he continued. 'What is this? Amateur dramatics night?'

'Feels like it,' mumbled someone. 'Nothing like the smell of chip fat to make you realise you've made it to the big time.'

'Do you think it gets any better?' he demanded, turning round to address the general area of where the mumbling came from. There was silence. 'Well, do you?' he demanded again.

'I'd like to think that Benedict Cumberbatch isn't distracted by fried food when he's preparing his Hamlet,' piped up the headless dormouse.

'Do you want to know the difference between you and Benedict Cumberbatch?' Tom asked the defiant mouse.

'About four stone,' offered Tweedledum. He was still wearing the dormouse's head.

'Fuck off and give me my head back,' said the dormouse, turning on him and scrabbling at his head.

'The *difference*' – Tom spoke loudly over the din until the dormouse fell silent – 'is that Benedict wouldn't give a damn about what his dressing room is like. It's irrelevant. None of this matters,' he said, waving his arms around so much he nearly fell off his saucepan. 'All that matters is what happens out there.' He pointed to the stage. 'All that matters is what your *audience* sees, not what you see. Put your energies, your emotions, your feelings out there on the stage, not in here. Now grow up the lot of you and let's stop wasting our time with petty quibbles about backstage. You are professionals. I know that in this room is the potential for the most amazing show this park has ever seen. So start acting like it. Anything to add, Amy?'

Amy was staring up at him with her mouth open as if in a trance.

'Actually there is,' she said, giving herself a little shake and then legging herself up on to the stainless-steel table. She had grabbed a cane from the tarot card. 'You've got big dreams,' she said, slowly rotating herself round so she could address the entire cast, pointing her cane. 'You want fame? Well, fame costs and right here is where you start paying' – she slammed the end of the cane down on the counter – 'in sweat. And I wanna see sweat!' She slammed the cane down again. 'Do you understand?' she demanded at the top of her voice.

'Hell yeah,' came a cry from Carly, peering between the curtains.

'Hell yeah,' everyone chanted back to her.

'You heard Tom,' continued Amy. 'Energy, emotions and feelings are required on that stage in five minutes, fully dressed and made up. Now go!'

Tom heard the dormouse mumbling behind his back about his inability to sweat in a temperature of just five degrees as he held his hand up to help Amy down from her makeshift stage.

'Impressive,' he said, nodding to her.

'Just thought they needed a few more words of encouragement,' she replied. 'For fuck's sake, Richard,' she shouted over Tom's shoulder, 'the tights go over your underwear not underneath them. A zombie would hardly be seen sporting Mickey Mouse pants, would he?'

She pushed past Tom to go and rectify any other wardrobe malfunctions.

Tom blew out his cheeks. He'd better go back out to the front and prepare for what he suspected would still be an appalling first dress rehearsal. He just needed to pass on a couple of notes to Carly though, if he could find her. He walked over to the flimsy divide and peered round the corner asking the nearest person if everyone was decent so he could go in.

'Tom wants to come in,' shouted Jessy, a stalwart member of the department. 'Has anyone still got their tits out?'

'I'll check, shall I?' Tom heard a male voice shout back. 'No, don't worry, girls, it will be my pleasure.'

What the hell, thought Tom. Was that who he thought it was? He pulled the curtain back sharply and searched the room.

'Jerry!' he exclaimed. 'What are you doing back here? You shouldn't be in the girls' dressing room.'

'Oh, don't worry, darling,' said Jessy, touching his shoulder. 'He's fine. We don't mind Jerry being here, do we, girls?'

'No,' came back a chorus of approval.

'He's been really helpful,' added Jessy. 'Look, he's put all these mirrors up and proper lights. He and Will have been a godsend.'

Tom looked over to the back wall where Jessy was pointing. In contrast to the chaos of the men's dressing room the ladies' area was organised and calm. A row of mirrors had been attached to a blank wall and his brother was halfway up a ladder attaching a string of high-powered lights above them.

Jerry came ambling up to him grinning like an overweight married man who'd just spent the last half-hour in a room with semi-naked women.

He went to embrace Tom and hissed in his ear. 'Time of my fucking life. I want your job. You get to spend time with this?' He cast his arm around the room as various girls looked up and smiled and waved at him.

'That isn't why I do this job,' Tom hissed back.

'Well, it should be. Might stop you being so fucking miserable about it half the time.'

'Why are you here exactly?' asked Tom impatiently. He didn't really have time to deal with Jerry's adolescent behaviour just now.

'Carly called me,' said Jerry with a shrug. 'Said the show couldn't possibly go on without decent mirrors and lighting for these adorable women to get ready in front of. How could I refuse? They were damsels in distress in hardly any clothes. I had no choice but to come running to their aid. And guess what? They're all really grateful. They keep calling me their hero. Especially that one over there. The brunette with the extremely long legs. What's her name? I'll be her hero any day of the week, I tell you.'

'Must I remind you that you are married?' said Tom.

'Am I?' Jerry suddenly frowned.

'Yes,' urged Tom. 'Remember? To Hannah? I didn't waste all that money on a stag do for you to throw it away on someone half your age.'

'We stayed in a caravan in Blackpool,' said Jerry. 'It was a lot of money back then.'

'If I remarried I'd have a stag do in Vegas,' said Jerry wistfully.

'What are you talking about?' asked Tom. 'You're not getting remarried.'

Jerry turned to him looking uncharacteristically sad. Jerry's pint was always half full. Typically Jerry didn't know what half empty meant.

'So what do you make of this?' he asked. 'I come home with a seven-foot-long inflatable crocodile from the pub—'

'And Hannah wants a divorce? Understandable,' interrupted Tom.

'It was a surprise,' continued Jerry. 'I've booked us a round-the-world trip including a week on my brother's vineyard in Australia and do you know what she said?'

'Get that enormous waste of space out of my sight?'

'The crocodile had come to a sticky end having dive-bombed off the landing at that point.'

'I meant you!'

'Cheers. I'm trying to have a conversation here, buddy.'

'OK,' said Tom, looking at his watch. The cast had now had well over their allotted five minutes to get ready. 'So what did she say?'

'She said, and I quote, "I'll think about it." What in heaven's name is that all about? I'm offering to take her to the ends of the earth and back and she needs to think about it. You'd think I'd offered to replace the hoover. I don't get it, Tom. There was nothing. Not a hint of a smile, or glimmer of excitement. What do I have to do to make my wife look like she's pleased she married me?'

'She's probably chuffed to bits. Just not showing it.'

'Oh, she'll be worrying about the cost, I know she will. She doesn't know how to sit back and enjoy what we've achieved. What's the point of working like a dog when you don't get to make the most of the rewards? If only she'd just live a little, let go, have some fun. What's wrong with that, I ask you?'

'I have to say that Laura is no barrel of laughs either at the moment,' said Tom. 'She's very short with me. I must have done something wrong but I've no idea what it is.'

'Do you think it's the menopause?' asked Jerry.

'They're not old enough for that yet, are they?'

'I don't know.' Jerry shrugged. 'Not even sure what the menopause is, to be honest. Do you know? Do you think we should know?'

'Something to do with hormones, I think.' Tom shook his head. 'Not really sure though, I have to admit.'

'Are you allowed to travel if you're going through the menopause? Perhaps that's why she doesn't want to go to Australia. She can't because of too many hormones or something? Shall I ask her if she's got too many hormones?'

Tom looked at Jerry. 'Somehow that doesn't feel like a question that it would be wise to ask.'

'Shall I ask her if she's menopausal then?'

'Again, Jerry, I'd steer clear if I were you. Perhaps she's pregnant? Have you thought about that?'

'Bah. There's no chance of that. To be honest it's partly why I booked this holiday, get her away from that bloody dog. The damn thing is ruining my love life.'

'What are you talking about?' asked Tom.

'It sleeps in the corner of the room and if I make one move, just one, it growls. I'm not kidding. It's like trying to have sex whilst your mother's listening.'

'My mother's listened to you having sex?'

Jerry paused.

'Possibly,' he said eventually.

'What!' exclaimed Tom. 'When?'

'When we went to your mum's caravan when we were eighteen and I brought those girls back with us on the Friday night, do you remember?'

'Yeah.'

'And your mum and dad came to join us on the Saturday.'

'Yes.'

'They lied. They'd arrived on the Friday night whilst we were out. They just pretended they'd arrived on the Saturday because they were too embarrassed to admit they'd had to spend all night listening to us shagging.'

'Wow,' replied Tom, reeling.

'Point is I'm not getting any. I either need to hire a hit man for the damn dog or get my wife out of the country and neither is looking likely at the moment. Now, will you tell me what the name of that brunette is?'

Chapter Eighteen
Laura

Laura pulled her skirt down and recrossed her legs, feeling the unfamiliar sensation of nylon against nylon between her thighs. Why on earth had she decided to wear a short skirt and her new knee-high leather boots, thus making it unavoidable that she wear tights? She knew it was inevitable that the crotch would end up halfway down her thighs whilst the waistband would remain determined to hang on just beneath her breasts. Both unattractive and uncomfortable. Why was she putting herself through this?

She looked up as a couple of brightly uniformed young lads strolled through the reception of Wonderland totally ignoring her. She pulled her skirt down over her knees again. She was embarrassed that she'd made such an effort for her meeting but it was all part of her attempt to spruce up her image in retaliation to the glamour that Carly had bought to the house. After Tom's rejection and her late-night chat with Hannah, Laura had headed back to bed with the intention of waking her husband up and demanding the services of his body. But when she'd looked in the bathroom mirror and caught sight of her wine-stained teeth and hideous tangled mass of hair she'd convinced herself that waking him would only lead to another knock-back. Instead she'd vowed to 'glam up', and promptly went out and purchased knee-high boots and a short skirt but so far they had not had the desired effect on her husband.

She sighed and looked at her watch. Archie from Guest Happiness was running ten minutes late. She could have predicted that. When she'd spoken to him on the phone she'd realised very fast that Archie was probably not the type of client she was used to dealing with. She actually wouldn't normally have come to this meeting, she would have sent her assistant as it was all very straightforward and Laura was used to dealing with more senior clients. However, for some reason she felt compelled to be involved and as she lived so close to the theme park it made logistical sense for her to call in on her way home to have a quick meeting and work out the details.

'Hiya,' said a lad leaping into view. She'd met plenty of Archies when she'd worked here before. Young lads whose dream-come-true was to work at Wonderland. Keen, enthusiastic, lovely, totally on another planet and totally clueless. He was a car crash from head to toe. The badly dyed jet-black hair didn't suit his pale skin and served only to draw attention to his acne-ridden face. He was wearing a shirt and tie no doubt in an effort to make him look older than twelve but the gravy stain down the front gave away that he was barely out of bibs. He had every reason to be miserable and yet he wasn't. The truly beautiful and truly ugly should not be allowed to be happy, thought Laura. It's the middle-of-the-roaders like me who need the happiness. The pretty ones don't need it and the ugly ones just make you feel bad because they have dealt with their shortcomings way better than you have.

'Welcome to Wonderland,' announced Archie. 'Your happy place.'

Laura already wanted to punch him.

She stood up and smoothed down her too-short skirt. Archie's youth and exuberance made her feel like a sad old desperate cow.

'So I've booked Laughter for our meeting.' Archie grinned. 'Chuckles was free but Laughter has a much nicer feel to it even though everyone says that you can't beat Chuckles for successful one-on-one. Follow me.'

Laura's heart sank. Either he fancied himself as a bit of a comedian, or he'd been on some dubious substances around the back of the Cantering Carousel. She tramped down a long dark corridor watching the black curls on the back of his neck bounce over his stained collar.

'Would you like a coffee?' he shouted over his shoulder about halfway down.'

'Yes please,' she replied on autopilot.

He abruptly turned left into a small kitchenette as Laura paused awkwardly by the door. She watched as he picked a mug out of the washing-up bowl and switched on the cold tap. He swirled water around inside it then banged the mug down on the counter without drying it.

'Do you take milk?' he asked. 'I've run out but I can nick someone else's. No one minds if it's for a guest.'

'I'll have it black,' replied Laura.

'Sugar?'

'OK,' she said slowly, worried that she might be leading him into further theft.

'We share the coffee and sugar,' he said, pouring boiling water into the mug and then adding the coffee powder afterwards. 'How many?'

'Just one,' replied Laura, mesmerised.

Archie extracted the spoon and plunged it straight into the sugar bowl. It emerged with damp, claggy, coffee-stained sugar clinging to it. After a vigorous stir he tapped the rim of the mug with the spoon and hurled it into the washing-up bowl.

'Shall we go and make ourselves comfortable in Laughter?' he said, smiling and shaking his head as though amazed by his mirth. 'We've renamed the meeting rooms. They used to be numbered but now we have Laughter, Joy, Happiness, Chuckles and Giggles. Cool, hey?'

'Genius,' said Laura, following him down another dark corridor at the end of which it seemed unlikely there would be anything approaching laughter, joy, happiness, chuckles or giggles.

They eventually entered a beige room, with beige carpet and beige chairs and a beige table, which instantly made you feel quite depressed. Blu-Tacked to the door was a sheet of A4 paper with a large pair of red lips on it and underneath 'LAUGHTER' spelt out in capital letters.

Laura sat down and tucked her new shiny boots under her chair, as far away from Archie as possible. She pulled a notebook and pen out of her bag.

'So?' she said, looking expectant. 'You said on the phone that you needed a piece of bespoke research formulating to monitor the effectiveness of the *Malice in Wonderland* Halloween Show.'

Archie nodded enthusiastically but said nothing.

'OK,' said Laura, writing *Give me strength* at the top of her piece of paper. 'So do you have any particular measurement in mind?'

'Not really. We just want to know if it's any good or not, which of course it will be because everything we do at Wonderland is utterly amazing.'

'OK,' Laura said again, writing *Shoot me now* on the next line down.

'I know,' Archie squeaked, looking very pleased with himself. 'Why don't we ask if watching the show makes them happy!'

'Happy?' asked Laura.

'Yes.' Archie nodded vigorously. 'It's one of our brand objectives. To make everyone happy. We aim to be the leading family brand for happiness.'

'Yes,' said Laura. 'Just not sure if the right way to judge a Halloween show is how happy it makes you.'

'Mmmm,' said Archie, frowning for the first time.

'Might I suggest that we keep it simple? That we ask the same sort of questions that we use on the overall park survey.'

Archie was still frowning.

'We could ask people to rate the show out of ten just as we do for all the other attractions. Then we will at least have something to compare it to.'

Archie nodded.

'We could also ask people if they would recommend the show to other visitors. That can be an effective way of asking in a different way if they enjoyed it.'

Archie nodded again.

'What about asking if having a show is more likely to make them come back to visit next Halloween?'

Archie continued to silently nod.

'So shall we do all that then?' asked Laura.

'Sounds brilliant. Great. Look forward to seeing the results,' Archie said, getting up as if to leave.

'Whoa,' cried Laura. She couldn't believe it. That wasn't a meeting. It was a mother telling her son how to do his homework. She took a deep breath. 'You need to tell me who you want asking, how many you want to ask, when you want it doing, when you want the results, all that sort of stuff.'

'Oh, we will need the results straight away,' replied Archie. 'My boss said Phillip was very clear about that. Like immediately. Head Office are coming up or something so it's really important.'

'Right. So it's really important we get this right then, isn't it?'

'Of course.' Archie looked at his watch. 'But you can sort all that out, right? That's what a research agency does, isn't it?'

'Yes, but I need you to be absolutely clear on what you want or else we could do the research and it would be a total waste of money,' she said, feeling exasperated. She watched as Archie's eyes widened in fear. 'If you tell me the wrong thing or if what we agree here doesn't give Head Office the information they want then all there will be to show for it is a bill from us. Not sure anyone would be impressed with that, are you?'

Archie looked at his watch again, then nervously up at Laura. He wasn't smiling now.

He swallowed. 'What do *you* think we should do?' he almost whispered.

'I think we should pretend this meeting never happened,' she replied, closing her notebook emphatically. 'I'll email your boss with a draft set of questions first thing in the morning with a suggestion of how it should be administered.'

'Good idea.' Archie nodded eagerly.

'Now would you be kind enough to take me to where the show is being staged so I can assess where the researchers might stand.'

'OK,' he muttered, his attention drawn to his watch again.

'Don't worry, you don't have to wait with me,' she said, putting her notebook in her bag and getting up. 'Just let me on to the park and then you can go and meet your girlfriend.'

'What!' he said, jerking his head up. 'How do you know I'm meeting my girlfriend?'

'Your aftershave is, er… very present, and you keep checking your watch. And guys like you always have a girlfriend. I bet she's just like you too,' she said.

Archie blushed. 'People do say that we are like peas in a pod,' he admitted. 'We do everything together.'

'Does she work here?' asked Laura, already knowing the answer.

'Oh yes,' said Archie. 'We get to work together and at Wonderland, the best place on earth. It's brilliant.'

She smiled at him. She envied him. She wished her life were that simple and that she were that happy.

Five minutes later Archie had let her through a side door and then scurried off to meet his girlfriend. He'd told her she was called Delilah, was utterly bonkers (obviously), almost as bonkers as him (obviously), and they were meeting in the Enchanted Forest area of the park to take photographs of each other sitting on the giant toadstools which they were then going to turn into their joint Christmas card.

'We're dressing up as elves,' he'd reassured her when she gave him a concerned look.

'Oh, right,' said Laura. 'I get it now. That's just so hysterical.'

'I know. We're going to have such a laugh. It was Delilah's idea. She is proper mental.'

Laura nodded. 'She must be.'

'Well, she'd have to be to put up with me!' Archie laughed.

They'd had an awkward handshake that somehow moved into a polite peck-on-the-cheek moment. She watched him stride off in the direction of the Enchanted Forest. Oh to be young again and thrilled to be taking pictures of each other dressed up as midgets.

It was already getting dark as she made her way along the pathway towards the main guest entrance to the park. She felt overwhelmed with nostalgia as she passed the Haunted House, which was, as far as she was concerned, the most romantic place on earth. It had been the end of the summer season and the last day of her contract before she returned to university. Her shoulder had been well and truly soaked by Tom as he'd grieved for his lost relationship with Natalie. They'd taken to going to the pub for a quick drink after work where Tom would sit nursing a pint going over and over the break-up, trying to make sense of it whilst Laura patiently listened, stretching out her vodka lime and soda for as long as possible. She didn't mind hearing about Natalie night after night. Anything to spend time with him. Anything to see her thigh sit alongside his; anything to have

the chance to gaze at his perfect face, which gave her
goose bumps if he ever deigned to flash a smile. She
didn't feel used, she felt like the luckiest girl alive.
She was sitting having a drink with Tom Mackintyre.
She was the chosen one he was pouring his heart out
to – who cared if his heart was full of someone else.

After a couple of weeks of melancholy moan-fests
in the snug of the Green Man, Laura chanced her
arm at lightening the mood. The grief appeared to
be drying up slightly; the anguish was coming out at
a drip rather than a gush, leaving the odd opportunity in conversation to talk about something else.

'By the way,' she'd said casually one night, when
they'd sat in silence for a few moments, 'have you
heard about Rob?'

'Who's Rob?' he asked.

'You know Rob – he runs the Pirates of the Cajun
Chicken restaurant over in Stormy Seas Land.'

'Oh yeah.' Tom looked totally uninterested.

'Well, his boss told him he wasn't getting enough
customers and he should think about having a Jack
Sparrow lookalike outside to attract people in.'

'Right,' said Tom, barely nodding.

'Well, Rob is such a doughnut, all he heard was
"sparrow", so he went to Wardrobe to ask if he could
borrow a bird costume. They only had a giant yellow budgie so Rob put it on to give it a try and managed to push over a child by mistake. The dad went
ballistic apparently and punched the budgie to the
ground. So Rob's boss walks by and instead of Jack

Sparrow outside the restaurant there's a budgie flat on its back, acting dead.'

'Oh my God,' said Tom, his eyes wide, an inkling of a smile at the corner of his mouth. 'What I would have paid to see that!'

'I took a picture,' said Laura, quickly getting her phone out of her pocket. She leant into him so he could see the tiny screen and the photo of three men in park uniform crowding around an enormous yellow bird outside a pirate-themed restaurant.

'That's hilarious,' he said, grinning for the first time in ages. 'You could make a whole show with a giant yellow bird appearing in really odd places. Can you imagine?'

'Oh yeah,' agreed Laura. 'It would be like a real life *Where's Wally*.'

Tom paused for a moment, looking at Laura. She self-consciously ran her tongue over her teeth in case she had lipstick on them.

'You are brilliant,' said Tom, his face suddenly lighting up. 'Do you know what we could do?'

'What?' asked Laura.

'Not sure it would work though,' he said, his smile disappearing.

'What, what, tell me,' begged Laura.

'Well, we could do Where's Wonderbear. Rather than your normal meet-and-greet type stuff, which is so boring now, we could set up a game of Where's Wonderbear for kids when they arrive. Give them a clue sheet or something and they have to write down every time they see Wonderbear. We could be totally random and pick really weird places so they think it's really funny.'

'Like posing with the statues in the gardens or pretending to be a dinosaur in the T-Rex Terror ride?'

'Or acting dead in the Haunted House, then suddenly coming alive like some weird bear zombie,' he added, looming over her with scary eyes.

'Cool,' shrieked Laura.

'Then we could do a meet and greet at the end of the day and all the kids could come and tell me where they'd seen me and I'd shake my head like this.'

Tom shook his head in an *I'm-amazed* fashion. Laura could only imagine how good Tom would be at acting like a bear in denial.

'Let's tell Bill tomorrow,' he said, grasping Laura's hands. Laura stared down at his hands over hers and then looked up.

'Yes, let's. I can show him the photo of the dead bird to give him an idea of what we mean.'

'This is going to be hilarious,' he said, wrapping his arms around her but then pulling back all too soon. 'Can you come in early and bring your phone?'

'I guess so,' she replied when really she meant, of course, I will do anything you ask me to.

'Let's go round the park early with me as Wonderbear and take lots of *Where's Wally*-style pictures to show Bill what we mean.'

'Brilliant,' replied Laura. 'That's a great idea.'

Tom grinned. 'Shall we go mad and have another drink and sit and think of the funniest places we can put Wonderbear in?'

'Absolutely,' agreed Laura. 'Let's not lose momentum now. We need to carry on with this until we've nailed it. It could be a long night.'

Yes, they had a lot to thank Wonderbear for, thought Laura as she approached Tom, who was standing in front of the temporary stage at the exit to the park. It was five-thirty and the park was deserted having shut at four now that the nights were drawing in. Suddenly the park music went off and all that could be heard was the low rumble of generators powering spotlights that flooded the stage with light. Laura didn't really need to see the area in order to put together her research proposal but she'd promised Tom she'd call in and say hello and tell him how the meeting had gone. Not that there was anything to tell him other than Archie really should use deodorant.

'Where's Wonderbear?' roared Tom as she walked up behind him. Wonderbear didn't appear on the empty stage. Tom turned to say something to Amy, who was standing next to him. He didn't look happy.

'I will ask one more time,' Tom shouted at the top of his angry voice towards the stage. '*Where's Wonderbear*?'

'Maybe he's playing dead in the Haunted House – or he could be peeping out of the photo booth at the top of the last drop on the Log Flume?' offered Laura from right behind him.

Tom swung round. He smiled in instant recognition. 'Playing dead in the Haunted House was the most fun I ever had as Wonderbear.'

He remembers, thought Laura. He remembers their first kiss in the Lurid Library whilst screaming teenagers whizzed past them with only a zombie in a coffin to shield them.

'You were Wonderbear,' said Amy in amazement.

Tom nodded. 'Oh yes. In fact Laura and I made Wonderbear who he is today. Without the massive success of Where's Wonderbear, then I'm afraid Wonderbear would no doubt have been relegated to the rejected theme-park mascot graveyard in the sky.'

'We invented Where's Wonderbear,' said Laura when Amy looked confused. 'Kids loved it.'

'We got into places that Wonderbear never should have been,' continued Tom, winking at Laura.

Laura felt herself blush. Where's Wonderbear proved to be an overnight success with kids clamouring to visit the park in search of their new hero. Laura and Tom were given free rein with the game, putting them in many a tight, intimate spot together as they tried to trick their followers. Squashed together behind a zombie in the Haunted House, Tom had said he needed air. He took his bear head off and with lips inches apart it seemed rude not to kiss, then snog for what had seemed a wonderful eternity, until Tom had finally pulled away and said, 'I hope

Wonderbear's not watching?' They'd both glanced at the floor to see the blank eyes of the bear gazing back up at them. Screaming in delight they'd run out of the building into the sunlight hoping that no one would see a headless bear chasing a petit brunette out of the Haunted House.

'Do you remember the time behind the giant gnomes in the Secret Garden?' asked Tom.

Laura felt herself go bright red.

'Disgusting,' announced Amy before turning around. 'Where the hell is Wonderbear?' she shouted at the top of her voice. 'If you don't come out on this stage right now I will personally chop off your furry balls.'

'We're trying to rehearse the Twisted Tango – you know, like Carly and I showed you the other night?' Tom told Laura.

'I remember,' said Laura through a forced smile, her nostalgia bubble deflating fast.

As if on cue Carly dressed as Malice Alice tottered on stage.

'Speak of the devil,' said Amy, looking right at Laura and raising her eyebrows.

She knows, thought Laura. Though what Amy knew she wasn't sure. Carly crouched at the edge of the stage, making it impossible to avoid looking up her skirt.

'Crotch,' Amy said, nodding at the offending exposure.

'Oh, sorry,' replied Carly, not looking the slightest bit embarrassed. She jumped down to join the three of them on the floor. 'Hello, Laura,' she said.

Laura nodded back.

Carly turned to Tom. 'Do you want the good news or the bad news?'

'Bad news,' said Tom. 'Get it over with.'

'Well, the bad news is Wonderbear man has a cold and hasn't been seen all day, which apparently – I'm reliably informed, in theme-park Entertainment Department speak – means he's gone to audition for the pantomime in town.'

'Happens every year,' said Tom, shaking his head. 'The sniff of another job at the end of the season and they're off. No bloody loyalty. So what's the good news?'

'Apparently he's crap so he won't get the part and will return to work tomorrow,' she replied.

'Unbelievable,' cried Tom. 'And we are expected to welcome him back.'

'Um…perhaps Amy could stand in just for tonight?' said Carly slowly.

'No can do,' said Amy instantly. 'Tom needs me out here, don't you, Tom?'

For a moment Tom's face had brightened but it fell at Amy's response.

'Of course,' he was forced to agree. He put his head in his hands. 'This is a shambles,' he muttered. 'I really needed to see Wonderbear in the number tonight so we could plot where he's going to be. It's like a little homage to Where's Wonderbear, you see,' he said to Laura. 'He's going to appear at odd times, in odd places – really get the kids going. You know, just how we used to do it.'

Laura could feel it coming. She wasn't quite sure which direction it would come from but she could feel it dropping on her like a big fat trap.

'Laura, could stand in,' cried Carly, as if she'd just discovered the cure for cancer.

If Tom had asked or even Amy then it might have been palatable. Acceptable even. But Carly asking her to don the ugliest, heaviest costume you have ever seen, on the same stage where Carly would be prancing about as sexy Malice, was just too much.

'Genius!' cried Tom. 'Oh, thank you, Laura, that would be so brilliant. And you know all the moves and everything. She used to stand in for me all the time, you know,' he said to Amy. 'She'd have made a great costume character if she had stuck at it.'

Laura was shaking her head but nothing was coming out.

'No, really,' she eventually managed to sputter out. 'I can't remember how to do it.'

'You put on the costume and you act like a moron,' said Amy. 'Like I say to all our costume characters: if I could get hold of them, I'd pay monkeys to do it.'

'No, really,' said Laura again. 'I have to get back. I have to write up my notes from the meeting.'

'Quarter of an hour, that's all we need,' pleaded Tom. 'Just to do the Twisted Tango. Please, Laura. Can't tell you how helpful it would be. Like old times, hey? Me, you and Wonderbear.'

She swallowed and closed her eyes, knowing what she was about to say was the wrong answer.

'OK,' she spat out. 'Fifteen minutes and that's it.'

'Wow,' said Amy, shaking her head in wonder. 'There is no way I'd put on that stink-bucket of a costume after Duncan has let off in it all season.'

'Amy,' shouted Tom. 'Not helpful.'

'Sorry,' Amy muttered.

'Carly, why don't you take Laura backstage to put on the costume,' said Tom, 'and we'll get cracking, shall we? Tell the rest of the cast they are on stage in five minutes for the Twisted Tango, and I want it faultless.'

'Yes, sir,' said Carly, giving him a salute and grabbing Laura's arm. 'I've got my perfume so we can spray the costume to make it smell better if you like,' she whispered as they trotted off. This did not make Laura feel any better.

Minutes later Laura was standing in the girl's side of the makeshift dressing room wondering what terrible thing she must have done in her past to deserve the situation she was currently in.

'You'll have to take your skirt and top off,' Carly had said casually, leaving Laura with the awkward problem of having to follow the instruction without a clear path to covering herself up again. She had never felt more mortified as she stripped off in a room full of skinny young singers and dancers until she was left standing in the least flattering garment of all time: tights. And Tom hadn't even noticed the skirt and the boots so the whole thing had been a catastrophic waste of time and money. Carly was busy undoing buttons on the huge fur teddy body as the girls tried desperately hard not to stare at her. But Laura could feel all eyes on the roll of undesirable belly forced out by the supposedly magical tummy flattening control panel. She must have been an extraordinary sight to this image-obsessed crowd.

'Here you go,' Carly said eventually, bending down to allow Laura to step into Wonderbear.

Laura tugged the costume up as fast as she could, for once relieved to look like a furry sumo wrestler.

Carly fastened her up at the back and then carefully put the headpiece in place. 'You OK in there?' she asked with a sickly grin.

Laura was nearly choking on Carly's perfume and trying hard to resist the desire to punch her. She nodded and turned, knocking over a chair.

'Whoa,' said Carly, 'easy does it. Why don't you take my hand and I'll lead you out.

Laura felt Carly reach for her furry paw and had no option but to let Carly lead her out on to the stage where she found herself standing in front of her husband dressed as an obese teddy bear next to their glamorous young lodger dressed as a sexy Malice in Wonderland.

'Doesn't she look great?' Carly shouted over to Tom.

Ten minutes later and Laura was having the time of her life. She'd forgotten how much fun you could have inside such a costume. For some reason, because no one can see your face you feel like a different person, and you can get away with absolute murder and not be blamed.

'All you need to do is,' Tom said to her as she pulled hideous faces at him from inside Wonderbear's head, 'two or three times during the number, appear in an odd place, to add that element of surprise and cheekiness for the kids. I thought maybe you could hide behind one of the playing cards and when they do a tango turn you suddenly appear. You know, stuff like that. You know how Where's Wonderbear works. I'm sure you can pull it off. Is that OK?'

Laura nodded her head and gave a thumbs up whilst blowing a raspberry from behind Wonderbear's mouth.

'Great. Now, everyone in position please. Two run-throughs of the Twisted Tango and we'll call it a night,' Tom shouted out to the crowd milling around on stage. 'That is unless you are all a disaster, then we will be here until midnight.'

Laura ambled off to hide in the wings and await an opportunity to appear during the routine.

As she sat alone in the dressing room afterwards, having been ordered to leave the stage by her husband, she was utterly horrified by what she'd seen and heard whilst she'd been hidden inside the grubby theme-park mascot costume.

CHAPTER NINETEEN
TOM

Tom gasped in horror.

Amy burst out laughing.

The music carried on but everyone was frozen to the spot on stage, including Laura inside the Wonderbear costume.

Tom stood rigid, incredulous at what had just happened. Laura stared blankly at him, unblinking.

Carly gave a low moan from where she lay crumpled on the ground having fallen off the front of the stage following a dramatic collision with Wonderbear. Tom noticed she was clutching her ankle. This could be catastrophic.

Tom stared back at Laura as she raised her hands to Wonderbear's mouth in mock horror. This was no time for Laura to be fooling around.

'That was bloody funny,' declared Amy, still laughing. 'We should keep that in the show.'

'Carly, are you all right?' asked Tom, suddenly realising that everyone was waiting for him to react.

He leapt to her side and put his arm around her shoulder. 'Where does it hurt?'

'My ankle,' moaned Carly, burying her head in his shoulder.

Oh my God, thought Tom, starting to panic. This could spell disaster. He couldn't afford to lose his best singer and dancer to an injury. What should he do? He looked towards Amy, who was still doubled up with laughter. How could she be the best and the worst assistant all rolled into one?

'Right, Carly,' he said. 'I'm going to try and get you up to see if you can put weight on it and then let's get you to Medical and get some ice on it to stem any swelling. OK?'

Carly nodded. She crumpled up her face in pain. 'It really hurts,' she cried.

Tom noticed there were no real tears. Perhaps it was the shock of the incident that was causing the anguish rather than any real damage. He bent down towards her, put her arm around his shoulders and then hoisted her up on to one leg until she could gingerly press down on her other foot.

'Ow,' she yowled, flinging her other arm around him. Tom scooped her up into his arms, feeling her shivering against him. He should get her inside in the warm as quickly as possible.

'Amy,' he barked. 'You take over and run through the number again with everyone. Charlotte, you stand in for Carly. Do you think you can do that, Amy?'

'Of course, boss,' said Amy, looking indignant that he would think otherwise.

He turned to go, but then remembered Wonderbear. 'Laura,' he called out. 'You can go home.'

He walked away, carrying Carly in his arms.

Chapter Twenty

Laura

Laura was aware of the rest of the cast staring at her as she stood in the middle of the stage and realised she was in their way. In everybody's way apparently.

She walked back to the dressing room with her Wonderbear head drooping low, slumped into a chair and stared at her furry reflection in the mirror not knowing whether to laugh or cry.

It had been a total accident. It had all been going so well. Tom was giving her lots of thumbs ups as she popped her head around the corner of the enormous rabbit hole at the back of the stage and then skulked behind the Mad Hatter as he strutted backwards and forwards. She was actually starting to enjoy herself being anonymous and yet right in the centre of things, able to slink away and disappear when she felt like it.

But then Malice arrived on stage and all eyes turned to her as she sang in the most beautiful velvety voice in the build-up to the Twisted Tango. Laura was distracted for a moment by how good she was; but when she caught sight of the look on Tom's face, it was like a knife to the heart. He was gazing at her in adoration. Laura kicked into action, doing star jumps across the back of the stage until Tom waved crossly. Clearly Where's Wonderbear should not distract from the star of the show.

As the rest of the cast started to fill the stage, the music built to a crescendo and suddenly Laura was caught in the middle of a whirling, swirling melee of bodies. She tried to escape but dancers continually obstructed her path until Laura decided it would be fun to join in and pretend to be part of the routine.

She put herself in the correct hold just as Tom had taught her in their kitchen and headed towards the front of the stage, her aim to reveal herself to the crowd and then dive off to allow the routine to continue without her. When she arrived directly in front of Tom and Amy she did a very swift tango-style turn, which she thought even Tom would be proud of. What she was unaware of, however, was both the width of her fur-enhanced body and the fact that Malice and the White Rabbit were right behind her. Sadly her rapid, perfectly executed turn somehow managed to knock Malice clean off the front of the stage on to the cold hard block paving below.

Laura was still in full costume when the Cheshire Cat and the Queen of Hearts came in behind her.

'Are you all right?' the Cheshire Cat asked her.

Laura nodded her big furry head.

'Is this your first job?' she asked. 'Newbies always get put in Wonderbear. It's like some really bad initiation.'

Laura nodded again, too tired to explain.

'Well done you,' said the Queen of Hearts, cackling behind her. 'Carly has been cruising for a fall ever since she got here. You only did what most of us have been dying to do for ages, isn't that right, 'Chelle?'

'God, yeah. Acting as if she owns the place and she's only been here five minutes. Just because she's shagging Tom doesn't give her the right to think she's better than us.'

Wonderbear's head swivelled at hyper speed to look at the Cheshire Cat grinning back at her.

'She is so shagging him,' she confirmed. 'Got to be. She waits for him every night. I've seen her getting in his car and I've seen her arrive with him in the morning.'

Laura shook her head. They didn't know, did they? He was just bringing her home.

'And you can see the way they look at each other,' joined in the Queen of Hearts. 'I know lust when I see it. I have a lust radar. And there is serious lust between them, I'm telling you.'

Laura swivelled her head again. The Queen of Hearts was a girl of generous proportions who had the biggest cleavage Laura had ever seen. With that chest Laura could believe that this girl did know lust when she saw it.

'And he brings her a coffee to every rehearsal, just her, not the rest of us. Talk about favouritism.'

'Talk about "Thanks for last night," you mean,' cackled the Cheshire Cat.

'Casting couch definitely springs to mind,' added the Queen of Hearts. 'Honestly, sometimes this business is a disgrace.'

'He's married, isn't he, Tom?'

The Cheshire Cat shrugged. 'He is quite old.'

'Probably then.'

'Shit, we'd better get back on stage before Crazy Amy comes after us. Don't beat yourself up, eh,' she said, squeezing Wonderbear's shoulder. 'Cheered everyone up no end.'

'Apart from Carly and Tom,' said the Queen of Hearts.

'Oh yeah,' she laughed. 'Apart from Carly and Tom.'

CHAPTER
TWENTY-ONE
TOM

'How's my superstar stage-director mate?' asked
Jerry when he picked up the call on his mobile
from Tom.

'Fucked,' said Tom.

'Lucky you. I'd give my eyeballs for that at the
moment.'

'Eye teeth I think you mean, Jerry.'

'Eye teeth? What the fuck are eye teeth?'

'No idea.'

'So why would I be giving them away?'

'I don't know, Jerry.'

'You don't know what they are and you're telling
me to give them away?'

'I didn't tell you to give them away.'

'But I wanted to give my eyeballs away – which I
would, quite frankly, at the moment for a shag – and

it was you who told me to give away something else but you don't even know what it is.'

'Did you not hear me, Jerry? I'm seriously screwed.'

'Do you really have to rub it in?'

'I'm not kidding. I'm in A & E at the moment.'

'Oh my God,' exclaimed Jerry. 'Why didn't you say? What happened? Are you all right?'

'It's not me, it's Carly. Laura might have broken her ankle.'

There was silence at the other end of the phone for a moment.

'Carly and Laura are hurt?'

'No, listen. It's Carly who's hurt because Laura might have broken her ankle.'

'Why's Carly hurt if Laura's broken her ankle?'

'Because Laura knocked her off the stage.'

'Knocked who off the stage?'

'Carly! For goodness' sake, what is wrong with you tonight?'

'It's not me, it's you trying to confuse me. Just start again and tell me exactly what happened.'

'Laura came up to watch the rehearsal because her company is doing the research.'

'Is that the thingy-majiggy scores that Phillip wants?'

'That's it,' replied Tom. 'But our guy who wears the Wonderbear costume had let us down so Laura offered to stand in.'

'Laura in the Wonderbear costume,' said Jerry. 'Strangely alluring.'

'You really need to have sex with your wife if you are fantasising about Wonderbear.'

'I know, I know. Not for want of trying, mate.'

'Anyway, so Laura's on stage dressed as Wonderbear and knocks Carly flying off the edge of the stage, dropping about four feet on to the ground.'

'I know how high the stage is, Tom, I helped build it.'

'It's a nightmare,' exclaimed Tom. 'I had to carry Carly to Medical. They weren't sure what she'd done but said she should go and get an X-ray just in case. We've been here three hours and she's only just gone in. What if she's broken it, Jerry? We'll have to cancel the show. She's the only good thing in it.'

'What!' It was Jerry's turn to shout in horror. 'You can't cancel the show. As your producer I'm telling you: You cannot cancel the show.'

'Producer? Where did you get that idea from?'

'A producer,' said Jerry, clearing his throat, 'is the person who makes it all possible, brings it all together. That's what I've done, isn't it? I have pro-duced your show.'

'You got some blokes to build a stage and you bought some mirrors. That hardly makes you Harvey Weinstein.'

'Us producers all have to start somewhere, my friend. This project has given me a taste for it. I'm enjoying investing money in the arts. I think it's an extremely worthwhile thing to do and it's giving me enormous satisfaction.'

'And you get to spend time with young women who treat you like a hero.'

'And why do you think Harvey Weinstein does it?'

'Because he's brilliant at it.'

'I'd also like to point out that he's no looker but he still gets to hang out with the best-looking women on the planet. He's one smart man.'

'All right then,' said Tom. 'If you are the self-appointed producer of this production what the hell do we do? We may have just lost our leading lady.'

'I'm on my way,' announced Jerry. 'I think Harvey would be holding a vigil by the bedside of his leading lady if he was in this situation. Carly needs me right now. I'll see you in twenty minutes.'

'No, Jerry,' said Tom. 'You'll just make things worse.'

Jerry had already put the phone down.

CHAPTER
TWENTY-TWO
LAURA

Laura had tried to text and call Tom, but had not been able to get through. She had no idea where he was, but was beginning to think that maybe he'd had to take Carly to hospital and was punishing her for what had happened by refusing to talk to her. She'd done her best to settle herself in front of the telly with a packet of Oreos and large glass of red wine but every time there was a creak or a bang or the slightest noise her heart leapt into her mouth and she braced herself for what on earth they were all going to say to each other when they eventually arrived home.

When nine o'clock came without any communication, time she'd also spent stewing over what the Cheshire Cat and the Queen of Hearts had told her, she decided she couldn't face them that night. She dragged herself up from the sofa, turned the television off and walked through into the kitchen to put her wine glass in the dishwasher and switched it on. The gentle hum signalled the end of the day and she felt a sense of relief. Tomorrow she would tackle him. Tonight she needed sleep and to wake up with a fresh head so that she could get to the bottom of what was happening once and for all.

It was gone ten when Laura became aware of Tom moving about their bedroom. The bedside light went on. He ambled around, undressing; then he reached under the pillow for his pyjamas. Eventually he fell into bed with a thump that bounced Laura's head at least twice. A thump that no one would sleep through. Laura kept her eyes tight shut. What was she going to say? She wanted to know that Carly was OK and the show would go on but she also couldn't forget the back stage tittle-tattle she'd overheard.

He wriggled next to her and then lay still.

She braced herself to roll over and talk to him, no longer sure if she could wait until the morning to air some of the thoughts that had been trapped in her brain for so long. What would she say? Would she ask him? Are you having an affair with Carly? Dare she say that? Dare she say that right now? Put an end to all this suspicion and distrust. Yes, she would do it now. Right now. She'd waited long enough.

She took a deep breath and then froze, unable to move. She could hear something. The very faint tinkling of bells, or music perhaps. What was it? She couldn't quite make it out. Then it dawned on her. Her husband had come home, having not told her where he was for the last four hours, and lain down in bed next to her, not to explain himself or hear her side of the story, but to play Candy Crush!

Laura clenched her fists in rage. She wouldn't speak to him now if he begged her to.

CHAPTER
TWENTY-THREE
HANNAH

'Just a very slight sprain apparently,' Laura told Hannah. 'Honestly, if you'd seen the way she was thrashing about you'd have assumed she'd broken it. Such a drama queen.'

Hannah wasn't listening. She was staring at the middle-aged woman sitting opposite them in the Jacuzzi in an attempt to make her feel so uncomfortable that she would leave. She hadn't come to the Radcliffe Hotel Spa with Laura today to relax. She had work to do but she couldn't get on with it until the other bloody woman chose to go.

'So she's just got to rest it for a couple of days,' continued Laura. 'Thank goodness she'll be all right for when the show starts. Tom said she knows her part so it's not ideal but she can afford to sit out of rehearsals until then.'

'Mmmm.' Hannah nodded. She coughed loudly, hoping to disrupt the tranquillity of the peaceful, blue-tiled room.

'I told him it was an accident,' added Laura. 'I apologised. I don't think he was listening though. It was like I wasn't even there. His head is so full of this show that anything beyond it may as well not exist.'

'Did you see they were giving away vouchers for a free massage at the reception desk when we came in,' announced Hannah loudly. 'I grabbed us two as there were hardly any left.'

Before Laura had a chance to respond the other woman rose from the bubbling water, glided up the steps of the Jacuzzi and then set a fast but dignified pace out of the room towards reception.

'Great,' said Laura, sinking her shoulders down into the warm water. 'A massage is just what I need.'

'Come on, quick,' said Hannah, leaping up. 'Before anyone else comes in.' She got out of the tub and reached for the fluffy white dressing gown hanging on a peg on the wall. She took a tape measure and phone out of the pocket. 'Here, hold this,' she said, holding the end of the measure towards Laura.

'Really! Are we doing this now?'

'Yes. Now hurry up.'

Laura dragged herself out of the water, grudgingly took hold of the tape and then walked towards the far wall.

'Great,' Hannah called once she'd tapped the measurement into her phone. 'Now the other wall.'

Hannah watched as Laura lumbered towards the adjacent wall. Hannah didn't know why her friend was in such a sulk. Hannah had made the reason for their visit very clear. 'OK, now just stand there, so I can take some pictures.'

'You can't take pictures. It's not allowed.'

'Watch me.' She held her phone up taking some shots with Laura in them to give her a sense of scale; then she moved to get close-ups of all the fixtures and fittings. She was just photographing the intricate Moroccan-style tiles bordering the Jacuzzi when the door to the room flung open and in walked a security guard.

'I have never been so humiliated in my life,' Laura told Hannah as they were escorted out of the building half an hour later.

'Yesterday you pranced around on stage dressed as a teddy bear. This is nothing,' replied Hannah, searching around in her bag for her car keys.

'Thank you for reminding me,' said Laura. 'I thought that today might bring a sense of peace and tranquillity and perhaps a little perspective to the nightmare I seem to be living at the moment. Yesterday I get ordered off the stage in a bear costume by my husband and today I manage to get myself banned from a spa.'

Hannah shrugged. She didn't understand what Laura was making such a fuss about.

'Now I've been in one I don't get what the big deal is anyway,' she said, unlocking the car. 'Strikes me as a lot of sitting around, semi-naked, bored out of your mind whilst a bit damp. Too much like school swimming lessons if you ask me.'

'Well, it's the first time I've ever been in one and I have to say, Hannah, you ruined it.' Laura disappeared, plonking herself in the passenger seat.

Hannah sighed and opened the driver's door to join her. 'You knew we weren't there to enjoy ourselves,' she stated.

'I know,' Laura said. 'And it was very kind of you and Jerry to offer to pay for me to go in with you but I assumed, particularly as I've taken the morning off work, that we were going to really enjoy the facilities before we did Jerry's spying for him. Besides, if all you needed were a few measurements, why didn't Jerry go himself?'

'Are you mad?' exclaimed Hannah. 'Jerry in a room full of semi-naked women? That's not good for him. He'd be more likely to come back with syphilis than measurements.'

Laura buried her face in her hands. 'I'm so embarrassed,' she moaned though her hands.

'We'd have got away with it if it hadn't been for the CCTV. Surely it's illegal to have cameras in a spa?'

'I'm not sure that your argument about surveillance being an invasion of your privacy was a good one when you were standing there with a camera taking pictures of their light switches and measuring the dimensions of the room.'

Hannah shrugged. 'All builders do it. We're always spying on each other – no big deal. Robinsons are getting all the contracts for spas at the moment. We're just trying to work out why.'

'People were trying to relax, forget the stresses of their everyday lives and you were frantically snapping pictures like some Japanese tourist at the Taj Mahal.'

'I needed a picture of the tiles,' said Hannah. 'They've obviously found a really cheap supplier somewhere but I can't work out who they are because I don't recognise the tiles.'

'Oh, call the fire brigade, you don't recognise a tile.'

Hannah turned to her friend. 'What has got into you?' She wasn't sure she had it in her to calm Laura's ruffled feathers today. She vaguely remembered Laura saying something about Carly and Tom's visit to hospital last night whilst they were in the Jacuzzi – perhaps that was winding her up. 'So he took her to A & E. Big deal. What choice did he have?'

Laura gave her a wounded look. Hannah sighed. No, she definitely didn't have room in her brain to cope with anyone else's emotional problems. She was too busy trying to ignore her own.

'We're heading for divorce, I just know it,' declared Laura and promptly burst into tears. 'I watched him carry her off,' she sniffled. 'He never carries me anywhere, does he?'

'No,' said Hannah carefully. 'But you can walk, so he doesn't need to.'

'Even the rest of the cast think they are having an affair. They told me.'

'Really, to your face?'

'No. I was still in costume. They didn't know who I was.'

Hannah tried not to smile at the image of Wonderbear hearing such news.

'Just idle gossip,' Hannah said dismissively. 'You know it is.'

'He spent *four* hours in hospital holding her hand and couldn't even be bothered to tell me where he was.'

'But Jerry was there. Best passion-killer known to man or woman.'

'Don't you care?' asked Laura, suddenly angry. 'Don't you care that both our husbands care more about *bloody* Carly than they do us?' She had clenched her hands and was pounding them on her knees.

Hannah swallowed. What could she say? That no, actually, she didn't care? She didn't give a monkey's what Jerry did and that was just as difficult for her to make any sense of as it clearly was for Laura to work out what was going on between Tom and Carly.

'I don't understand how you can turn a blind eye,' continued Laura. 'They're all over her. Why doesn't it get to you?'

Hannah racked her brains for a reasonable answer rather than the truth. She couldn't even admit the truth to herself, never mind Laura.

She shrugged. 'Jerry's always been like that, hasn't he? His head always has been turned by a pretty girl. I knew that when I married him.'

'When me and Tom got married…' said Laura, pausing to take a deep breath, '…he was still on the rebound from Natalie, wasn't he? We should have waited but I was so over the moon that he'd proposed that I shut all thoughts of Natalie out. I wanted to marry him as quickly as possible before he changed his mind. But I knew deep down it was a mistake, really I did.'

'It wasn't a mistake,' Hannah consoled her. 'He was over Natalie by the time you got married.'

'She sent us a card, you know. When we got married. We got back from honeymoon and opened all the wedding cards and there it was, congratulating the happy couple. Tom stared at it for a moment, and then tore it into tiny pieces. Really tiny little bits. He was angry, you could see it by the size of the shreds,' she said to Hannah.

'Right.' Hannah nodded. 'Really small shreds. I get it.'

'That's when I knew that he wasn't over her,' mumbled Laura as the tears began to roll down her cheeks again. 'He still loved her.'

Hannah put her arm around her friend. She sniffed, horrified that tears were pricking her eyes too.

'You get married and that should be it, shouldn't it?' said Laura, holding her sodden face up for a moment. 'Your love life should be straightforward from then on. That's why you get married, isn't it? To get away from all this crap.'

'Yes,' replied Hannah, pulling Laura back into her shoulder before Laura could spot the tear trickling out of her own eye. 'If you're lucky.'

CHAPTER TWENTY-FOUR
TOM

'Bollocks,' said Tom. 'Bollocks, bollocks, bollocks, bollocks, bollocks.'

He sat on the toilet with his head in his hands trying to compose himself when he felt that all around him was falling apart.

'Tom. Are you in there?' Jerry's voice echoed around the otherwise empty toilet block.

'No,' he shouted back.

'Mate, you've got to come out and look at this.' Tom heard Jerry stride to a stop right outside the cubicle he was hiding in.

'I'm busy,' he said through gritted teeth.

'I'll wait,' replied Jerry, starting to whistle. 'Oh my God, I've just looked in the mirror,' he cried. 'I'm killing it today. Come on, mate, you seriously have got to get out here and take a look at what they've done to me.'

Tom sighed. He had no choice. He'd have to emerge. He got up, unlocked the door and walked out.

'Are you not going to flush that thing?' asked Jerry. 'You are disgusting.'

'I've not used it.'

'What you doing in there then, texting?'

'No.'

'That's what I do. Forget where I am sometimes.'

'Why are you orange?' asked Tom, noticing Jerry's face.

'That's what I wanted to show you,' he replied, admiring himself in the mirror. 'Bianca has set up a tanning booth in the dressing room. Said she'd do me. How could I refuse? A young lady spraying my body all over? Too good to miss.'

'All over?' asked Tom.

'No, sadly. I did tell her I didn't like tan lines and I didn't mind taking my undies off but she admitted she's a little shy and offered to get Gavin to do it. But I've seen Gavin giving me the eye and I didn't want to encourage the poor lad.'

Tom nodded. 'Denying your manhood to anyone is extremely cruel.'

'Too right. Anyway, do you like it? Sets me up to look like a proper local down under in a few weeks I reckon.'

'Oh yeah,' said Tom, 'you'll fit right in. If you're in an *orange* grove.'

'Well, I want it to last, don't I? Don't want it to have faded to nothing by the time we go.'

'You'll be lucky if it's faded to the shade of an orange highlighter pen.'

'Bah, you're only jealous.'

'You are still going, are you? Thought you said Hannah was showing a lack of enthusiasm.'

'I'll talk her round, you wait and see. Now, I wanted to ask you about reserved seating for VIPs at the premiere of the show tonight.'

'It's a Halloween show at a theme park, Jerry, not the next James Bond movie.'

'I know, I know, but it's my first production so it's special to me. I want to be front and centre cheering you on.'

'I wouldn't bother,' mumbled Tom. 'It's going to be shit.'

'What?' cried Jerry. 'I thought Carly was OK, just a very light sprain.'

'It is, but to make sure she's OK for tonight she's had to rest it so we haven't been able to rehearse with her. That's fine for her, she's going to be great, but her leading man is a moron. I've been trying to rehearse him all morning and he's diabolical. He could ruin the whole show.'

'Stop stressing, man,' said Jerry, putting a hand on his shoulder. 'It's Carly they'll all be looking at, not him. No one will notice if he cocks up – she's the star of the show by miles.'

'Maybe,' Tom sighed. 'But it's not just him. We've got proper crotch-popper problems.'

'Crotch-proper problems?'

'No, proper crotch-popper problems.'

Jerry looked blank.

'One of the costumes is a black all-in-one leotard thing with poppers at the crotch. The dance routine they do is so energetic that the poppers pop open leaving them exposed.'

'Jeez, terrible,' said Jerry.

'We are currently sewing up the crotches of three black cats.'

'Painful.'

'*And*, to top it all, we thought it would be hilarious if the lead zombie had a Welsh accent.'

'I can see that.' Jerry nodded. 'You don't get many Welsh zombies.'

'Yeah, it's funny all right – or it would be if Zack could do a Welsh accent. At the moment he sounds Pakistani, which Guest Happiness have said could be misconstrued as racist. They're worried they'll get complaints.'

'But it's OK to make fun of the Welsh?'

Tom shrugged. 'Apparently.'

'What about Brummie? Can you make fun of them? Could he do *that* accent do you think?'

'I don't know. We could ask him to try but we'd have to ask Guest Happiness if Brummies are fair game first.'

'Birmingham's not that far from Wales, surely that would be OK?'

'I have no idea,' said Tom, throwing his hands up in the air. 'I tell you what, doing comedy on the stage is an utter minefield these days. It has never been so difficult to decide who you can take the piss out of.'

'Well, I'm confused.'

'And we've not done a technical run-through yet because our tech guys haven't connected all the speakers because they are too busy chatting up the dancers. Trying to focus young lads whilst semi-naked young women are about is like trying to herd cats. It's a bloody disaster. Tonight will be a shambles. I'm just warning you, Jerry.'

'Do you need more electricians? I can get you electricians. Your brother for a start.' Jerry reached for his phone and started to tap at the screen. 'Why didn't you say that's what you needed? I'm your producer, remember, here to help. I'll get you electricians and, as a special favour to you, I will personally keep the dancers away from them so they can concentrate on getting your lighting up. No, don't thank me,' said Jerry as Tom was about to protest. 'You need my help and I am only too happy to give it. Ah, Will' – he turned his back on Tom – 'I need you over at the stage pronto. Your brother is in a right state.'

Tom was still nervous. In fact he didn't think he'd ever been more nervous in his life. The day had flown by and yet they'd barely fought all the fires that had presented themselves. And now it was half an hour until show time and he didn't know which of the fires still raging he should be panicking about the most.

He was currently holding a ladder for Will as his brother fixed up a speaker in the dressing room so the cast could hear what was going on on stage and wouldn't miss their cues. Probably not the most productive use of the show director's time at that moment, but at least he was doing something of value rather than standing around thinking about the potential catastrophe to come.

There was an enormous bang and Tom braced himself for another disaster but it was only Amy slamming a saucepan on the steel bench to get everyone's attention.

'Listen up, guys,' she hollered. 'Thirty minutes to show time. Let's take a roll call to check you are ready for the first number. Ten technicolour rabbits, ready?

'Yes,' came the chorus of replies.

'Three black cats, ready?'

'Yes,' came three shouts.

'Are your crotches secure?'

'Yes,' they repeated.

'White Rabbit, ready?'

'No, I'm late,' someone shouted.

'What the fuck—' started Amy.

'For a very important date,' Nathan continued in a singsong voice. 'No time to say hello goodbye, I'm late, I'm late, I'm late. I'm late.'

'Are you trying to be funny?' asked Amy, seeking Nathan out in the crowd.

'No, I'm in character,' stated Nathan.

Amy glared at him. 'You are in the shit, is where you are,' she said. 'We don't have time for this. See me afterwards.' She looked back down at her clipboard.

'Zack, have you decided which regional accent you're using tonight?'

'I'm from Buuuurrrrrrmingham,' he replied in full grim zombie costume. Several of the cast burst out laughing. Even Amy raised a smile.

'Have you been to Guest Happiness and checked what impact doing a Brummie accent might have on complaints?'

'The general consensus appears to be that Brummies have a sense of humour and don't tend to complain. Overall it was concluded that Brummie was relatively low risk.'

'Excellent,' replied Amy.

'Finally, Alice, you ready?'

'Yeah,' came a quiet voice at the back of the room. Tom strained to look over the rest of the cast to see where Carly was. She had her back to the room and was staring into a mirror.

'Right, that's it from me. Don't fuck it up, OK?' said Amy. 'Now let me hand over to Phillip who wants to say a few words.'

Jesus, thought Tom. What's he doing here?

Phillip got up on the table but, just as he was about to start to speak, Amy interrupted him.

'Phillip is the General Manager, by the way. The boss, just so you know. So no arsing about. All yours,' she said, turning back to Phillip before jumping off the table.

'I just wanted to say that all eyes are on you this evening. We have visitors from Head Office who are here to see what a good job we do of entertainment at Wonderland, so don't let me down. We are also conducting market research on the show and we will be getting a reaction straight from those that matter. Our guests. So I look forward to seeing some amazing scores. You are representing the high standards we have here at Wonderland so get on that stage and ... what do you say ... break a leg?'

Inappropriate, given the circumstances, thought Tom, although he'd not shared the incident of the star of the show being knocked off the stage with Phillip for fear of him having a heart attack. Tom grabbed hold of a passing zombie and asked him to hold the ladder, so he could chase after Phillip and do some managing of expectations. Or more crucially make sure he was aware that first nights were always tricky. Things always went wrong and Phillip had been an utter idiot to invite anyone important along. It was asking for trouble.

He dashed across the room after him but was stopped in his tracks by Carly, who was white as a sheet. Shit, he thought. She was in pain. Medical clearly hadn't given her enough drugs. What were they thinking?

'I can't do it,' she said firmly.

'I'll get you more drugs,' he said quickly. 'Whatever you want, just say.'

'It's not my ankle,' she replied. 'It feels fine.'

'Then what is it?' he said urgently. Where was Amy? He needed her ready to get whatever Carly needed. Blue smarties – whatever. The show had to go on.

'I'm not good enough,' she said, looking away and biting her lip. 'I'm going to let you down. I can't go on stage.'

Oh, for fuck's sake, thought Tom. He did not need this now. 'You are good enough,' he said, putting his hands on her shoulders and looking into her eyes. 'You are brilliant and are going to be brilliant out there. Believe me, I know.'

'Really?' she said, looking back at him with puppy-dog eyes.

Tom sighed. 'Yes,' he said firmly, then bent low to whisper in her ear. 'You knock the socks off everyone else here. You know that, don't you? When you're up there, there might as well be no one else on the stage. You're utterly mesmerising.'

'Am I?' she said, her lip starting to tremble.

He pulled her into his chest. 'Of course you are, silly,' he said into her hair.

She leant back, leaving her face and lips frighteningly close to his. Shit. He could feel some kind of panic rising again.

'Can I ask you something?' she said. He could feel her breath on his cheek.

'Yes.'

'Do you think Laura deliberately pushed me off the stage?'

'What? No!' he exclaimed, pushing her away. 'Of course she didn't. Whatever would make you think that?'

'Well, she hasn't said a word to me since. Do you think she might be jealous of me?' continued Carly.

What was she talking about? Jealous? Jealous of what? He so didn't understand women.

'No, no way.' He shook his head. 'She was really upset about what happened.' He vaguely recalled Laura fretting about it the morning after they got back from hospital but his head had been so full of how to make the best use of rehearsal time now Carly was out of action that he'd barely listened. 'She's just busy – you know, stressed.' He shrugged. 'She goes quiet when she's got too much on her plate. She'll start talking again soon. Mark my words. Now,' he said, taking a step back. She was a mess and he had to act fast. He took her arm and led her back to her chair in front of the mirror. 'Look' – he pointed at her reflection – 'you've ruined your make-up.' He picked up a bottle of cleanser and a ball of cotton wool and poured some on. Then he reached forward and started to wipe the stage make-up off her face. She stared back at him mesmerised.

'Look,' he said gently. 'You can't give up now. This is your time. You are young and you are the star of the show. I would give anything to be in your shoes.'

'You would?' she murmured.

'Of course. You are about to go out on stage in front of hundreds of people. Isn't that what you always dreamt of?'

She nodded.

'Enjoy it,' he said sternly. 'Enjoy it whilst it lasts. Because it's the best feeling in the world.'

'Do you miss it?' she asked.

He sighed. 'Every day.'

She smiled at him, letting him stroke her face with the cotton wool.

'There we go, all gone,' he said. 'Now, I'm not so good at putting the make-up on so can I leave you to make yourself beautiful and we'll see you on stage in fifteen minutes?'

She nodded. 'Thank you,' she said.

'You're welcome,' he replied, turning away in relief. Time for a final crotch check.

CHAPTER
TWENTY-FIVE
LAURA

Laura turned around from her front-row seat to scan the audience behind her. A large crowd had gathered, stamping feet and blowing on hands as they eagerly awaited the finale to their day: 'The all-singing, all-dancing *Malice in Wonderland* Halloween Show guaranteed to thrill and excite the entire family'. Well, that's what the flyer had said when it was stuffed into their hands on arrival that morning. What better than to watch a show before they began their journey home? Ten minutes to go and the square was alive with chatter as the anticipation built.

Laura had done one last check to make sure all the on-park hosts conducting the research were in the right spots and were properly briefed. She'd been asked to come in and supervise the first lot of research when Archie had been forced to admit he didn't know how to use the in-house software

Wonderland had paid a lot of money for. She'd said she'd show him how to use it for the first show then he would be able to do it himself after that.

She settled herself into a seat next to Jerry, who was wearing a shirt and tie as though he were father of the bride. He'd seated himself in pride of place next to Phillip, who was doing his best to avoid small talk with Jerry so that he could look after the visitors from Head Office.

'This is so exciting,' Jerry had hissed at Laura before the show was due to start.

'We'll see,' said Laura, already noticing that people were starting to leave, as they got bored of waiting. Eventually the stage lights went up ten minutes after the show's official start time and there was a small, disheartened cheer. Alice wandered on to the stage and opened her mouth and the audience went absolutely quiet. Laura couldn't help but be impressed again with her obvious talent. How could she compete with that? Carly could sing and Laura was good at adding up. No contest.

Jerry nudged her, a massive grin on his face. 'Wow,' he mouthed.

Laura tried to smile back.

Unfortunately that proved to be the first and last wow moment in the show. The idea was actually brilliant. All the characters in *Alice in Wonderland* were weird and a bit freaky anyway so putting a Halloween spin on the story was inspired. But a desperately disillusioned lad called Theo was absolutely appalling as the Mad Bad Hatter. He was so bad he was almost funny. Almost, but not quite. He forgot his lines, he sang out of tune and during the Twisted Tango, the grand finale of the show, he managed to trip Malice up twice and eventually tip over an entire row of tarot cards. The smoke machine went into overdrive, which Laura strongly suspected had been ordered to mask the bun fight that was going on on stage. Unfortunately it also swamped half the audience, causing them to retreat from the stage. Most never returned, using the mist to spirit them away from the carnage of a performance.

Jerry's exuberance died down not long after the Mad Bad Hatter took to the stage and by the time the Twisted Tango had finished he was slumped in his chair, shaking his head from side to side. Laura actually felt sorry for him. His dreams of a Hollywood-producing career seemed already doomed.

Once the smoke had settled, but before the cast had finished taking their bows in front of a rapidly escaping audience, Phillip and his guests got up from their seats. The guests trooped off but Phillip paused next to Laura, looking grim.

'How soon can you get me the research scores?' he asked, squatting down next to her chair.

She looked at her watch. 'They'll be collecting data for another half an hour, I would say; then it will take me about another half-hour after that to run it through the software.'

'Can you bring it up to the boardroom as soon as you have it? I'd like to see what we are dealing with.' He got up, tweaked his trousers and strutted off.

'What did he say?' hissed Jerry.

'He wants to see the scores in his boardroom in an hour,' she replied.

Jerry nodded slowly. His lively demeanour evaporated. 'Shall I tell Tom?' he said.

'I guess so,' she replied. 'I'd best go and check how they're getting on.'

'OK.' Jerry grabbed her hand. 'We will get through this, you know,' he added seriously.

'I hope so,' replied Laura, trying hard to rid herself of the vision of her husband tenderly removing Carly's make-up. She'd thought it had been the right thing to go and wish them good luck back stage. Take the moral high ground. She wished she hadn't bothered.

Laura could hear voices raised in the boardroom as she followed Archie down the corridor. He turned to look at her as they hovered outside the heavy wooden door.

'Why don't you tell them the scores,' he said nervously. 'It'll be better coming from you.'

She had to keep reminding herself that this spotty youth was the client and her job was to take instruction from him.

'If you really think so I will, but are you sure?'

Archie nodded vigorously before opening the door and pushing Laura in front of him. She took a deep breath and threw her shoulders back, trying to remember that she was here as a representative of Harvest Research and not as Tom's wife and must act like the professional she was.

Laura nearly bumped into Jerry, who was pacing up and down the room. She hadn't expected him to be there – or Amy, or Carly. She spotted Tom sitting next to Phillip at the end of the table; he was looking grim. He turned to look at her, searching her face for an indication of which way the scores had gone.

'What's the verdict?' hissed Jerry before she could even sit down.

'I will ask you to leave, Jerry,' said Phillip firmly, 'if you don't calm down. You are lucky even to be in this room.'

'Sorry, Phillip,' said Jerry, plonking himself on the nearest available chair.

Laura sat herself down, feeling all eyes on her. She tapped at her iPad as silence fell and the whole room held its breath.

'So the scores are in,' she said, and then coughed as the numbers lit up her screen. 'When asked on a scale of one to ten how good they would rate the show with ten being excellent and one being very poor the respondents scored you an average of...' Laura looked up. '...five.'

'What? No way!' said Jerry, getting up and pacing the room again. 'It wasn't that bad. Who are these people answering these questions? Idiots?'

'They are what are known as guests,' said Amy. 'We deal with the morons every day.'

'Sit down, Jerry,' said Phillip.

Jerry slunk down into his chair. Tom had his head in his hands. Carly was fighting back tears.

'Continue,' said Phillip. 'What about the other scores?'

Laura glanced back down at the iPad. 'In answer to the question, "Would you come back to next year's Halloween to watch the show?" eighty-three per cent said no.'

'Thirteen per cent, that's a start,' cried Jerry. 'Something we can build on.'

'No it's not,' said Amy.

'Yes it is,' replied Jerry.

'It's seventeen per cent,' said Amy.

'Even better,' said Jerry.

'This is an unmitigated disaster,' said Phillip. 'We haven't even picked up any additional food and beverage spend. I saw Gillian on the way up and she said spends were down six per cent on the same time yesterday when we had no entertainment on. This is not the good news story I was hoping to give Head Office, Tom.'

'No,' muttered Tom, still looking down. 'I'm sorry. I thought I could pull it off. I was wrong.'

Laura gazed over at him. He looked broken.

'What the hell?' said Jerry, leaping up. 'Please don't tell me to sit down again,' he warned Phillip. 'What did you tell me this morning, Tom? You said first nights

STRICTLY MY HUSBAND

are always shit. Well, there you go. We've got it out the
way. It'll be brilliant tomorrow, won't it, Tom?'

Tom didn't answer.

'It's me,' said Carly. 'I'm no good, I told you I
couldn't do it.'

'No!' chimed Tom, Jerry and Phillip.

'It isn't you,' Tom added, putting his arm around
her. 'You were brilliant.'

'You were amazing,' said Jerry.

'The only decent thing in it,' agreed Phillip.

Amy and Laura exchanged glances.

'You mustn't blame yourself,' said Tom. 'You
stood out a mile. It's the rest of the cast who were
woefully under-rehearsed.'

'I suppose I have had more experience than
them,' said Carly. 'I've been in a lot of shows and
done TV.'

'You posted a letter in Albert Square,' interrupted
Amy. 'You haven't done TV, your left hand has.'

'I don't think we need to raise this just now, do
we, Amy?' said Tom, his arm still around Carly.

Amy and Laura exchanged another glance.

'It's all my fault,' Tom told Phillip. 'I was too
ambitious. I got carried away. I should have realised
our limitations. I'm sorry.'

Phillip nodded in agreement as an awkward
silence descended on the room.

'So what are your next steps?' asked Laura, drill-
ing her gaze into Tom. Come on, she willed him. You
need to respond.

'What?' said Tom, glancing over to Laura; he almost seemed to have forgotten she was there.

'What is your action plan?' she pressed. She'd had enough of this self-pitying navel-gazing and his sickening comforting of Carly. This was supposed to be a business meeting but everyone was behaving as though they'd just lost the final of *Britain's Got Talent*.

'I've presented the research,' she said slowly and deliberately, 'so now is the point at which we work out what the solution is.'

Tom was staring at her as though she were talking in a foreign language.

'Why don't we take it right back to what your original objectives were,' suggested Laura.

'Objectives!' cried Amy. 'What the hell have they got to do with it?'

'It can help,' said Laura, desperate to get them talking about solutions rather than failure.

'The objectives were to deliver entertainment that was seen by over sixty-five per cent of park guests, achieve an average of eight out of ten for enjoyment and increase secondary spend by five per cent,' said Phillip, leaning forward. 'The worst thing is that I reckon over sixty-five per cent of guests *did* see that wreck of a show and left with an extremely bad impression of Wonderland.'

'Right, good,' said Laura, ignoring Phillip's troubled frown. 'So how do we improve that satisfaction score then? Tom, what would improve the show? Give me one thing.'

Tom shook his head, bewildered and desperate. 'Getting rid of Theo and at least ten hours' more rehearsal,' he said.

'Excellent, do that then.' She leant back in her chair. Finally some progress.

'We can't, Laura. That's the point,' replied Tom, looking exasperated. 'There is no one to replace Theo and we can't rehearse on the stage during the day because there are visitors around. It's useless.'

'There is no one in the cast who can take over the male lead?' asked Laura. She willed Tom to get on the same wavelength as her. Come on, I'm trying to help you here! At least *try*, she thought.

'There is, but they would be worse than Theo, believe me.'

'I've got a brilliant idea,' Carly said, her eyes suddenly wide with excitement.

'I very much doubt it,' muttered Amy.

'Tom could do it,' Laura cried. She couldn't let Carly steal her thunder. 'You'd be brilliant.'

'Fuck me,' said Jerry, leaping out of his chair. 'You are a genius,' he said, kissing Laura on the cheek. 'Of course Tom can do it. He knows all the lines; he knows all the moves. I'm telling you, Phillip, I've seen Tom and Carly do that Twisted Tango together. It brings tears to my eyes.'

Laura sat motionless, staring at Tom. He wasn't saying anything, too stunned to speak. Clearly the option had never crossed his mind.

'You were only just saying how much you missed performing,' said Carly. 'How much you loved it. Come on, you and me on the stage together: it'll be brilliant. You must do it. Say you'll do it?'

Laura watched as Carly draped herself around Tom's neck and begged him to dance with her. He turned to look at Laura.

'Do you think I can?' he asked her, his brow furrowed.

Laura hesitated. In spite of knowing she had made exactly the right suggestion her entire body wanted to say no. Her stomach needed her to say no to get rid of the awful sick feeling that was rising up through her body. But she nodded her head and silently mouthed yes.

He smiled back at her and then turned his face towards Carly. 'Let's do it,' he said, grinning.

Carly practically leapt on to his knee. 'This is going to be the best show ever!' she announced. 'Seriously,' she added, turning her head to Phillip. 'We are going to knock it out of the park now, you wait and see.'

Laura swallowed. She needed to get out. She wasn't sure she could maintain this professional persona any longer. She glanced down at the notes she'd made and turned to talk to Phillip whilst Tom and Carly began to discuss how they could make the Twisted Tango even better.

'You should consider cancelling the show for tomorrow night,' she said to him as if on autopilot. It had been plain to her whilst watching the show that they needed more rehearsal time to have any chance of getting it halfway decent. 'Give them tomorrow night after the park shuts to rehearse and get it right.'

'Good idea,' agreed Phillip.

'And one last thing,' she said, starting to gather her things together. 'You need to take hot food and drink out to the guests. Everyone was cold and hungry but couldn't be bothered to go and hunt out food.'

Phillip nodded.

'Maybe even a bubbling Halloween broth or something? If you themed a hot drink I bet you could charge a fortune.'

'Thank you,' he said. 'I'll tell Commercial to get on to it straight away.'

'They'll be able to do the research without me the next time,' she said, standing up. 'I've shown them what to do.'

'Well, I really appreciate you coming in tonight,' said Phillip, following her to his feet. 'Your contribution has been very worthwhile.'

Laura nodded.

'I'm glad the Research Department has been of use,' said Archie, holding his hand out to Phillip. Laura had forgotten he was even there.

'Who are you?' asked Phillip.

'No one,' he mumbled and scurried out of the room.

Laura shook Phillip's hand, then turned and walked out, leaving the excited chatter behind her.

CHAPTER TWENTY-SIX
HANNAH

'Why?' asked Hannah, staring straight ahead.

'Why what?' replied Jerry, flicking his indicator on the side of the steering wheel of his Range Rover.

Hannah stared ahead into the gloom of the autumnal early-evening. She actually knew why, but she wasn't fond of the conclusion she had come to. Maybe she should give him the benefit of the doubt.

'Why the cigar?' she asked, turning to watch her husband casually flick ash out of the narrow slit in the driver's window.

He shrugged. 'Dunno. Just fancied giving it a go.' He took another draw and gave a small cough.'

'Does Harvey Weinstein smoke cigars?' she asked.

He shrugged again. 'Might do.'

'Do you think smoking cigars will make you look more like a Hollywood movie mogul?' she asked.

'Might do.' He smiled, looking pleased with himself.

Hannah turned away to stare out of her window. 'Ridiculous,' she muttered to herself.

'What did you say?'

'I said: *Ridiculous*,' she repeated a bit louder.

'And what's that supposed to mean?' he asked, taking his cigar out of his mouth and waving it around in a grand gesture.

She turned back to look at him, his stubby fingers held in a rigid V shape around his latest accessory, his fake-tanned tangerine face poking out from behind a spotted cravat that he'd deemed appropriate to drag out of the depths of his wardrobe for this evening's occasion. She sighed. She couldn't help it.

'I mean you look ridiculous,' she said.

His only reaction was a slight furrowing of the brow.

'What do you mean I look ridiculous?' he asked eventually.

'What do you think I mean?'

'I have no idea,' he replied, sticking his cigar firmly back in his mouth.

'It means that I don't get the cigar, I don't get the cravat, I don't get the fake tan, I don't get it and I think you're making a fool of yourself.' Hannah sat back in her seat and tried to control her breathing, which out of nowhere was suddenly very fast. What had got into her? She was being mean but sometimes Jerry irritated the hell of her and it made her want to scream. Was this normal? she wondered. Were all marriages like this? A continuous challenge to ignore the inevitable irritations of living with the same person every day of your life whilst constantly trying to recall the reasons why you'd agreed to do it in the first place?

'I'm just upping my game,' Jerry defended himself. 'Everyone has put so much effort into getting the show back on track for tonight that I thought the least I could do was look the part.'

Hannah shook her head in disbelief.

'Why don't you try it?' His hand clutching the cigar appeared in front of her face. 'Smithy got them for me. They're proper Colombian ones. The real deal. You don't get these down Super Cigs, I can tell you.'

Hannah shoved his hand out of the way, not trusting herself to speak.

'We could come back from Australia via South America, you know? How do you fancy that?' he asked. 'Actually I quite fancy Rio. I've always wanted to go to Rio. That's the one with the massive statue of Jesus, isn't it?'

'Christ the Redeemer,' muttered Hannah, leaning her head against the side window.

'That's the one. I'd like to see that, and that Sugar Puff Mountain.'

'Sugar Loaf Mountain,' said Hannah.

'That's what I said. The really weird-shaped one. I'd like to see that. Wouldn't you like to see that?'

Hannah didn't reply.

'Hannah,' he repeated. 'What do you reckon? Do you want to go and see Big Jesus and the Sugar Puff Mountain?'

'Not really,' she replied.

'Oh,' said Jerry, 'OK then. So where would you like to see? Or shall we just stay in Australia? We could, I suppose. Be a bit of a waste, though, don't you think? If we are halfway across the world we might as well see some other stuff as well. Where would you like to go?'

'I don't want to go,' she said quietly.

'Don't want to go where?' asked Jerry. 'To see Big Jesus? I know – you said that. But where would you like to go?'

'Nowhere,' she said, sitting up straight in the seat and staring forward out of the front window. She braced herself.

'What do you mean nowhere? Do you mean you just want to stay in Australia?'

'No,' she said, feeling exasperated and desperate and petrified all at the same time. 'I mean I don't want to go anywhere.'

'Anywhere at all?'

'Yes.' She faced him. 'I don't want to go anywhere at all on holiday.'

He glanced over at her and then back at the road ahead. They were almost at Wonderland.

'Why not?' he asked. She detected a slight wobble in his voice.

'I just don't,' she said, turning her head away.

'You don't want to go on holiday?' he asked again.

'No.' Christ, did she have to spell it out? She could hear Jerry breathing heavily next to her. She couldn't look at him. She didn't want to see his face.

'Then what *do* you bloody want, woman!' exclaimed Jerry as he slammed his hand on the steering wheel.

Hannah jumped out of her skin. She'd crossed a line. She knew it. He was the most cheerful man she had ever met. He had never once during their eleven-year marriage got cross with her.

'Tell me,' he demanded, banging the wheel again. 'Just tell me what you want, will you?'

Hannah felt tears prick the back of her eyes and she gasped, trying to hold them in check. She couldn't answer that question. As hard as she tried, she just couldn't answer it.

'I don't know,' she whispered.

Jerry pulled the car up in the staff car park at Wonderland. They could already hear the tinkling of the park music in the background – it was sharply at odds with the tense mood in the car. Jerry switched off the engine but didn't move; he just stared straight ahead. Hannah held her breath, totally at a loss as to how to move forward. She felt paralysed. Everything felt paralysed: her body, her brain, her heart.

They sat for what seemed like an eternity but in actual fact was only a few seconds. Suddenly Jerry reached across to open the glove box, making Hannah flinch. He took out a packet of cigars, sat back in his seat and looked over to Hannah. She looked back, fearing what he might say.

'It's show time,' he said firmly; then he turned and let himself out of the car.

Hannah tried to concentrate but the last place she needed to be right now was watching a Halloween Show at a theme park. But what do you do when your best mate calls and asks you to go and observe her husband whilst he cavorts on stage with an attractive younger woman.

'No,' had been her answer, but Laura didn't appear to have taken that in.

'Why don't *you* go?' Hannah had suggested then. 'Go and see for yourself.'

'I can't, I've got research groups every night this week out in Chesterton,' replied Laura. 'But I need to know. I need you to tell me how they perform together.'

'As in: how good they are in the show?'

'No, not really. Just how they look together on stage?'

'I don't understand what you are asking me.'

'You can tell, can't you?' said Laura. 'You can tell when a couple dances together if they are in love?'

'You want me to watch Tom and Carly dance together and tell you if I think they are in love?'

'Yes.'

'No way. I'm not doing that.'

'Why not?'

'What if I get it wrong? No, Laura, you can't ask me to do that.'

'But I need to know.'

'It's a performance, Laura. You know that. They are performers; it's all an act. You can't make a judgement on a performance.'

Laura was quiet for a minute and Hannah heaved a sigh of relief. Hopefully she'd got herself off the hook.

'But there's the moment, isn't there?' continued Laura.

'What moment?'

'The moment. The moment after the dance has finished. When they are not acting, when they are themselves. You can tell in that moment exactly what the relationship is. You can tell by the look. You can tell by the body language. You tell by the spontaneous embrace. You can just tell, Hannah.'

'You might be able to, but not me.'

'Just try,' begged Laura. 'Please.'

Hannah sighed. How did she get herself into these situations?

'I'll try but I'm not promising anything,' she eventually said.

'*Yes!*' hissed Laura. 'I'll call you as soon as I've finished the research group. You are such a star. Let me know if I can return the favour in any way, won't you?'

'Of course, Laura,' Hannah replied. 'If I ever need someone to spy on my husband, you will be the first person I call on.'

'It's not spying.'

'Then what is it?'

'It's data collection.'

To Hannah's amazement she really enjoyed the show. Jerry had told her what a car crash the first night had been so she wasn't expecting much but she was entranced by the stunning array of freaky costumes, the clever twists on the *Alice in Wonderland* story but most of all the beauty of Carly's voice. You literally could have heard a pin drop in the large crowd that had gathered to watch the show in the darkness when she hit the high notes on her opening number.

In fact Hannah was so swept away by it all that she completely forgot to concentrate on what may or may not have been going on between Carly and Tom on stage. As the crowd erupted with delight, and she joined them in a standing ovation, she realised she hadn't checked what they were doing at the end of the final number and had no idea whether or not they'd shared a moment – whatever that was. It was clear, however, that they'd fixed the catastrophe from two nights ago. From the roar of the crowd it sounded to Hannah as though they had a huge success on their hands.

She watched as Tom and Carly took their bows. They were holding hands and looked extremely happy – did that count as some kind of moment? Or were they justifiably pleased with the reaction they were getting? Tom took a step back, prompting Carly forward to take her turn in the limelight as the cheers increased. She picked up the edge of her blue skirt and did a sweeping curtsey before stepping back and pushing Tom in front of her. He shook his head in a modest fashion and then dipped down in a further bow, doffing his hat. Tom and Carly retreated to let the rest of the cast bask in the ongoing glory and then easily and comfortably they joined hands again and skipped off into the wings and out of sight. Hannah studied them carefully throughout but was still none the wiser as they disappeared.

'We smashed it,' cried Jerry, flinging his arms around Hannah. 'We smashed it,' he repeated right in her face, their earlier awkward conversation clearly erased by the excitement of being the supplier of the stage to a successful theme-park Halloween show. He embraced her in a bear hug and she hugged him back, carried away by his euphoria. Eventually he pulled back and gazed into her eyes. He looked so happy. So happy it almost broke her heart.

'It's all going to be all right,' he said, grinning. 'Everything is going to be all right.' He lunged forward and kissed her full on the mouth. She kissed him back. She couldn't remember the last time they had kissed like this. Lips, tongues and in public. She pulled away. It was wrong, all wrong. He beamed at her and reached inside his pocket and pulled out a cigar and flicked it up to his mouth. He missed; it fell on the floor. He shrugged, his grin not fading; then he bounded off, leaving Hannah gazing at the discarded cigar lying amidst the post-show debris.

CHAPTER
TWENTY-SEVEN
LAURA

'What are *you* doing here?' gasped Laura, nearly spitting out a piece of homemade flapjack. She'd just settled herself into the lounge of a very nice five-bedroomed detached house on the brand-new upmarket estate on the edge of Chesterton and was quite looking forward to picking the brains of half a dozen women in the 'Successful Suburbs' demographic. This was supposed to be a focus group comprised of previously high-earning mums with one or more pre-school-aged children, which under no circumstances included someone like Karen.

'Ooh, I remember you,' said Karen, settling herself into the enormous corner sofa. 'You were at the last one I did – you know, the one about...'

'Incontinence pants,' said Laura.

'Yeah, that's right.' Karen leant forward and grabbed a piece of flapjack.

'What are you doing here?' asked Laura. 'This is a research group for young mums, not, er ... '

'Yeah, I know, don't rub it in. But I fancied a look round one of these posh houses and my sister-in-law said that if I told you I had four grandchildren under five then that would be OK.'

'Your sister-in-law?' asked Laura.

'Yeah – Liz. She recruits for these things,' replied Karen, flapping her hand around the room.

Laura tried to stay calm. 'Well, I'm sorry but I'm going to have to ask you to leave,' she said, standing up. 'I'm afraid your sister-in-law was very wrong. I can't allow you to participate in this group. You don't fit the criteria. For many reasons,' she added.

'I can't go,' countered Karen without missing a beat. 'Neil dropped me off and he won't be back for an hour and there are no buses. I checked.'

Laura sat back down, speechless.

'You wouldn't chuck an old woman out in the cold, would you?' asked Karen, taking another bite of flapjack.

Laura seethed inwardly. She was stuck. Karen was right; she couldn't chuck her out. She couldn't even ask the host if they could shove her in a different room; it wouldn't be fair on the host and goodness knows what snooping Karen would get up to if left alone.

Luckily for Karen the rest of the participants arrived at that point, distracting Laura as she got them settled on to the various sofas and chairs scattered around the room and supplied them all with name badges. She was careful not to sit anyone too close to Karen.

'So I wondered if you could all introduce your-selves and share how many children you have and what ages they are?' Laura asked after she'd been through the usual introductions. 'Could we start with you?' She indicated a very smart-looking woman to her left.

'Hello, everyone, I'm Charlotte and I have a two-year-old called Oliver.'

'Hi, I'm Fran and I've got Isla who's three and Evie who is thirteen months,' carried on the lady sit-ting next to her.

'Ooh, is it me?' apologised the next woman with a white stain down her shirt in the midst of cramming flapjack in her mouth. 'My name is Vicky and I have twin boys aged two and a half.'

All the women assembled nodded in apprecia-tion of her challenges.

'So I'm Philippa and I've got Isaac who is four, Tilly at eighteen months and another on the way.'

There were several sharp intakes of breath.

'I'm Rachel. Chloe was eighteen months last week.'

Karen looked Laura's way as it approached her turn. Laura glared back, willing her not to take her usual disruptive stance.

'Karen,' announced Karen, nodding to the group. 'I had Leo when I was nineteen followed by

Cindy when I was twenty-one. Their dad left three years later so it was just the three of us for about five years. Then I met my Neil and we had our Sean followed by our Sammy. Of course they've all left home so now the house is full of bloody grandkids. You're never shot of them, I tell you!' She grinned, leaning forward to help herself to yet another flapjack.

Laura was very aware that the inhabitants of the room were staring at Karen in silence. She needed to fill the gap but she didn't quite get there in time.

'I tell you what,' said Karen. 'They do a better class of biscuit here than they do at your office.' She held up a half-eaten piece of flapjack and scrutinised it.

'Karen happens to have been to a research group before,' Laura informed the rest of the group. 'Something we don't encourage. However, there appears to have been a mix-up in the recruiting.'

'Oh, don't mind me,' said Karen. 'I'm quite happy sitting here. Please continue.'

'Right, OK,' said Laura, taking a deep breath. She should just plough on, she decided, get it all over with as quickly as possible and then she could get home and call Hannah to see what was going on down at Wonderland.

'So I'm hoping that you're going to really enjoy this group as I'm here to give you a sneak preview of some possible TV and cinema advertising campaigns that my client is considering running. They are really keen to get your reaction, and your thoughts and opinions could help shape the campaign that finally makes it to the screen.'

'Excellent,' said Charlotte. 'That actually sounds quite interesting. I was worried we were going to sit around for ages talking about baby products.'

'Me too,' agreed Vicky. 'I'm only here to escape the potty training; last thing I need is a discussion about nappies.'

'Nappies, nappies, I'm sure I dream about nappies,' muttered Philippa, shifting her pregnant belly in her chair and looking as though she might doze off at any minute.

'Then it's fortunate that it's not a baby product we're discussing tonight,' said Laura, reaching over the back of her armchair and pulling out several large pieces of card. 'I'm going to show you what's known as a storyboard, which is just a series of pictures that illustrate the story of the advertisement.'

'I know what a storyboard is,' said Charlotte, leaning forward eagerly. 'In my previous life I was a sales director in London. I used to get shown these things all the time.'

'Great,' said Laura. 'I'll talk you through the first concept and would welcome all your thoughts at the end, whatever they are. Please be as honest as you can even if it's a different opinion to others in the group. There are of course no right or wrong answers.'

'Gosh, this is quite exciting,' said Philippa, suddenly perking up. 'Better than being stuck at home doing bedtime.'

Everyone nodded silently in agreement.

'I've never been involved in a TV campaign before,' added Karen. 'Wait until I tell Diane next door. I keep telling her to get in on these research thingies. She's a bit lonely and could do with getting out and about and meeting people. And, as I told her, the coffee and biscuits are free. Who needs Costa, eh?'

'So if we are all ready and everyone can see, I'll take you through the first concept,' said Laura, deciding her best policy was to ignore Karen throughout the session. She twisted the first board around to face them and began her spiel.

When Laura looked around the room less than two minutes later she knew instantly that she'd lost them. She was greeted with at best blank looks and at worst cold stares. This was quite common when testing advertising. Creative agencies often tried to be too clever in their desire to create a masterpiece, which resulted in a failure to communicate anything whatsoever about the product. Laura didn't think this was the case here, however, as the storyboard had seemed very straightforward to her. Charlotte was the first to enlighten her on the hostile reaction.

'Washing powder?' she asked. 'You brought us here to talk about washing powder?'

'Well, yes,' replied Laura. 'What do you think of the concept? What do you like or not like about it?'

'Quite frankly I couldn't give a monkey's,' replied Charlotte, leaning back in her chair and folding her arms. 'I couldn't give a toss about washing powder. I ran a team of forty-seven sales reps two years ago and now the only thing that my opinion is valued for is washing powder? No. Not interested.'

'I quite liked the pink kittens in the pink jungle,' muttered Philippa, looking around nervously. 'Didn't anyone else like the pink kittens in the pink jungle?'

'Not really,' said Rachel, screwing her nose up. 'It was a bit...well, actually extremely patronising.'

'Of course it damned well is,' exclaimed Charlotte. 'Everything aimed at mothers is. Don't you think? Clearly advertisers believe that having children extracts all intelligence therefore they must speak very slowly and use pretty colours and cute animals in order for us to understand their message.'

'Is that how you feel?' asked Laura.

'Yes,' said Charlotte, looking exasperated. 'I had a child not a lobotomy.'

'Do any of the rest of you feel like that?' asked Laura. 'Do you feel patronised by advertisers now you have become a mother?'

Many heads nodded.

'Not really thought about it,' announced Philippa. 'Too tired.'

'Do you want to know what is really patronising about it?' added Charlotte. 'I don't see any dads being asked their opinion on the pink kittens in the pink jungle.' She looked round the room.

'You're right,' Laura had to agree.

'Do you want to know what my husband did today?' said Charlotte, leaning forward and throwing her hands out in exasperation. 'He got on a plane to Istanbul to speak at a conference. And here I am being asked what I feel about washing powder.'

'I'm really sorry you feel like that,' said Laura sympathetically.

'Oh no, no, don't be. It's not your fault.' Charlotte shook her head and sighed. 'It's the first time he's been away since Ollie was born and … well, to be perfectly honest I'm as jealous as hell. Don't get me wrong, I wouldn't be without our son for anything, but I used to do stuff like that and somehow it doesn't seem fair that my husband still can, just like that, without a backwards glance.'

'I know what you mean,' chipped in Rachel. 'My other half got offered last-minute football tickets tonight. I told him I was already going out, but who had to organise a babysitter? Me. Never even crossed his mind.'

'My husband moaned because I was going out,' muttered Philippa. 'Said he wanted to watch the match on telly and it clashed with bathtime.'

Karen cackled with laughter in the corner.

Laura's heart sank. This was clearly not a laughing matter.

'Let me share something with you, girls,' Karen said, leaning forward. 'You're a mum now and that is how the world sees you. You may as well have your kids' faces tattooed on your forehead. Same isn't true for dads, of course. But the worst thing you can do is try to hold them back. You very quickly become the bore at home and it won't be long before they find something new and shiny and sparkly. Believe me, it happened to me with my ex. Set them free if you want to keep them, that's my advice.'

Laura forgot where she was for a moment as she took in what Karen was saying. All she could think about was Tom, performing on stage right now – something he'd given up to provide them both with more stability. Had she become the bore at home who'd stopped him doing the very thing he loved? Worse than that, had she got in the way of him following his dream? If Karen was right then the only way of holding on to her marriage was to set him free; but she wasn't sure how to do that or, indeed, whether she could.

'Hi,' said Hannah when she finally picked up the phone.

Laura had arrived home, flung her handbag on the kitchen table and immediately called Hannah. She'd wrapped up the session early, knowing from years of experience that she was unlikely to get much sense out of the group in relation to washing powder. Instead she allowed the assembled mothers to let off steam regarding their demotion in society since giving birth whilst she simmered over Karen's depressing speech.

'So,' said Laura, 'how was it?'

'The show?' asked Hannah. 'To be honest it was excellent. I was very pleasantly surprised. I really enjoyed it.'

'Thank goodness,' sighed Laura. That was good news. 'And how was Tom?'

'Oh, he's still got it, Laura. Really he has. I'd forgotten how good he is. The crowd went mad for him.'

'Great, that's good, that's good … I think; and what about, you know, him and Carly?'

'Well …' Hannah hesitated. 'From what I could tell they were, you know, doing what they were supposed to do.'

'What do you mean, what they're supposed to do?'

'They were performing. They were dancing, they were holding each other, they were touching, but I can't say I saw or felt this mythical moment you keep going on about. Nothing about it struck me as different to any other time I've seen dancers and actors on stage. They're always lovey-dovey and all over each other, aren't they? That's just what they are like.'

'Well, yes, but you can tell if there's more going on behind all the air-kissing and back-slapping.'

Hannah sighed. 'I'll say it again, Laura. I think you are looking for something that isn't there. I really do.'

Laura allowed herself to breathe out. Perhaps she just had to let it go. She was imagining things purely because they danced together. Maybe she was being unfair.

'Well, thanks for going anyway, Hannah,' she said.

'You're welcome,' replied Hannah. 'Like I said, it's a great show. You should be very proud of your husband. Perhaps that's what you need to focus on.'

'Yeah, I'll try,' she answered. But she was not entirely sure Tom's triumphant return to performing made her feel any better.

CHAPTER
TWENTY-EIGHT
TOM

Tom and Carly struggled to get Jerry's sozzled bulk through the front door. It was past ten and Tom had no idea where the time had gone. Jerry had come backstage immediately after the show, jumping up and down as though the production had just won an Oscar. He went round the entire cast slapping them on the back, handing out cigars like candy canes and somehow miraculously produced bottles of champagne until the dressing room resembled some dodgy drinking den in the back streets of Soho.

'Don't you think this is a tad premature?' Tom had said to him. 'We haven't had the scores in yet.'

'Fuck the scores,' cried Jerry, handing Tom a bottle to swig from. 'It was a triumph – anyone could see that.'

'I think I'll wait, if you don't mind.' Tom pushed the bottle away. 'Until we know for sure.'

'Suit yourself,' said Jerry, helping himself to another mouthful.

Tom looked at his watch. Archie had promised he'd come backstage as soon as he had the results of the research. Although Tom knew that the show had been much better, he also knew that he was in no position to judge. It was the audience that mattered and what they thought.

Carly came up behind him. 'It'll be OK,' she said. 'We rocked it out there. We were on fire!'

'You never know,' said Tom, shaking his head. 'It felt good but it might not have felt good out there in the crowd.'

'If it felt half as good as it did on stage, we have nothing to worry about.' Carly grabbed his hand and squeezed it. He smiled back gratefully.

The truth was he was frightened how good it felt. It was like a drug that he was both euphoric and regretful to have been reunited with. What if he never felt that way again? He dropped Carly's hands and ran his fingers through his hair. Where was Archie? He couldn't stand the suspense any longer.

As if on cue a small tornado burst through the door, black hair flapping and sweat pouring down his sideburns.

'Archie,' shouted Tom. 'Over here.'

Archie looked up and wove his way quickly across the dressing room. Carly clutched Tom's left bicep hard with both hands as Archie approached.

'Seven point six,' he breathed, clutching his sides.

'Right,' said Tom, nodding whilst trying to work out how he felt about that.

'You wanted it to one decimal place, right?' asked Archie, when Tom failed to give any further response.

'Yeah,' replied Tom. He'd thought one more decimal place might just help somehow.

'So it's definitely seven point six,' repeated Archie. 'I checked it three times like Laura showed me. I'm sure it's seven point six.'

'Which when you round it up is actually a score of eight out of ten,' interrupted Jerry, appearing out of nowhere. 'Bloody eight out ten! You cracked it, right? That's the score Phillip was after.'

'But...but...what about the decimal point?' said Tom, struggling to take it in. When Archie had started his declaration of the result with a seven it had thrown him. His heart had sunk immediately. They weren't quite there yet.

'Fuck the decimal point,' cried Jerry. 'Who needs decimal points anyway? Stupid invention, if you ask me. You scored eight out of ten. It's a fact. Either way it's a miraculous turnaround from two days ago. Come on, mate, cheer up. This is good news. Here, have a cigar.'

'I guess you're right,' Tom replied. 'It was a lot better than Saturday's show, wasn't it?'

'A lot better!' exclaimed Jerry. 'It was different show, mate. You and Carly? Enough to make a grown man cry, you two were.'

'But it could be better,' said Tom. 'We need to keep making it better.' He didn't want a whisper of a seven in his scores, decimal place or no decimal place.

'Of course you do.' Jerry slapped him on his back. 'Now can you please put a smile on your face and let's get down that pub and do some celebrating.

It had all been a bit of a blur since then. Jerry had insisted on taking the entire cast to the pub where he'd proceeded to get drunk as he enjoyed the company of his new-found young female dancing friends. Tom had popped outside at one point to call Laura and share the improvement in the scores but she was on the phone and he'd got dragged back into the pub by Tweedledum and Tweedledee, who wanted to settle a bet as to how old he was, which took them forty-five minutes and two pints of lager to drag out of him.

By nine o'clock Tom could see that things were on the verge of getting out of hand. The Halloween cast had now taken over the entire pub, having frightened the regulars into heading across the road to more peaceful surroundings. Someone had started a game of blindfolded darts whilst one of the girls had set up an impromptu stage-make-up class for the incompetent male members of the cast and was currently using Jerry's face to show them how to create the perfect zombie.

When Zack pulled down his trousers to show his pearly white bottom and asked Michelle if she could make a zombie out of that, Tom decided to take action. He grabbed hold of a chair and stood on it and shouted for quiet.

'Go home,' he bellowed.

'Booooooo,' everyone hissed back at him.

'Get down, you misery,' shouted Jerry.

'You have a show to do tomorrow,' Tom continued. 'And if you score below eight because you're hung-over, you're all fired. Do you understand?'

Jerry leapt up out of his chair and pushed Tom off his perch.

'Listen to the man,' he yelled from behind his half-zombie, half-man make-up. 'What the bloody hell are you all doing in here? Tom's right. Get home to bed this instant. I want to see a nine tomorrow. Do you understand?'

There was muttering but no one really moved.

'I'll ask you again. Do you understand?' he bawled.

'Yes, Jerry,' everyone shouted and slowly but surely they all drained the last of their drinks and trickled out of the pub as Jerry stood guard at the exit telling each and every one of them he personally wanted to see them bright and breezy the next day.

Tom knew there was no way Jerry was going to be full of beans the following morning as he and Carly dropped him on to the sofa in his lounge. Jerry grunted, somewhere between barely awake and a blissful haze.

'I think I'd better get you a coffee,' said Tom. 'You want one?' he asked Carly.

'I'm fine.' She followed him into the kitchen; after a moment she said: 'We were amazing up there.'

Tom nodded, his mind a jumble of different emotions. He felt euphoric that it looked as though he'd pulled it off – that he'd managed to deliver a knock-out show. But he'd never in a million years expected to be up there on stage again.

'You were brilliant,' said Carly. 'Honestly, I'm not just saying it.'

'Thanks.' He grinned. 'I didn't do too badly, did I?'

'Too badly!' exclaimed Carly. 'You were seriously good. You know what you should do, don't you?'

'What?'

'You should come with me after we finish next week. They're auditioning for a new show, a massive one, a big new musical. They want singers and dancers and there are some pretty big parts going from what I've heard. They've described it as an ensemble piece so not just a handful of main parts and the rest is chorus-line shit. Lots of really good roles. Why don't you come and give it a go? You never know, do you?'

'Where is it?' asked Tom, struggling to suppress a familiar spark of hope that he thought had long been extinguished.

'London,' Carly continued excitedly. 'It's West End, Tom. How exciting would that be? I'm heading down the day after we finish. Why don't you take the day off and come with me? You'll never know unless you try!'

Tom looked down at Carly. She had never looked so young. She was glowing with success and hope for the future.

'I'll think about it,' he said, carrying a cup of coffee back into the living room for Jerry.

'It's a shame Laura wasn't there tonight,' said Carly, flopping down into an armchair. 'What happened?'

'Oh, she had to work. She's got evening research groups all week. It happens sometimes. In fact she planned them for this week knowing that I'd be on park late every night. She didn't realise then of course that I would actually be in the show.'

'She must be gutted she can't come and see you.'

'Yes, yes,' replied Tom, looking away. 'Of course she is. I'm sure she would have been there if she could.' He sighed and looked at his watch. 'Now it's time to get some beauty sleep,' he said, holding out his hand to Carly and pulling her out of the chair; only he pulled her too hard and she over-balanced, falling into him.

'Sorry!' She laughed, staring up into his eyes.

'It's OK.' He smiled and kissed her on her forehead.

'Get on that stage and sock it to 'em,' mumbled Jerry in his sleep, making the pair of them jump.

Tom pulled away. It was definitely time to go to bed.

CHAPTER
TWENTY-NINE
LAURA

She knew this would happen. It was Friday night and Tom's fifth performance in the show and Laura and Hannah were sitting at the dining table waiting for everyone else to arrive back from the theme park for dinner. Tom and Laura had barely talked to each other all week, passing like ships in the night. She'd been leaving for work before Tom got up and he was coming home later and later: staying behind after every show to work out further improvements to what had clearly become his pride and joy. But he'd said he'd be back in good time tonight. Now it was edging towards nine o'clock and Tom, Jerry, Carly and Will were nowhere to be seen. Laura sighed and reached up to open some more wine.

'So just show me on your face how Tom looked at Carly after the Twisted Tango,' she asked Hannah again as she topped up their glasses.

'I can't!' pleaded Hannah, lifting her glass to take a gulp. 'I didn't see anything other than a really good show and everyone seemed delighted. That was all there was to it.'

Laura wasn't convinced. 'So what do I do now, Hannah?' she asked.

'About what? I can't see what there is that you need to do something about.'

'You think he loves her, don't you?' Laura pressed. 'That's why you won't say anything. You know I'm right. He loves her and he's going to leave me.'

'I didn't say that,' said Hannah.

'Then bloody well say *something*. I don't know what to do. I need you to help me.'

'I don't know what you should do,' snapped Hannah. 'Why are you asking me? I've no idea about these things. What do I know about love and happiness and all that claptrap? These looks you keep harping on about, these *moments*. It's all bullshit. Romantic bullshit. I don't get it.'

Laura stared at Hannah. Hannah was close to losing her temper, she was swearing and slightly slurring her words: a combination she never would have associated with her friend.

'Of course you get it,' said Laura. 'When you fell in love with Jerry, you remember those feelings, those moments, those looks. I remember it like yesterday with Tom. I know it fades, gets worn away by domestic stuff and the day-to-day crap you have to deal with. But it's still there. Somehow it keeps you welded together. That is until you see that look again on your husband's face, but this time staring at another woman,' she finished bitterly.

Hannah shrugged and drank some more wine. What the hell was wrong with her? thought Laura. She could get more response by trying to talk to a man about this stuff.

'I married Jerry because it was good for business,' Hannah suddenly announced.

'Fuck off,' said Laura, realising suddenly that perhaps she'd had too much to drink as well.

Hannah shrugged. 'I did. It was my dad who fell in love with him, to be perfectly honest. Treated him like the son he never had.' She threw back some more wine. 'He was the one who started sending Jerry out to drum up business he thought we had no chance of getting, just to train him up. But he kept getting the deals. He was a natural and when he asked me to marry him ... well, we couldn't lose him to a rival firm by then, could we?'

Laura was speechless. She'd never heard Hannah talk like this.

'But ... but there must have been more to it than that,' she said eventually. 'You make it sound like you were courting in Victorian times or something.'

'Oh, don't get me wrong. I was besotted with him in the beginning.' Hannah shook her head and stared down into the bottom of her wine glass. 'No one like Jerry had ever shown any interest in me and I fell for it, hook, line and sinker, like the desperately insecure teenager I was. Thought I was lucky to grab a catch like Jerry. Thought I was the type to be left on the shelf. But it was relief I felt when I married him, not love.'

'I don't know what to say,' said Laura, pouring more wine for both of them.

'There's nothing to say. I made my bed and I've got to lie in it.' Hannah took a gulp of wine and Laura thought she detected a glistening of tears in her eyes.

'Why haven't you said anything before?' asked Laura, leaning forward and putting her hand over Hannah's.

She shrugged. 'To be honest, I never really thought about it before now. Kind of shoved it to the back of my mind. Jerry's not a bad man, is he? We have a good life. It's not a bad marriage.' Then Hannah caved and allowed a single tear to slip down her cheek.

'Oh, Hannah.' Laura squeezed her hand. 'I'm so sorry.'

'I thought it didn't matter, the love bit. There were so many other good things about us being together, I thought I could live without love until…until…' began Hannah.

'We have champagne!' came a cry from the hallway and the crashings and bangings of the four latecomers arriving for Friday-night dinner.

Hannah snapped her hand away from Laura's, threw back some more wine whilst simultaneously wiping away her tear.

'Ka mate, ka mate, whoaah,' shrieked Jerry as he burst through the dining-room door and stood with his legs wide apart, his hands raised, eyes bulging and tongue hanging out of his mouth in some vague interpretation of the New Zealand haka tribal dance. 'Ka mate, ka mate, whoaah,' he repeated, stamping his feet.

'So sorry we're late,' said Tom, bustling past the chanting beast that Jerry had become as if what he was doing was quite normal. He rushed over and planted a kiss on Laura's forehead. 'Will has put up a roving spotlight to follow me and Carly during the Twisted Tango. It took a bit longer than expected.'

'All those wires,' said Carly, kicking off her shoes and slumping down in a chair. 'Will is some kind of genius. I have no idea how he works it all out.'

'It was trickier than I thought it was going to be,' admitted Will. 'I'm really sorry we kept you waiting,' he said to Hannah and Laura. 'I needed a particular sort of screw that took me a while to find.'

'There are times when we all need a particular kind of screw,' said Jerry, wrapping his arm around him. 'Eh, lad? Do you know what I mean?'

Laura glanced nervously between Jerry and Hannah. Hannah looked furious. Will looked uncomfortable.

'Aah, leave him alone,' piped up Carly.

'He knows I'm only messing,' replied Jerry. 'I tell you what though, Will, I noticed quite a few of those dancers giving you the eye when you were up that ladder. You were making them all silly. You should get in there, lad.' Jerry winked at Tom, who had returned from the kitchen with three cold bottles of beer.

'Ooh, yes,' Carly squealed. 'I meant to tell you. Elspeth was asking me all about you. She really likes you, Will.'

'You lucky bastard,' cried Jerry. 'She is H.O.T., hot. You have to get in there, mate.'

Will shook his head. 'No really, I—'

'Is she coming to the after-show party here next week?' Jerry asked Carly.

'I presume so,' she replied.

Jerry rubbed his hands together in glee. 'I repeat, you lucky bastard. Oh, to be free and single – no offence, Hannah,' he said, waving his hand in her vague direction. 'Would you like me to allocate you one of the guest rooms now?' he asked Will.

'No, Jerry,' said Will, suddenly raising his voice.

Everyone went silent.

Will grabbed a beer from Tom and took a swig.

'All right, keep your hair on,' said Jerry. 'I was just trying to help you out, that's all.'

'I don't need any help,' said Will, showing uncharacteristic signs of losing his temper.

'Well, it looks like you do from where I'm standing.' Jerry chuckled, glancing round at everyone. 'You'll forget how to use it if you're not careful.'

'Jerry!' Hannah cried out, nearly knocking her wine glass over as she stood up abruptly.

'What?' Jerry threw his arms out wide in surprise. 'It's only what you're all thinking,' he said. 'We're worried that you're not getting enough sex, Will.'

'You are disgusting,' breathed Hannah.

'You don't have to—' started Will, shooting a concerned look in Hannah's direction.

'Oh yes I do,' she continued. She took a step forward and stood between Will and Jerry, looking in Will's direction. 'I must apologise to you for my husband.' Tears pooled in the corners of her eyes. 'He has no right whatsoever to tell you how to conduct your love life and you deserve so much more than the stupid pointless sex he is suggesting.'

She turned to give Jerry the most disdainful look imaginable and then picked up a bottle and her wine glass from the table. 'Utility room?' she said to Laura.

'Absolutely,' replied Laura, following her out of the dining room.

Half an hour, another bottle of wine and a moan-fest later, Laura and Hannah staggered out of their hiding place.

'Where's Carly?' slurred Laura.

'Where's Will?' slurred Hannah.

Jerry stood up from the table and put his arm around Hannah's shoulder. 'Will went home,' he said. 'I apologised,' he added when Hannah looked at him accusingly. 'We're all good. Honestly. Now let me take you home. I think it's time you went to bed, isn't it?'

Hannah looked at him for a moment; then she sagged against his shoulder, nodding. 'S'pose,' she agreed, closing her eyes.

'Right,' said Jerry brightly, turning to Laura and Tom. 'I'll get this lush home now she's let off some steam. Sorry about dinner, Laura. I'll make it up to you. See you all soon.'

Laura said nothing until she heard the front door slam behind them.

'Where's Carly?' she repeated, grabbing the back of a chair to stop herself swaying.

'Oh, she went to bed,' said Tom. 'Wanted to get her beauty sleep ready for the weekend's performances. And we're going in early to practise a new lift for the end of the Twisted Tango. It's really complicated so I'm not sure we can do it but if we could just perfect...'

Laura zoned out; the alcohol was making it difficult to concentrate and she really couldn't bear to listen to what Tom and Carly were going to do together the following day.

'...tomorrow?' was the next thing she registered Tom saying.

'Sorry, what did you say?' she asked.

'You'll tell me what you think tomorrow, won't you?' said Tom. 'Tell me if you think we are right putting that extra lift in when you come and see the show.'

'I'm not coming,' she blurted out without thinking.

'What do you mean?' He looked hurt.

'I … I … ' She didn't know what to say but she knew she had to put off seeing the show for as long as possible. She couldn't bear the thought of seeing them dance together and then having to live under the same roof knowing the inevitable was coming and her marriage was doomed the minute they walked off stage for the final time. She'd rather not know until the end; then at least it would all be over quickly. 'I'm going to wait and come on your last night. I don't want to put you off,' she said. 'And I, er, want to make sure I see it at its best and share in the glory of your final night.'

'Oh.' Tom did not seem convinced. 'Are you sure? I was really looking forward to you finally seeing it tomorrow.'

'I'm sure.' She nodded vigorously. 'I'll be there on closing night. I promise.'

'OK,' he replied, nodding slowly in his turn. 'If that's what you really want to do?'

'Yes. Can't wait. Now if you don't mind I'm off to bed.'

She turned and narrowly avoided banging into the doorpost before crawling up the stairs.

CHAPTER THIRTY
LAURA

'So you are definitely coming to see me later, aren't you?' Tom asked as he got up to clear the table after Sunday lunch. She watched him shuffling between table and fridge and dishwasher, putting everything in the wrong place, of course. Carly had gone to Wonderland early to prepare for what would be their final show that evening and so they had had a meal alone for the first time in a month.

'Of course,' she said, getting up and flicking the kettle on. She stood with her back to him so he wouldn't see her face. 'I'm really looking forward to it.' Over a week had passed since the disastrous dinner party and her announcement that she wouldn't go and see the show until the final night. Tom hadn't mentioned it again but she could tell he was confused by her decision. To her relief it meant he'd avoided any discussion about the show with her all week.

But standing here in the kitchen now, knowing she was just hours away from having to face Tom and Carly in all their splendour on stage was making her feel sick. She wasn't sure how she was going to cope, especially following the discovery she'd made in the garage that morning: a massive bouquet of flowers with a card attached saying: 'To my favourite leading lady'. All her fears and suspicions had lit up inside her and there was nothing she could do to quell them. All she could do was wait until that evening when she was certain all would become clear.

'I really want you to be honest about what you think of the show,' said Tom, turning his back to her at the sink and switching on the taps.

'You don't need me to tell you how brilliant you are,' she replied, bending down to pretend to search for teabags in the cupboard.

'Yes I do,' he said.

'No you don't.' She stood up to rearrange the mugs next to the kettle.

'I do,' said Tom, twisting around to face her, up to his elbows in suds.

She took a breath trying to calm her frustration at his neediness. 'Look, even from the first performance I could see what a great show it was. You just needed to sort out the teething problems, that's all. Not give up just because you screwed up casting the lead male.'

Tom looked startled; he paused before he replied.

'Is that what you think? That I screwed up?' he asked.

'Well, you did, didn't you? He ruined what was otherwise a brilliant show.'

Tom stared back at her as though she'd just told him he was adopted.

'Well, thanks for that.' He slammed a saucepan on to the drainer.

'You would have given up at that point, wouldn't you?' she continued. 'Admitted defeat. The slightest problem and you throw your hands in the air, down tools and go into a massive sulk.'

'No I don't.'

'Yes you do. You do it every time. You dream big and then when someone puts the slightest obstacle in your path you give up.'

Tom looked stunned. She was pretty shocked herself. Her current turmoil was clearly driving out some home truths she'd harboured for some time.

'Your dreams are brilliant, Tom,' she continued more gently, noticing his crestfallen face. 'I could see all your ridiculous, funny, amazing and utterly bonkers dreams up there in the very first performance. It's why it's such a great job for you. You get to put your dreams up there on stage. Where else would you get to explode a dormouse? I mean – seriously?'

Tom half raised a smile.

'Being an Entertainment Director is a job made in heaven for you,' she said.

'I hate it,' he muttered, turning to gaze through the window.

'No you don't,' said Laura. 'It's the failure you hate, not the job. But instead of facing up to it and doing something about it you blame other people, making yourself look like the victim.'

He turned sharply back towards her.

'Phillip keeps cutting my budget so my shows are rubbish,' she continued, mimicking his pained-looking face. 'My leading man can't dance for toffee so my shows are terrible. I've decided to hate my job because I'm too bloody scared of making a success of it because then I might just be happy and what a disaster that would be, because this wasn't what I thought would make me happy. The mighty Tom Mackintyre couldn't possibly be happy being an Entertainment Director at a theme park in his home town with an unglamorous, boring wife who stares at numbers all day and couldn't do a paso doble if her life depended on it.' Her voice had risen to a squeak and her heart was hammering.

'That's not true,' said Tom, wide-eyed at her outburst.

'Which part?' demanded Laura. She'd never been this honest with her husband. 'I can assure you that I cannot, will not ever be able to do the paso doble to save my life.'

'None of it's true.' He lifted his hands out of the washbowl and picked up a towel. He was silent as he dried his hands, looking at the floor.

'There's an audition,' he said quietly.

'A what?' asked Laura, thinking she'd misheard.

'An audition.' He looked up. 'It's a musical. They're looking for men my age who can sing and dance. Really good parts. Carly told me about it.'

Laura felt all the air get sucked out of her body. He couldn't be saying this. He really couldn't be saying this.

'Where?' she managed to ask.

'London,' he said. 'It's the West End, Laura.'

'Carly told you about it.'

Tom nodded. 'She's trying for a part too. She said I should go and give it a go.'

'What do you expect me to say?' she asked after an uncomfortable pause.

'I want you to tell me after you see the show today if you honestly think I'm good enough,' he said. 'I need to know what you think I should do? Whether it's a stupid idea. I mean, I know I won't get it, I'm nowhere near good enough, but maybe I should give it a try, right? You never know, do you? And if I did get it, which I won't, but if I did then we'd work it out, wouldn't we? I'd come home when I can and if it looks like a long run then you could move down. There must be loads of jobs in market research in London.'

Laura looked down at the teabag in the bottom of her mug. She so should have married an engineer or even a plumber. Anything but the torture of this.

'What do you think I should do, Laura?' he asked again. He was chewing his nails now.

She looked up at him. 'So you agree that I'm a boring, unglamorous wife who stares at numbers all day then, do you?' she asked.

'I never said that,' cried Tom. '*You* said that. You're twisting things. You're not boring or unglamorous, you're – well, you're Laura. You're my Laura.' He stepped forward, flinging the towel on the table, and took her in his arms. She breathed him in and couldn't stop the tears from falling.

'Don't cry, please,' he said, looking down and wiping away a tear. 'You're Laura. You're wise, you're funny and you're my best mate. You know that. What would I do without you?'

She wished he'd said she was beautiful, thought Laura. She buried her head in his chest.

'I don't know what to do,' he said to the top of her head. 'I don't know what to do to make us happy.'

She could hear his heart beating very fast. She felt his arms curl tighter around her. She put her arms around him and pulled him in tight as the tears soaked through his shirt. She listened to his heartbeat as they held each other in the middle of the kitchen, dishes half stacked in the dishwasher, saucepans still soaking in the washing-up bowl, the scraps of Sunday lunch strewn over the table and the floor.

She pulled away and looked up at him. His eyes were rimmed red.

'You just have to listen to your heart,' she said. 'That's all you can do.'

She walked around him to the sink and began scrubbing a saucepan.

CHAPTER
THIRTY-ONE
HANNAH

Who the hell was it this time, thought Hannah, hurrying to the front door, Sherlock hot on her heels. She'd spent all day answering the door to all shapes and sizes of delivery men as Jerry's excitement at hosting the wrap party for the *Malice in Wonderland* cast members materialised into complete and utter over-indulgence.

Hannah watched horrified as a tall skinny man carried in Jerry's order from Waitrose. Crate after crate after crate was paraded through the marble-tiled hall to her kitchen. Bag after bag after bag was lifted out as it dawned on her that despite Jerry's promise to be solely responsible for the party she didn't want them to have, it was going to be left to her to put away the enormous amount of food, as he seemed to have completely disappeared.

Why? she thought as she attempted to jam the second ham joint into their enormous American-style fridge-freezer. She had told Jerry when he was ordering the food: They're performers, they don't eat. A few bowls of crudités would be more than enough, she'd said. Ten minutes later and he'd come to find her to say that Waitrose didn't sell crudités; he'd done a search and everything. She couldn't be bothered to tell him that he was only looking for raw vegetables. She told him to go and buy whatever he thought best and he'd skipped off rubbing his hands together. She knew it had been a mistake. First it had been Marks and Spencer's, then Majestic Wine, followed by Amazon, who had dropped off several large boxes. God knows what he had hiding in there. There couldn't be any more delivery companies that could be involved in a party could there? But knowing Jerry anything was possible. After all, he was the man who'd bought a seven-foot-long inflatable crocodile to announce a holiday in Australia.

Hannah flung open the door with a scowl. She'd tried to contact Jerry to tell him his six bags of ice would be melting on the under-floor heated tiles in their kitchen but he was either screening her calls or somewhere without reception.

'Oh,' she said when Will appeared on the front-door step, toolbox in hand. Her scowl instantly dissolved. 'What are you doing here?'

'Jerry sent me round,' he replied, wiping his boots on the mat. 'He wants some more disco lights downstairs plus all his speakers connected to the main system. All the other lads are busy so I said I'd do it.'

'Right, right,' she said. 'Come in. Can I get you a coffee?'

'If you have the time,' he replied. 'He also said I had to put a smile on your face.'

'Oh, why?' she flustered.

'He said you were cross with him and I had to come over and cheer you up so he dares come home when you're in a better mood.'

'I'm not cross really, it's, er, just, er...' she stuttered.

'Just Jerry,' offered Will.

Their eyes met. They hadn't spoken since she'd stuck up for him at the dinner party over a week ago.

'Yes, exactly,' Hannah acknowledged after an awkward pause. 'Just Jerry.' She looked away and turned to head towards the kitchen. 'Come and look at the food mountain that he calls a party,' she shouted over her shoulder.

'Bloody hell,' breathed Will when Hannah had shown him the supplies that had arrived throughout the day. 'How many has he invited?'

'God only knows,' said Hannah. 'I'm not sure whether he's expecting me to sort all this food out either. He's a great starter, but not the best finisher.' She ran her fingers through her hair. The sight of all the food was actually starting to make her feel sick.

'I could do with a hand,' said Will. 'If you need to get out of the kitchen, that is?'

'Oh yes,' she said instantly. 'Definitely. Quite frankly I'll go anywhere I can't see cheese puffs floating in front of my eyes.'

'Well then, follow me,' he said, grabbing his toolbox and heading towards the basement door.

'Are you coming tonight?' asked Hannah from the bottom of a set of steps whilst Will balanced on the top, trying to screw up a set of disco lights.

'Oh yeah,' said Will. 'Jerry's asked all the sparkies and the builders who helped with the stage. It's the hottest ticket in town over on the building site.'

'Why?'

'Are you kidding me? A party with singers and dancers? Tradesmen don't get invited to parties like that.'

'Oh, right,' said Hannah.

'The plumbers aren't too happy though. They've been offering to fit loos, showers, bidets, full spas, you name it, just to get a look-in. One of them is thinking of retraining to be an electrician if that's the type of job opportunities you get.'

'So did you enjoy it then?' she asked.

'What?'

'Working in show business?'

He laughed. 'It was all right,' he said. 'Best bit was seeing Tom working, really. Made me so proud to see him put that together. I could never do anything like that.'

'But what you do is amazing too, you know – it takes so much skill. You really underestimate yourself. You should blow your own trumpet a bit more.'

'Maybe,' he said. 'But I'm not in Tom or Jerry's league, am I? They're the real high-achievers. Confidence just oozes out of them. Oops, sorry.' Will's screwdriver clattered to the floor. Hannah went to retrieve it and handed it back to him. They smiled at each other. Hannah resumed her position at the bottom of the steps.

'It can be hard being close to someone who's really confident and outgoing, can't it?' she said. 'It can make you feel like you pale into insignificance a bit. I'm sure next to Jerry I look like the grumpy, quiet one who holds him back.'

'No,' said Will, looking down at her and shaking his head. 'That's not true. No one sees you like that. Honestly. You can't think like that.'

'I think Jerry thinks like that,' said Hannah.

'I think Jerry thinks he's a very lucky man,' replied Will, holding his hand out to her. 'Screw, please?' he asked.

Hannah silently handed him a screw. Will started humming as he battled with his screwdriver.

'Do you want to know what I think?' Hannah said eventually.

'Go on then,' said Will. 'I'm coming down by the way.'

Hannah stood back from the stepladder to let him down.

'They aren't as confident as you think, Jerry and Tom,' she said. 'I know they both come across that way, brimming full of it, like they could do anything.

But they're just like you and me really. I reckon every-one's the same underneath. Exactly the same.' She paused, looking straight at him as he got to the bottom of the ladder. 'We all spend our lives trying desperately to say what we mean and hardly ever having the confidence to go through with it.'

The room had somehow gone really quiet and still. Will's expression didn't change. She had no idea whether he understood what she'd said. She held his gaze.

'I think that's pretty much how most people live their lives,' she added.

Will hadn't looked away. She couldn't look away either.

'You make life sound very depressing, when you put it like that,' he said eventually.

'It can be,' said Hannah. She swallowed. She couldn't believe what she was doing. She felt a bit faint.

'Did you ever tell her?' she asked.

He flinched but said nothing.

'The woman you said you wanted,' she continued. 'Did you tell her?'

Will shook his head. She watched his Adam's apple travel all the way up and down his neck.

'You should just do it,' she said quickly.

He blinked several times, swallowed and then took a step back.

'We should really test these lights and these speakers,' he said slowly, his brow furrowed.

'I suppose so,' she sighed.

'Stay here,' he said. 'I'll just go and try the music and ... and flick some switches. Don't move.'

Hannah gazed after him, rooted to the spot. She felt hot, then cold, then hot again as she watched him disappear behind Jerry's bar and fiddle with the state-of-the-art sound system. A song Hannah instantly recognised came on and all of a sudden she was plunged into total darkness.

'It's all right, don't panic,' she heard Will shout.

She wasn't panicking. Sure, her heart was thumping really fast but she didn't think that was panic.

Suddenly her face was illuminated by floating coloured lights as the disco spots Will had put up burst into life. The glitter ball above her head started to swirl, casting sparkles at her feet. She thought she might burst into tears.

And then there he was standing next to her, looking white as a sheet but with a determined look on his face. Hannah held her breath. What was she doing?

'So we need to test these lights,' he said, holding out his hand.

'What do you mean?'

'The only way to test disco lights is to dance underneath them, isn't it?' There was a slight quiver in his voice.

She allowed a small smile to touch the corner of her mouth. 'But I don't dance,' she replied, and then instantly regretted it.

'Neither do I,' said Will. He took a step forward and delicately picked up her hand. She could feel the slight roughness of his tradesman's fingers. Her smile extended to the both corners of her mouth.

He swayed gently and she found herself mirroring him. They danced like that, smiling at each other, with just their hands touching for most of the Ed Sheeran track. Their eyes roamed each other's faces, searching, checking for reassurance that this was really happening. As Hannah sensed the tune rising to its conclusion she felt her heartbeat accelerate. Their dance was already coming to an end and still they had only touched with their hands. Dare she take it further, lose herself in the music just for a moment, try it and see what it felt like?

Yes, she thought, stepping forward at precisely the same moment as Will, who dropped her hands and folded his arms around her shoulders, drawing her into his chest. She sighed with relief as the cotton of his shirt pressed against her cheek, making her feel instantly at home. She slotted her feet in between his and they continued their soft swaying beneath the sparkling glitter-ball lights. She could hear that the song was about to call time on their first dance. But would it be their last? Her breath caught in her throat at the thought of it. Panic gripped hold of her and she jerked her head up to look into Will's eyes before the tune ended. She had to know whether this was their first or last dance.

She took one look in his eyes and knew the answer. There could only be one answer.

'You are listening to Radio Cornerstone, and this is me, Colin Campbell, bringing the magic straight to your ears,' boomed out of the speakers. Will and Hannah sprang apart at the surprise interruption but remained gazing at each other.

'That was "Thinking Out Loud" from Ed Sheeran and hopefully it's got you in the mood for our next guest, award-winning organic pig farmer, Mike Robson, who's here in the studio with his prize-winning sausages and with his pigs. Yes, you heard me right, we have pigs live in the studio. Straight after all your local traffic news from Sandra Shephard.'

'That fucker Mike Robson is always on the fucking radio,' came a voice from the bottom of the stairs.

They turned in horror to see Jerry's arms piled high with boxes, staggering towards the bar. How long had he been there?

'And his sausages are shit.' He dropped the boxes on the floor and then straightened up, stretching his back. 'Hiya, Will, mate,' he called over. 'Where's the number of that osteopath, love? I need some serious knuckles on my spine, if you know what I mean?'

Chapter Thirty-Two

Laura

The show was drawing to a close now and the entire cast was in the midst of delivering the Twisted Tango. Tom and Carly flicked and kicked their way through the complicated routine. They were so in tune with each other that Laura couldn't help but admire their flawless synchronicity. Their faces were fixed and rigid as they expressed the intensity of the dance. Their bodies slipped and slid all over each other and Laura held her breath as the music built to a crescendo. This was it. This was the moment she had to see but couldn't bear to watch.

Tom and Carly were alone at the front of the stage, the rest of the cast having lined up as a row of playing cards at the back, forming an impressive backdrop to the couple's finest moment. Tom and Carly curled and swooped and bent around each other, casting striking shapes and patterns until the music ended with a dramatic flourish and the cards at the back of the stage tumbled over in perfect formation. The

Mad Bad Hatter caught Malice up in his arms and swooped her on to his right shoulder in a triumphant final pose.

Laura could feel and hear the delight of the crowd behind her. They stamped their feet, clapped their hands and cheered and cheered while the performers held their final positions on stage.

Tom carefully slid Carly back down to the floor. Their eyes met as her feet made contact with the stage. They were nose to nose, oblivious as the cheers continued to echo around them. Tom grinned first, then Carly, and then they embraced, there on stage in front of hundreds of people. Tom buried his face in her neck and lifted her feet off the floor and swung her around before they fell apart and smiled from ear to ear at each other again.

Laura pulled her long coat around her and wrapped her arms protectively around her chest. The icy wind bit into her cheeks as she hurried away from the stage, pushing through the crowd of delighted theme-park goers, stamping their feet and cheering as the final curtain came down on *Malice in Wonderland*. She'd seen more than enough.

CHAPTER THIRTY-THREE

TOM

That was it. They'd done it. It was all over. One hand supported Carly's legs on his shoulders whilst the other was stretched out to his side. He fixed his broad grin for a count of eight, trying to absorb the reaction as much as he could until he assisted Carly to the floor and they wrapped themselves around each other in pure joy. If he weren't on the stage he would have fallen to the floor and sobbed his heart out, such was the emotion tearing through his body right now. Instead, he took Carly's hand from around his neck and led her to the front of the stage where they took their bows, the roar of the audience ringing in his ears.

They rose back up again and Tom gave himself a moment to commit the scene to his mind. A sea of kids in scarves and hats on grown-ups' shoulders bobbed up and down, smiling, laughing and cheering. A small army of theme-park staff stood at the back, wolf-whistling and waving, having been allowed by Phillip to come and see the final performance of the show. The rumours had spread that it was actually something Wonderland should be proud of, which caused quite a stir among the rest of the staff, who were mostly cynical when it came to on-park entertainment. Right at the very front Tom could see Jerry on the verge of a nervous breakdown: jumping up and down, whistling, stamping his feet, his face bright red with excitement. He paused to give Tom a thumbs up, then blew him a kiss. Christ, thought Tom, Jerry was getting all theatrical on him. He was so taking this producer thing too far. Then he stopped. Where was Laura? He'd been so pleased to see her sitting next to Jerry when he'd first stepped out on to stage. He'd flashed her a massive grin and then thrown himself into his performance. He was determined to go out with a bang. But now, he could only see Jerry. The seat where Laura had been sitting was empty. Where on earth had she gone? Tom spotted Phillip with a couple of suits from Head Office completing the front-row line-up. His heart sank. Phillip hadn't mentioned anything about VIPs. He should have learnt from bringing them to the first show that it was a bad idea. One was whispering something in Phillip's ear so Tom couldn't see his face; but he was clapping, Tom noticed. That had to be a good sign. Surely they couldn't fail to be impressed by what had become the best show Tom had ever been involved with.

Every day it had improved. Every day Tom had made Amy sit in the audience and then give her opinion on the performance. In true Amy style she'd pulled no punches, but instead of shrugging his shoulders and not doing anything about it, Tom had done his best to fix the mistakes. Every day he made the cast come in early to listen to Amy's review and they'd agreed on how they could improve things until eventually even the cast members were coming up with their own enhancements without being asked. The buzz in the dressing room was no longer about the stink of chip fat or the lack of mirrors, but about how they were going to top the previous night's show. The cast had grown into a company who all wanted the same thing: to deliver the best possible show they could.

Tom and Carly stepped back and allowed everyone else to take their last bow in the limelight. Tom took his opportunity to look in the wings to check if Laura was waiting for him there but she was nowhere to be seen.

One last glance at the delighted crowd and he signalled for the tarot cards to start shuffling off the stage. The stage lights lowered and the security lights emerged on full beam to guide the guests back to the exit and their journey home.

The cast bounced off stage, whooping and hollering into the blackness of the wings and back out into the real world again. A world not dominated by rehearsals and performances and costumes and make-up, fuelled by nerves and adrenaline.

Usually, when the curtain closed on a theme-park season Tom experienced a feeling that can only be described as dullness edged in failure. Another year wasted delivering lacklustre entertainment with only the prospect of a few months' planning another load of lacklustre entertainment for the following year to look forward to.

But there was no dullness this evening. He felt on top of the world, alive and happy. Really happy. A happiness that was bursting inside him and which he had to try his hardest to grab hold of because any minute he knew it would deflate leaving a shell of remembered joy.

He bounced into the dressing room, leapfrogged over Tweedledee who was undoing his shoelaces and leapt straight on to the steel bench.

'Shut uuuuuuuuup,' he shouted at the top of his voice above all the post-show hubbub. As if by magic Amy appeared and banged the bench very loudly with a frying pan. Everyone immediately shut up.

'Thank you,' he said, throwing his arms wide. 'I just want to thank you all for the most amazing experience! I've dreamt of doing a show like this for so long and you guys made it happen.' Jerry gave a loud cough at the back of the room. 'And especially you, Jerry of Camberwells Construction. The best mate any man could have. A mate with tradesmen at his fingertips.' Everyone laughed. 'This happened because of you too, mate.' Tom thought Jerry might burst with pride. He watched him cast his head round to make sure everyone knew exactly who Jerry Knight was. He looked back up at Tom and then took a step forward and Tom realised that Jerry was going to try and join him on his makeshift stage and possibly make a speech. He decided he had to wrap up quickly before Jerry could get to him but before he could do so Carly was hoisted up on to the workbench by Tweedledum and Tweedledee.

'Just one minute,' she said and grabbed an enormous bottle of champagne out of someone's hands. 'May I butt in?' she asked, turning to put her hand on his arm. 'Tom, on behalf of the entire cast of *Malice in Wonderland*, I would like to say that you have been bloody awesome.' She threw an arm around him, raising the bottle of champagne in the air with her free hand. Everyone stamped their feet and cheered. Jerry stopped in his tracks, realising this wasn't his moment.

'*Malice in Wonderland* is a brilliant show,' announced Carly. 'We all did our best to fuck it up for you – well, actually Theo did his best to try and fuck it up for you,' she continued as Theo turned bright red in his supporting-cast, tarot-card costume. 'But the truth is, even though you perhaps didn't always think so, there was no way it could fail. Your vision and creativity were far too strong for that. All we had to do was deliver it. And didn't we do just that?' she cried out to her appreciative audience.

The crowd roared and suddenly all the pots and pans in the place were pulled off the shelves and an impromptu conga line was formed, lids and spoons creating a rhythmic beat.

Carly turned and took Tom's hand. 'Shall we?' she asked.

'Don't mind if I do.' He grinned, and they sashayed around the workbench to the beat of kitchen-utensil music. When Carly nearly fell off, Tom grabbed her, pulling her in close.

'You did that,' she said to him, nodding at the demented crowd.

'I know,' said Tom, grinning back at her.

'Help me up, will ya?' came a cry from Jerry, standing behind them.

Tom laughed and held out his hand, hauling him up with all his strength.

'Looks like there's quite a party going on up here,' Jerry said, raising his eyebrows at Tom.

'Just telling your mate how brilliant he is,' Carly yelled at Jerry, trying to make herself heard over the din.

'What, him?' said Jerry. 'Utter fuck-up until I got hold of him. You know what they say, behind every great show there's a—'

'Man who knows an electrician,' interrupted Tom.

'Precisely,' agreed Jerry, slapping him on the back.

'May I interrupt just for a moment?'

Tom looked down and saw Phillip standing next to the workbench, surrounded by youthful debauchery.

Shit, the scores, he thought. Phillip had said he was going to get Archie to run off the show average for the whole run. He must have the result. He scrutinised Phillip's face. He was smiling although it did look as though it was through gritted teeth. But then again he was getting pummelled in the back by not one but two foam flamingo croquet sticks, which could explain his discomfort.

Tom fell to his knees and shouted in Phillip's ear: 'Did we manage it?' He knew the scores had been consistently good all week but it was never over until the fat lady sang. Particularly in show business.

Phillip offered Tom his hand, which Tom shook, thinking it was a tad over-formal.

'Pull me up, you fool,' Phillip said. 'Let's tell everyone, shall we?'

Tom grabbed his hand and hauled him up to join him, Jerry and Carly on the now rather crowded steel table. Phillip coughed politely as though that would be sufficient to grab the attention of the bawdy revellers. Tom searched the crowd for Amy to see if she could do the honours again and within moments there was a massive clatter of pots and pans. Phillip covered his ears in horror.

'Thank you,' he said when everyone had finally noticed the big boss was awaiting their attention. 'Before you all go off to goodness knows where now the theme park is shut I thought you might like to hear your overall average score for the show.'

'Ten, ten, ten, ten, ten, ten,' came a shout from the back of the room until everyone else joined in. The only person who could calm them was Amy.

'Will you all shut up and listen to the man,' she screamed. 'Oh, and by the way, for those of you who clearly failed Maths GCSE: there is no way we can get ten, as this is an *average* overall score. Can anyone tell me what an average is?'

Everyone stared back at her blankly.

'Thought not. You add up all the scores and then divide that figure by the number of days the show ran for. Do you understand?'

Still silence.

Amy shook her head in despair. 'In idiot speak, to achieve an average of ten, we would have to have scored a ten for every show, which we know we didn't.' Amy turned to address Phillip. 'May I offer my apologies for the stupidity of this cast? Numbers are not their strong point.'

Phillip looked out over the now silent crowd. 'Can I start by offering my congratulations to you all for a job very well done—' he began but Amy interrupted his flow by tugging on his coat.

'I'd get on with it if I were you. Just tell us the scores and you can go home.'

Phillip nodded, then reached inside his jacket pocket and pulled out a piece of paper.

'I'm delighted to announce that your average score for *Malice in Wonderland* has ended up as a whopping nine point two.'

The cast went wild, shouting and cheering. Tom embraced Carly and Jerry and they all started jumping up and down again, very nearly pushing Phillip from his podium.

'However...' Phillip shouted at the top of his voice.

Oh no. There's a however, thought Tom.

Everyone hushed.

'However, if you take out the first show's score, which we could in hindsight treat as an extended dress rehearsal...' he said, pausing to look at Tom.

Tom nodded enthusiastically.

'Then your average score from the guests of Wonderland Theme Park would be an extremely impressive nine point five.'

'Nine point five,' gasped Jerry. 'Round that up and it's a perfect ten,' he said, grinning at Amy. 'Ten, ten, ten, ten,' he chanted until the entire building was a vibrating cacophony of shouting tens, all pointing at Amy.

'No,' she screamed back. 'You can't claim a ten. The average can't be ten.'

Jerry jumped down from the table and with the help of Tweedledum and Tweedledee lifted a kicking and screaming Amy on to his shoulders. She bobbed about above the crowd and eventually had to force a smile and start chanting ten along with everyone else.

'Well done,' said Phillip, turning to Tom amidst the chaos. 'I wasn't sure this was all going to work out but it's been a massive success. Commercial spends are up fifteen per cent as well so Head Office are coming in for a meeting at the end of next week to find out how we did it. You're around next week, aren't you?'

'Should be,' he replied, glancing over at Carly.

'I think they might ask you to look at the entertainment offering at some of the other group attractions, so be ready for that.'

Tom nodded, but looked blank, struggling to take in what Phillip was saying.

'You understand this could be a big opportunity for you,' continued Phillip. 'They're very impressed with the reaction they saw this evening. They're rethinking entertainment and you could be a big part of that.'

'So they liked it?' asked Tom.

Phillip nodded. 'They really liked it. Especially the scores, of course.'

'Of course,' said Tom. 'So I still have a job then?'

'More than that,' said Phillip. 'This could lead to something much bigger, Tom. Seriously well done.'

'Thank you,' replied Tom, feeling a little dazed.

'So is Laura here?' Phillip asked, casting his eye around the room.

'Er, no. I don't know where she is actually. She disappeared after the end of the show.'

'Shame. I wanted to thank her too. We would have given up if it hadn't been for her, wouldn't we?'

'Probably,' Tom was forced to agree.

'Will you pass on my thanks? Tell her I'll be in touch soon. I've got some thoughts on a few other projects she can help us with. She's clearly got a good head on her shoulders, that one. No idea why she married you,' Phillip said with a grin.

'Neither do I,' replied Tom.

'Well, I'll leave you to it. Have a good night. You deserve it. See you tomorrow.'

'I've booked a day off.'

'Oh, right. Well, Tuesday then.'

'Yes. See you on Tuesday.'

CHAPTER
THIRTY-FOUR
LAURA

Laura was curled up in her pyjamas at home, trying to block out the turmoil in her brain by watching the *Strictly Come Dancing* results show, when her phone rang.

'Where the hell are you?' she heard Hannah whisper. 'Why aren't you here? I really need to talk to you about what's happened this afternoon. *I've had one*,' she hissed.

Laura looked at the phone in confusion. She'd assumed Hannah must be ringing to ask why she wasn't at the after-show party where Tom would be having the time of his life with Carly, his 'favourite leading lady'. She turned down the volume on the telly to make sure she could hear what Hannah was saying.

'What did you say?' she hissed back.

'I said I've had one,' Hannah whispered again and then laughed.

'What have you had?' asked Laura, pressing pause on the TV. She was starting to get impatient.

'Are you ready for this?' asked Hannah.

'I've no idea!' cried Laura. 'You rang me!'

'You are so not ready for it,' declared Hannah.

'If you say so,' said Laura sarcastically. 'Go on then, spit it out. I've got Claudia Winkleman hovering very strangely.'

'I really don't know how to tell you.' Hannah laughed again.

'Are you pissed?' asked Laura, suddenly feeling suspicious. She checked her watch. The party must barely have started.

'Possibly,' replied Hannah. 'I opened a bottle before everyone arrived. But, Laura, I feel so happy I could burst.'

Laura looked at her phone in amazement. 'Excuse me but I am speaking to Hannah, aren't I?'

'Yes!'

'You don't sound normal.'

'That's because my normal was bloody miserable,' Hannah said. 'Now I'm happy and hope very much that this will become my new normal.'

Laura picked up the remote control and switched Claudia off. Anything that made Hannah swear deserved her full attention.

'So what has brought on this dramatic change in personality?' she asked.

'You'll never guess.'

'For goodness' sake, just tell me,' screeched Laura.

'I had a moment *and* I danced with him, and now I understand all those things you've been going on and on about,' Hannah announced.

'What do you mean you had a moment? And you danced? But you never dance.'

'I do now. But only with Will of course.'

'Whhaaaaaaat!' exclaimed Laura. She dropped the remote control. 'What did you just say?'

'I said I've danced with Will,' she repeated.

'I don't understand,' Laura said when she'd gathered herself. 'What are you trying to tell me, Hannah?'

'We danced. In the basement. Me and Will, to Ed Sheeran.'

Laura racked her brains to try and understand what this could all mean. She still couldn't fathom what on earth Hannah was trying to tell her. Then something struck her.

'Did you dance to "Thinking Out Loud"?'

'Yes,' hissed Hannah.

'Oh my God,' Laura screamed.

'It was a moment, Laura. A real moment. Just as he sang "People fall in love in mysterious ways".'

Laura was speechless.

'Have you taken drugs?' she asked eventually. 'Did one of the dancers give you something?'

'Of course not. I'm not stupid.'

'You're married and you danced with Will on the dance floor you told your husband was a waste of money. Stupid could be relevant at this point.'

Hannah went quiet for a moment.

'I think it's the most sensible thing I've ever done in my life,' she said solemnly.

'But...but...Will?' asked Laura. 'Since when? How the hell did that happen?'

'I don't know,' said Hannah. Now she sounded bewildered. 'Well, I guess I had a kind of inkling when he told me about that other woman.'

Laura gasped. 'You're the other woman?' she exclaimed.

'I guess I must be,' replied Hannah, sounding almost as shocked as her friend was.

'Did he tell you at the time that it was you? Why didn't you tell me?'

'No, no, of course not. He wouldn't tell me who it was but I do remember he looked at me strangely,' continued Hannah. 'I just brushed it off then, thought perhaps he was hung-over from the night before or something. Wasn't feeling well. But every so often since I've caught him looking at me in the same way. And I've found myself looking at him in that way too.'

'Why didn't you tell me any of this?'

'Because I didn't know for sure, did I? I couldn't really believe it. I didn't think you could tell anything from just a look.'

'But you can,' cried Laura. 'Haven't I been telling you that?'

'I know, I know, but I didn't really believe it until today.'

'So how did it happen?'

'Well, he came round to fix some more lights up for Jerry. I was helping him and we got talking and all this stuff came out, Laura. I kept banging on about how most people spend their lives miserable because they never actually say what they mean and then Will put Radio Cornerstone on.'

'I bet that killed the moment.'

'It didn't. Ed Sheeran was on and we just looked at each other and, well, we started dancing.'

'It was a moment?'

'It was a moment.'

'Wow.'

'I know. It was amazing, Laura, really. It felt so right. I've never felt like that before.'

'Then what happened?'

'Jerry came home.'

'What?' cried Laura. 'Did he see you?'

'I don't think so. He was carrying an enormous box down to the basement ready for this party. I don't think he could see past it.'

'He can't have done. I'm sure Jerry would have a lot to say about finding his wife having a moment with his electrician in the middle of his beloved dance floor.'

'He's not just an electrician, you know.'

'Bloody hell, you really have got it bad if you're defending his occupation.'

'I love him, Laura,' she said quietly.

Laura blew out her cheeks and pulled the phone away from her ear to stare at it in amazement.

'So what are you going to do?' she asked finally.

'Well, I'm going to start by telling Jerry tomorrow that it's over. I'd tell him tonight if I could but I can't ruin his party for him. I'm hoping then he'll still go to Australia. Give him some time to adjust. Then when he gets back we can see what happens next.'

'And what about Will? Are you going to tell Jerry about him?'

'Let's see what happens, shall we? The important thing is to be honest with Jerry about our marriage. He can't be happy either, so I don't think it's going to be that difficult.'

'Oh God,' groaned Laura.

'What, you don't think I should tell him?'

'It's not that. But I think Tom is leaving me.'

'Oh, come on Laura.'

'But he's going for an audition in the West End with Carly. It's all coming true, Hannah. I saw the way he looked at Carly this evening, and I know he's going to ditch me for her.'

For the first time Hannah was quiet on the end of the phone.

'Do you remember what I said to Will?' she said eventually.

'No,' said Laura grumpily. 'I didn't think you did much talking, it was all about the moment.'

'What I said to Will was that most people spend their entire lives being miserable because they don't say what they really mean.'

'And your point is?'

'Just talk to Tom, please, before you do anything stupid. Tell him whatever is in your heart or you will regret it for the rest of your life.'

'Are you sure you haven't taken any drugs?'

'One hundred per cent. You owe it to yourself and your marriage to get over here right now and sort this mess out.'

CHAPTER
THIRTY-FIVE
JERRY

The Queen of Hearts was doing his nails. Jerry thought he'd never been happier.

He was sitting on a bar stool having allowed Tweedledum and Tweedledee to take over the serving of the drinks to the happy bunch of thespians, singers and dancers sprawled all over his basement, either cuddled up on the enormous sofas deep in showbiz talk or doing dramatic formations on the dance floor. He felt totally at home amongst all the whooping and hollering and kissing and crying. He loved being around these hyped-up exaggerated human beings. It suited him. They were breathing longed-for life into what had been a sterile, emotionless home.

He took a sip of his margarita and smiled to himself.

'Do you remember Margarita Pracatan?' he asked Flora, the Queen of Hearts, who was carefully painting his middle fingernail in pink glitter.

'Who?'

'Margarita Pracatan. She used to sing songs and play the organ like a trouper on *The Clive James Show*.'

'Who's Clive James?'

Jerry laughed. So young, he thought. 'The man who made Margarita Pracatan famous.' He smiled. 'Ooh, Baby,' he said in a thick, vaguely Spanish accent.

'Was that her catchphrase?'

'It was. She had zero talent and was kind of crazy but boy was she entertaining. She really knew how to have fun.'

'She sounds cool.'

'She was. She made the most of herself – put it like that.'

'That's all this business is really,' said Flora, pausing to take a sip of Jerry's cocktail. 'It's ninety per cent confidence. I've seen people with loads of talent give up because they just aren't confident enough and I've seen utter numpties come alive on stage and bring the house down. You got the confidence you can be anything in life, I reckon.'

'Do you mind me asking how old you are, Flora?' Jerry asked.

'Twenty. Other hand?'

Jerry offered her his right hand. 'Will you promise me two things?' he asked.

'Mmm.' Flora nodded, concentrating on his thumbnail.

'Just go for it. Don't let anyone tell you you can't.'

'Mmm,' she repeated, still staring at the thumbnail.

'And have a laugh. Have fun. You've got to enjoy life.'

Flora looked up, smiling. 'Do you think we look like the kind of guys who don't have a laugh?' she asked. 'We're all Margarita Pracatans. Minimal talent, maximum confidence, up for a laugh. Sums most entertainers up really.'

Jerry nodded his head. He could get that. 'I think I'm a Margarita Pracatan actually,' he said contentedly.

'Of course you are. Why do you think you fit right in with all these misfits?' Flora said with another smile. 'I've never seen Margarita Pracatan but I just know you are the King of Margarita Pracatans.'

'I am!' agreed Jerry. 'I bloody well am. Will you do my face?'

'What do you mean, do your face?'

'Make me up. Really over the top.'

She shrugged. 'If you want.'

'Then can I borrow your Queen of Hearts dress?'

'Er, are you OK?'

'Absolutely. Never better. Top of the world. I think it's time everyone met the King of Margarita Pracatans.'

CHAPTER THIRTY-SIX
TOM

Why wouldn't she pick up the damned phone? thought Tom, putting his mobile away in frustration for the umpteenth time. He'd tried to ring her as soon as everyone had started to move on to Jerry's house. He wanted to know where she'd gone. He wanted to tell her what Phillip had said about Head Office wanting him to look at the entertainment offering in the other attractions. He wanted to talk to her about the audition. He wanted to tell her he had never felt on such a high in his life given how much of a success the show had been and he had never felt on such a low because she didn't seem to want to share it with him. In fact she didn't seem to want anything to do with him at all given that she was ignoring his calls and messages. God, she could be the most frustrating person in the world.

'Tom?' said Carly, nudging his elbow. They were sitting on one of Jerry's deep sumptuous sofas facing the dance floor.

'Mmmm,' he said distractedly.

'Would you get me another margarita?' she asked, holding out her glass.

'Sure.' Tom was glad to get up for fear he might fall asleep.

'And Elspeth?' she added, nudging her neighbour to hand over her glass.

'No problem.' He took both glasses and walked towards the bar. He heard them laugh behind him. It made him feel old.

He sneaked up behind his brother, who was leaning against a wall, still dressed in his electrician's overalls and finishing a pint. He turned when Tom put his hand on his shoulder.

'Oh, hello,' he said. 'How's superstardom?'

'You're only jealous,' replied Tom, giving him a good-natured punch on the arm.

'I'm not actually,' said Will, grinning as he looked down into the bottom of his pint.

'Can I get you another one of those?' asked Tom.

Will furrowed his brow and then looked up to survey the room. He appeared to be considering the request seriously.

'Er, no, actually. Better not. This might be your scene but it isn't really mine. I think I'm best out of the way for now – plus I've got an early start tomorrow.'

'Party pooper,' said Tom.

'Yeah, well,' said Will, handing his empty glass to his brother. 'I can't take too much excitement. You about tomorrow?'

'Er, well, possibly not.'

'You need a lie-down, do you, after your starring role?'

'Something like that.'

'Perhaps we could go for a beer tomorrow night,' asked Will, 'if you're not too tired, of course?'

'Sure,' said Tom, feeling puzzled. It was unlike his brother to instigate a night out and especially during the week. 'I'll call you if I'm free.'

Will nodded. 'Great. Be good to talk.'

'Yeah,' replied Tom, now even more bewildered. Will never suggested talking as a way of spending quality social time.

'See you then,' Will said, walking away quickly just as Carly snaked her way up towards them.

CHAPTER
THIRTY-SEVEN
LAURA

Oh no, thought Laura as she dashed up the steps to Hannah and Jerry's enormous oak door. Illuminated by a spotlight, a couple stood snogging the living daylights out of each other. Their hands were inappropriately positioned, forcing Laura to sneak past them whilst covering her eyes to avoid being accused of voyeurism. She pushed at the door only to find that it wouldn't open. She was forced to ring the doorbell, which – typical of Jerry – had the loudest chime available on the open market and alerted the amorous couple to her presence.

The man looked over and nodded, leaving his hand positioned somewhere up the lady's top.

'Didn't realise it was a pyjama party!' He laughed, casting an eye up and down her attire.

Laura looked down and realised to her utter dismay that she was still in pyjamas and Ugg boots, such was the fog she had been in when she left home. She pressed the bell again, praying someone would hear it above the throbbing music from the basement. What if nobody did? How would she stop herself punching the smirk off the young man standing next to her?

'Didn't realise it was an eighties party,' she said as at last she heard the click of the lock.

'It isn't,' he said, his smirk getting ever bigger.

'Oh, I thought being felt up outside a party was an eighties thing,' replied Laura, pushing the door open. 'You know: really uncool and crass and likely to end in a sexually transmitted disease.'

She smiled gratefully at the technicolour rabbit as she pushed past him into the hall but now she was here, her confidence failed her and she considered turning round and going straight back home. However, Hannah came dashing out of the kitchen and grabbed her by the hand, pulling her upstairs before she could change her mind.

'Hmm, pyjamas and Uggs, a great look for a wrap party,' said Hannah, thrusting a drink into her hand.

'I completely forgot what I was wearing!' wailed Laura. 'I've got no idea what I'm doing – or what you're doing come to that. I can't believe you're really going to leave Jerry. The world has turned upside down.'

'It's been coming for a long time,' said Hannah calmly. 'You know it has. We married too young and I'm sure Jerry thinks he missed out. I think he'd love to turn the clock back, act like an idiot, sleep around, especially now he's got the money to do whatever he wants. Once he's got over the shock he'll be delighted he doesn't have his buzz-kill getting in the way.'

'Buzz-kill?'

'It's what he calls me, to his mates. I've heard him when he thinks I'm not listening. To be honest, Laura, he'd have left me years ago had he been smart enough to think of it as an option.'

Laura didn't know what to say.

'Look at it from his point of view,' said Hannah. 'I'm giving him a free ticket to shag as many dancers as he flipping well likes.'

'Is that how you're going to tell him?'

'It's tempting. I think he might get that, whereas "I'm leaving you" may not compute for some time.'

'So what am I going to do about Tom?' Laura said quietly. 'Never in a million years did I expect *you* to do something like this. It's so confusing.'

'Just tell him. For goodness' sake, just talk to him and tell him what you are thinking.'

'No.' Laura shook her head. 'He has to decide.'

'But decide what? What do you mean?'

'Whether to go to the audition and leave me behind forever.'

'But he doesn't know that's what he's deciding, does he?'

'Well, he should. It should be obvious that's the choice he's making.'

'But he's a man, Laura.'

Laura looked up at Hannah. Hannah stepped forward and took her hand.

'Shall we both go downstairs, together,' she asked gently. 'Try and sort this mess out?'

Laura sighed. 'OK. I guess I've got nothing to lose.'

'Do you want to borrow something to wear?' asked Hannah.

Laura looked down at her pyjamas, which were held together with a safety pin. 'No,' she replied. 'If he's going to stay it has to be because of who I am, a slightly scruffy market analyst and not a glamorous young dancer.'

CHAPTER
THIRTY-EIGHT
TOM

'So I've been meaning to tell you,' said Carly excitedly, as they leant on the bar.

'Oh yeah?' said Tom, gratefully sipping a pint rather than the margaritas that he'd endured to fit in with everyone else.

'I've got us somewhere to stay tomorrow night,' she announced.

'Tomorrow night? What do you mean, tomorrow night?'

'Well, the call-backs for the audition are on Tuesday so we should stay down just in case. I don't want to jinx it or anything but best to plan for success, hey?' she said, raising her glass to his.

'Yeah, course,' he replied, pretending that he knew there might be call-backs. 'You're right. So where have you found then?'

'Oh, it's a girl I was in a show with a couple of years ago. She's got a bedsit in Hammersmith. She's rehearsing for pantomime in Carlisle at the moment so she said we could borrow it.'

'Right.' Tom took a long gulp of his drink. 'So she won't be there then?'

'No.' Carly shrugged, studying her glass hard. 'No, she won't be there.'

CHAPTER
THIRTY-NINE
LAURA

Laura felt sicker and sicker as she and Hannah descended the basement steps hand in hand. They could hear some absolutely dreadful karaoke singing winding its way up the stairs, interspersed with the haze from a smoke machine that must have been 'borrowed' from Wonderland. Laura wasn't sure what she expected to find at the bottom of the stairs but it certainly wasn't what greeted them once they reached the last step and turned the corner into the room.

Laura gasped and then laughed before Hannah dug her in the ribs and scowled. There sitting behind a Yamaha organ at the far end of the room was Jerry dressed in a glorious red frilly dress, towering red wig and gaudy over-the-top make-up. He was belting out 'Whole Again' by Atomic Kitten for all he was worth in some kind of dodgy foreign accent and at the end of every line he punched the air and shouted, 'Ooh, Baby,' at the top of his voice. A crowd had assembled round him, laughing and cheering, and he had never, in Laura's opinion, looked happier.

'I agree. You can't burst that bubble tonight,' said Laura to Hannah, who smiled resignedly.

'Laura!' came a cry from behind them and they both turned to see Tom and Carly fast approaching. Oh God, if only she could talk to Tom without Carly being constantly attached to him...

'Where've you been?' cried Tom.

'I, er,' started Laura. 'I, er...'

'Oh, it doesn't matter,' he said. 'As long as you are here now. There's something I need to do then I need to talk to you. Stand right there and don't move.'

Laura stood stock-still, trying to ignore Carly's semi-drunk smirk. This wasn't a position she had expected or wanted to be in tonight.

The next thing she knew Tom was striding across the basement, making his way over to Jerry with the flowers she'd seen in the garage earlier. Laura felt like crying. She couldn't do it. She couldn't stand there and watch her husband gush over another woman. She had to get out.

She tugged at Hannah's hand but her friend wouldn't let go. In fact Hannah gripped her even harder.

'I need to get out of here,' Laura hissed at her.

'Oh no you don't,' said Hannah grimly. 'We are in this together now. We are not leaving this room until your love life is sorted out.'

Tom was now attempting to take the microphone off Jerry, who was resisting.

'I'm performing,' protested Jerry. Tom gave it an almighty tug, causing Jerry to go flying.

'You can perform again in a minute,' Tom said crossly. 'There's something I've got to say.' He turned to face the revellers. 'Can I have your attention please, everyone?'

Everyone hushed and someone thankfully leant over and switched off Jerry's backing track. Laura thought she might throw up. She looked longingly at the exit.

'Before you all disappear I just wanted to thank you all again for what I can genuinely say has been the best thing I have ever done at Wonderland. Every single one of you pulled it out of the bag in the end and I could not be prouder. I must also thank again our wonderful benefactor, who has been kind enough to throw this fabulous party. Can you please show your appreciation for the one, the only, Margarita Pracatan.'

Jerry stepped forward, took a bow and blew kisses to his fans from magenta lips as everyone went wild. Soon the chant of 'Ooh, Baby' filled the underground room.

Tom signalled for quiet and everyone calmed down. 'There is, however, one person who I need to give my gratitude to who has so far not been recognised this evening. Without this very special woman we wouldn't all be standing here today celebrating our success. She always believed we could do it. She has stood by me through thick and thin and quite frankly we wouldn't have a show at all if it wasn't for her. She was the making of *Malice in Wonderland*.'

Laura tugged harder on Hannah's hand. She couldn't bear it. She had to leave. She couldn't watch Carly bask under the glow of her husband's praise. She cast her eyes sideways, unable to stop herself looking at Carly's reaction. Smug with a capital S was spelt out all over her face. Laura screwed her eyes tight shut. Perhaps it would help if she couldn't see, even if she had to listen.

'So as a token of my appreciation I would like to present these flowers to the ultimate leading lady in my life. My wife, Laura.'

Laura's eyes flew open. She'd heard that wrong, hadn't she? Being blind had played tricks on her. She looked at Hannah, who had finally released her grip. Hannah was clapping. Why was she clapping Carly? The traitor. What was she thinking? She looked up to see Tom watching her expectantly, holding up the dreaded flowers. Her head flew round, seeking Carly, but she seemed to have disappeared.

'What are you waiting for?' urged Hannah.

'What do you mean?'

'Tom's waiting to give you flowers.'

'Me?'

'Yes!' Hannah gave her a push. 'You.'

Laura walked like a zombie up to the front of the room, searching Tom's face for clues. She let him engulf her in a hug.

'I know I've been a real pain over the last few weeks, being so obsessed with the show, but knowing I have you to come home to has made it all bearable. And you were the one who made me face up to the failure I had on my hands and do something about it. I couldn't have done it without you,' he breathed into her ear. 'I love you.'

Laura pulled back and looked into his eyes. Was this his swansong, his way of saying goodbye? Thanks, you're amazing, now I'm off. He gripped her hand and turned back to his audience with a huge grin on his face.

'So all that remains to be said is ... ' He paused for dramatic effect. 'See you all this time next year!'

Everyone cheered and Jerry sidled in, setting the organ off again and beginning a terrible version of 'We Are the Champions'.

'Come over here,' said Tom. 'I need to tell you something.'

Laura let him drag her to the side of the room where they could be heard and not trampled by a flock of excitable performers.

So this is it, thought Laura, bracing herself. This is when he tells me he's going to the audition and it's all over.

'I saw Phillip earlier,' he said urgently.

Laura nodded mutely.

'Head Office are coming up next week to understand how we made such a success of the show and they want to talk to me about helping the other attractions in the group improve their entertainment.'

Laura looked at him blankly. She couldn't take in what he was saying. Where was the admission that he was off to London to find fame and fortune with the girl who looked like his ex-fiancée?

'Well, you could at least look happy for me?' cried out Tom.

'But... but what about the audition in the West End?'

'I'm not going.' Tom shrugged. 'It was a stupid idea. Should never have let Carly talk me into it. I mean, look at all this lot,' he said, casting his arm over the dance floor. 'What do they wake up to tomorrow morning? The thought of moving on to another strange place in the hope of another job and then doing that all over again at somebody else's whim. I don't want that. I want to wake up to you every day, not in some godforsaken bedsit with God knows who. I mean, a bedsit?' he said, shivering. 'I'm past all that. And it's made me realise what a great opportunity I have here. Well – you made me realise that. You and your bollocking over lunch.'

'Sorry,' said Laura, before she could help herself.

'Don't be,' said Tom. 'I needed it. You were right about everything.'

'Everything?' questioned Laura, feeling her stomach clench.

'Well, no, not everything,' he said, snaking his arms around her waist and pulling her in close. 'Not the bit about not living happily ever after with an unglamorous, boring wife.'

Laura couldn't breathe. He could so get this bit wrong. It wouldn't be the first time. And if he did, she feared they might never recover.

'I did live happily ever after with the most beautiful woman I have ever met.' He leant forward to kiss her.

She hesitated. Had he said enough? Yes he had. The most beautiful man that she had ever met had said she was the most beautiful woman he'd ever met. That was more than enough. They kissed and kissed and kissed until she felt she was floating.

'Can you say that again,' said Laura when they at last took a breath.

'Which bit?'

'The bit about me being the most beautiful woman you have ever met.'

'I thought that would be my winning line,' he replied with a cheeky grin.

She thumped him.

'Just because I don't tell you doesn't mean I don't think it every day,' he said, trying to fend her off.

'You should tell me more,' she said, sticking her bottom lip out.

'Tell you what I'm actually thinking?' said Tom.

Laura nodded. 'Yes.'

'Only if you promise to do the same.'

'Deal,' said Laura.

'Deal,' replied Tom. 'I do need to ask you something else though.'

Here it is, she thought. The kicker at the end. This wasn't going to end perfectly after all.

'Would you dance with me?' he asked, stepping back and then offering his hand.

She looked into his eyes. 'You want to dance with this?' she asked, indicating with her hands her scrappy ponytail, pyjamas and unsuitable footwear.

'Always,' he replied.

'Waltz?' she asked.

'Oh no,' he said, stepping forwards and grasping her around the waist. 'Tonight we do the dance of passion. Tonight we do the tango.'

Before Laura could respond Tom grabbed her hand and pulled her on to the dance floor, walking with such determination and speed that the party-goers, standing aside to let them through, paused their excitable chatter to check out what was going on.

Tom walked up to Jerry, who was still banging away on the keyboard, and shouted in his ear. She watched as he scuttled off to fiddle with his state-of-the-art music system. With a determined look on his face Tom pulled her to the centre of the floor, took both her hands and placed them in their dramatic starting position.

She looked up at him, trying to ignore the butterflies doing a quickstep in her belly.

'This' – he smiled down at her – 'will be my favourite tango of the night.' She felt the butterflies calm to a rumba. 'Because now I get to dance with my favourite partner,' he added.

She gasped as he pulled her in closer just as the opening bars of 'Eye of the Tiger' filled the room. Laura closed her eyes momentarily, trying to recall the opening steps, then opened them to see Tom gazing down at her, a look of pure love in his eyes.

She stopped thinking about the steps and let her emotions take over. She felt the music, she felt the rhythm and she felt Tom, her husband, masterfully guiding her around the floor.

She was aware of no one as she danced, other than her husband. Nothing mattered beyond the feeling of being in Tom's arms and dancing the night away. The explosion of applause and the stamping of feet as they struck their final pose was a huge shock. Laura felt jolted from a dream to be greeted by a sea of delighted faces, cheering and clapping and jumping up and down. She looked up at Tom, who was beaming back at her. He stepped to the side and she bowed to her audience, blushing as she did so. Then she turned back to her husband, who grasped her around the waist and spun her round and round; both laughed their heads off as they enjoyed their moment.

CHAPTER FORTY

LAURA

Laura looked across at her husband and smiled. They were sitting at the kitchen table in their dressing gowns at ten thirty on a Monday morning, sipping Buck's Fizz. She felt giddy. That could be due to the sex that they'd just had or the Buck's Fizz. Either way she didn't care.

Tom grinned back, holding his glass up. 'I could get used to this. Maybe we should take in more lodgers if they all leave us champagne when they move out.'

'No way.' Laura grimaced. 'That is the last time you bring home a lodger, understood? We'll manage without one in the future.'

'Understood.' Tom nodded. 'I'm sorry. I won't do it ever again. I promise.'

'Good,' she said, taking a glug.

'Morning, guys,' said Jerry, bursting through the back door. 'Aye, aye. What's this? Drinking in the morning? You trying to get Laura frisky or something?'

'No,' said Tom, getting up to find Jerry a glass. 'She needs no encouragement actually.'

Tom filled a glass with champagne knowing that Jerry might vomit at the thought of mixing it with juice. 'Carly left it for us. We woke up this morning and she'd gone. All her stuff and everything. Just left this, some cash and a thank-you note.'

'Blimey,' said Jerry, knocking back a large slug. 'Clearly it's a day for buggering off then,' he continued, staring for a moment into his glass. 'I've come to say goodbye actually. I fly out to Australia at seven o'clock tonight.'

'Tonight!' exclaimed Tom and Laura.

'Mmm-mmm,' confirmed Jerry.

'You and Hannah?' Laura asked tentatively. She hadn't heard from her since she and Tom had decided to make their excuses and leave the party early.

'No, just me,' sighed Jerry. 'Me and Hannah – well, we've decided to part ways.'

'What!' exclaimed Tom. 'What do you mean? No way.' He looked at Laura in bewilderment. She tried to look equally flummoxed.

Jerry nodded. 'It's not been right for ages. We both knew that. We've been flogging a dead horse, to be honest.'

'God, I'm sorry, mate,' said Tom. He looked devastated for his friend.

'Nah, don't be. It's definitely the right thing.'

'Are you sure you're both OK?' asked Laura.

'Yeah, we talked it all through this morning. We both want entirely different things. Hannah spelt it out really. She said to me, "Will you have more fun in Australia with or without me?" I had to admit, it would be without her. Makes it crystal clear, doesn't it? She told me to go and enjoy myself and she'll hold the fort whilst I'm away. The good thing about Hannah is she's as straight as a die. I know she's not going to diddle me. We'll sort the divorce out when I get back.'

Clever Hannah, thought Laura. She'd played it exactly as she'd said she would. Sometimes it didn't do to give Jerry too much information.

'It's still sad though,' said Tom.

No one said anything.

Then Jerry grinned. 'I'm going to fucking Australia! I can't be sad about that.'

'I'm not sure Australia is ready for you, Jerry,' said Laura.

Jerry grinned. 'Ooh, Baby,' he said.

'You're not taking Margarita Pracatan, are you?' asked Tom.

'Margarita goes everywhere with me from now on,' said Jerry, pounding his fist on the table. 'Now let's get some more champagne in these glasses and have a toast.'

Jerry held his glass high in the air when they had all been topped up. 'To a new lease of life,' he declared.

'A new lease of life,' chimed in Tom and Laura, grinning happily.

'And Carly,' continued Jerry.

Laura frowned. 'Carly?'

'Yes, Carly.' Jerry nodded thoughtfully. 'Carly who created chaos in our lives but has left us all behind the better for it.'

Tom and Laura glanced at each other.

Laura raised her glass. 'To Carly.'

'To Carly,' agreed Tom.

The End

Dear Reader

Thank you so much for reading *Strictly My Husband*, I hope you enjoyed it as much as I enjoyed writing it. I find it really useful to know what readers think of my books so if you could leave a review on Amazon I would be very grateful. I read them all, and although they can be as short as you like, they're helpful for other people who might be considering buying this book.

If you want to see what else I've been up to or wish to contact me, you can find me via the links below. Please do check out my Facebook page so you can see how I got on with learning the Argentine tango – it's not pretty! And if you 'Like' my page I will enter you into a draw to win a signed copy of one of my books.

Happy dancing and thanks again for reading,
Tracy Bloom

x

I am on Facebook at tracybloomwrites, on Twitter @TracyBBloom or on my website, tracybloom.com

PS: If you'd like to receive an email when my next book is out please sign up at this address: http://bit.ly/27vyn4u – I will never share your address and you can opt out at any time.

Tracy Bloom – The Low Down

Tracy Bloom was born quite a while ago, is average to short in height, buys clothes based on their ability to hide stuff rather than reveal stuff, has chemically enhanced hair and wishes she had kept her braces in longer as a teenager. But apart from that she really enjoys describing herself!

Tracy has always liked to say it how it is in her writing, right from when she began her first novel *No-One Ever Has Sex on a Tuesday* nearly ten years ago. This honesty and a desire to see the funny side of things, helped her to become a number one bestseller, published in over a dozen countries and twice winner of the Love Stories Award for Best Author-Published Romance. Not bad for a farmer's daughter from Derbyshire whose previous major achievements include winning a bottle of sherry in a raffle at the age of eight.

Other Books by Tracy Bloom:

No-One Ever Has Sex on a Tuesday
Single Woman Seeks Revenge
I Will Marry George Clooney (By Christmas...)
No-One Ever Has Sex in the Suburbs

ACKNOWLEDGEMENTS

Firstly thank you to all the dancers in my life. To Bruce who has always danced with me, even on crutches at a relative's wedding. You are my dancing hero. To Tom and Sally who are ever ready to crank up the tunes and give it some, and to my mum and dad who did learn ballroom dancing when they were young and can still show us youngsters how to do it.

Technical support on this book has come from Gary, a legend regarding all things research but please do not judge my portrayal as any reflection of his expertise. I must also thank Richard Swainson of Swainson Productions who provided me with many a useful anecdote but who also produces my book trailers, which you can find on YouTube. It is the best fun making them and you are a joy to work with.

The One Off have pulled it out of the bag yet again with a brilliant cover, spurred on by my daughter Sally's fantastic idea. My son Tom is, as ever, my right hand man when it comes to commercial decisions. I am very grateful for your input. I only wish you were as grateful for mine!

Finally, as always, I must thank Peta Nightingale and Araminta Whitley, my dynamic duo of agents who guide me through the difficult stuff. It's a pleasure doing business with you.

Printed in Great Britain
by Amazon